Críostóir MacCárthaoil

a leabhar

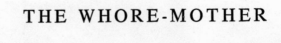

THE WHORE-MOTHER

SHAUN HERRON THE

Published by M. Evans and Company, Inc., *New York*
and distributed in association with
J. B. Lippincott Company, *Philadelphia and New York*

WHORE-MOTHER

Library of Congress Catalog Number 72-95976
ISBN 0-87131-112-7

Manufactured in the United States of America

Designed by Paula Wiener
0 9 8 7 6 5 4 3 2

For Shaun and Siobhan

THE WHORE-MOTHER

ONE

McMANUS folded the white margin of the *Irish News* along the line of the type, made sure it was straight, pressed the fold to a sharp edge with the nail of his thumb, and laid the page on the table.

He sat down to look at it. He was in fact looking at his hand which rested on the spread page.

Callaghan was watching him from the other end of the table. He had a mug of sweet tea cupped in his hands. "What're you playin at now?" he asked McManus.

"I want to see if I can tear it all the way up along the line of the fold," McManus said, and under cover of the talk raised his hand an inch off the table and spread the fingers. The hand was not trembling. He licked his lips.

"What's wrong w'your hand?" Callaghan said.

McManus turned it over slowly and examined it. "Where?" he asked stupidly and looked at Callaghan, turning the hand again. "What's wrong with it?" He felt in his head the comfort of a small triumph.

"You were lookin at it," Callaghan said irritably.

"Was I?" He didn't seem to understand. "No. I was looking at the fold. I'll try it."

He opened the fold and began to tear along it slowly, half an inch at a time.

Powers and Kelly, their feet on the old iron kitchen range, turned their heads to watch.

"Did you learn that sorta thing at the university?" Callaghan said.

Powers said, "Shut your gub."

McManus tore carefully and patiently at the thin page. Sounds came in from the street—a child's voice, a woman calling, traffic passing on the Falls Road at the end of the street. Four men watched intently as the white margin separated from the printed page with a little sound like a hamster shredding its bed. The lengthening tail of paper drooped over the edge of the table and wagged with the gentle movement of McManus's fingers.

Callaghan lifted his mug of tea to his mouth and slurped it. "You can't do it," he said.

Powers said, "Shut your gub."

McManus tore the last half inch. "I can't?" he said, and made a face like a grin at Callaghan. It took all his will to make the face and he was sure it looked false. He leaned back in his kitchen chair and tore a strip off the margin, about an inch and a half long. He went on tearing the ribbon of paper in equal lengths, with the mindless tranquility of a man killing time.

"What're you doin now?" Callaghan asked him.

"Tearing paper," McManus said.

Powers looked curiously at McManus for a long moment, then turned back to the fire.

Kelly snickered and glanced knowingly at Powers. "Ask a stupid question, get a stupid answer," he said.

McManus performed an odd little operation as he tore. Every other strip of paper was slipped into the crotch of the little finger of his left hand; the rest stayed in the thin stack forming between the thumb and forefinger of the same hand.

Callaghan watched the operation with hostile intensity. "What're you gonta do w'it when you get it all tore?"

"Burn it."

"Christ."

When his little enterprise was finished McManus closed his fist and put his hand into his pocket. The exercise relaxed him. He dropped the papers in the crotch of his little finger into the bottom of his trouser pocket, and folded the rest into his palm.

"You said y'were gonta burn it," Callaghan said in an aggrieved voice.

"When I'm ready," McManus said. "You should never hurry a therapeutic exercise."

"La-de-da," Callaghan said, and noisily drained his tea mug.

"What's a thera . . . thera . . . what sorta exercise, McManus? What for?" Powers asked, looking into the fire in the range.

"Therapy. Healing. It soothes the nerves." He knew he shouldn't have said it. That was the sort of thing that enraged them. He'd done it many times too often.

"You're sick?"

"No."

"You're afeareda the wee girl?"

"I'm not afraid. I'm nervous."

"What for?"

"I came here to fight soldiers, not little girls." He should keep his mouth shut. He wanted to. On this one, he couldn't.

"She's not a wee girl. She's a soldier-fuckin wee hoore."

No more, McManus told himself: Shut your stupid mouth. His accent and his vocabulary roughed their nerves and their patience. His attitudes inflamed them. "I know," he said, "I've never done it before, that's all." He had his envelope stamped and addressed in the foot of his sock. Now he had the paper for his letter in the bottom of his trouser pocket. All he had to do was write it and get it posted. The thought almost started him trembling. He could get it in the knees if they caught him. He collected himself, stood up, stretched, and tossed the papers in his palm into the fire. They were damp from the sweat on his hand. One scrap stuck. He gripped himself, picked it off his wet palm, and shook it from his fingers into the open range.

"That was a lotta work for fuck all," Callaghan said.

Powers said, "Shut your gub."

They sat in silence and immobility for five minutes and the ten-shilling alarm clock above the range ticked away the minutes with a tinny and irregular sound. McManus thought about writing his letter. It had to be done in bed, he decided, in the dark; he would read for a while, mark passages in a book to justify the pencil, put out the light, put one word on each piece of paper, and number each piece from its front edge. A letter written on scraps of newsprint would impress his sister with its desperate urgency.

But how could he get the stamped envelope from his sock to his pajama pocket? Callaghan was in the other single bed in his room, always watching, always listening, like a suspicious dog. Maybe that's what he was? Maybe they suspected his state of mind even more than he feared? If they did, he'd get it in the knees. Or the head. He closed his eyes tight and forced his mind back to the mechanics of the business. He'd keep his socks on so that he could get the letter into the envelope. "My feet are cold, Callaghan," he'd say. Callaghan slept in his shirt and underwear and socks. He'd see nothing strange about it. Go to the bog, he thought, and put the paper in your sock. That was it, do the whole thing in the bog. They couldn't come into the bog with him; he'd put everything in his sock, flush the bog, and come out looking casual. If he could.

It had to be done tonight. He had to know he was getting out. He couldn't know that till he started reaching out. His sister would do what he asked. England, for the love of God; he had to get to England. He'd be safer there, there'd be a place to hide there. His mind began to wander in that meadow: Irishmen and the poor dirty bloody English; Irishmen working in England or on the dole on English taxpayers' money; Irishmen hiding in England from other Irishmen; Englishmen hiding Irishmen from other Irishmen in England . . . a little shudder chilled him.

"Somethin botherin you, McManus?" It was Powers, strong Powers, single-minded Powers, Powers the leader; Powers the future martyr with his name on some martyr's monument and the television cameras showing it off to a grateful nation and an amazed and admiring world. . . . That was what Powers wanted—to die for Ireland and to be talked about forever. He wanted a ballad of his own.

"Just the girl. I'll get over it," McManus said.

"The university makes them soft," Callaghan explained with a malicious little smile.

"One of these days. . . ." McManus cut it off.

"Shut your gub and no morea that," Powers said strongly, like a master of men, and there was no more of that.

The alarm clock said half-past four. The girl worked in the city hall and would leave it at five o'clock. She would turn the corner from the bus stop into her street in Springfield at five-twenty or five-twenty-five. The bus could be a little late, but the girl's habits didn't change; home at the same time every day. She had her tea and if she was seeing her soldier that night she went out; if he was on duty she stayed at home. The man wasn't even much of a soldier—some sort of clerk. She was Irish, she was Catholic; he was English and that was political treachery and racial pollution. Her soldier was turning Catholic but that meant nothing. He was an English soldier. He was the enemy, she was a quisling, she had been warned, she had nobody to blame but herself. Examples had to be made, discipline had to be maintained, solidarity assured—and fear was part of the order of nature.

"Away on," Powers said, and led them out of the house into the street. Callaghan stood aside to make sure McManus went out before him. Like a watchdog, McManus thought, and his stomach sank. He wanted to run, full of fearful imaginings. He knew how far he would get. But they couldn't know what was in his mind? He had kept his nerve, given nothing away; he was sure he had given nothing away . . . the awful thought clouded his vision that maybe they weren't going to get the girl. Maybe he was the one? His brains scrambled. He stumbled.

"For the love of God, get a holt on yourself, McManus," Powers said contemptuously.

So much was done for the love of God.

TWO

T H E Y walked, two by two and almost heel to toe, in a defensive little square down the street away from the Falls Road into the warrens beyond. The car would be where it was supposed to be, the plates changed, keys in its ignition.

There were keys for every car that was made. Pick the car, locked or unlocked—these days people were locking them and a lot of good it did them—open it, drive it away, change the plates, leave it at a predetermined place deep in the district, and the men it was assigned to would come and get it when the time came. Plates were as easy to come by as keys and cars were alike: you only stole the look-alikes. It was the plates the police and the army looked for; who can tell one four-cylinder Vauxhall or Ford or Austin or whatnot from another? And who needed one for more than an hour or two? They went for their car with a fine sense of security. Very likely, they'd have dumped it or blown it up before the owner knew he'd lost it.

McManus scarcely saw the stringy street of flat-faced little houses, their brown blackened by generations of Belfast's industrial dirt. He knew people spoke to them as they passed, children greeted them, though not with the spontaneous exuberence of an earlier time, men saluted them with obedient deference, but these people were vague in the corners of his eyes. He stared ahead, clinging to the appearance of composure, and stopped when Powers stopped.

He shook his head free of the gauze that clogged it. He had to drive. He always had to drive.

He drove slowly, Powers beside him. There was plenty of time. These mean Belfast streets depressed him. They had been his home for nine months, though when he let the word home into his mind the idea that this place could in any sense have become his home repelled him. It had become his prison. The Antrim Road was his home, among Belfast's Protestant middle classes. The first thing he learned when he came here to the Falls—a young Ulster Catholic trying, as Conor Cruise O'Brien had put it, forever romantically to recreate the heroic past—was that he was an Ulster middle-class Catholic who was as distant from Ulster working-class Catholics as were the Ulster middle-class Protestants. The first undermining blow to his illusions of Irish Catholic comradeship was in his distaste for the coarseness and vulgarity of his comrades. They were urbanized peasants, without the earthy originality of the peasant, or the concrete poetry of his vocabulary. The second thing he learned was what he called "their single-minded mindlessness." The third was their righteous savagery. Christ, it was different from the heroic legends! He'd thought a lot about that in the past nine months—Finn McCuill and the Fianna, the ancient army of heroes; Cuchullian, the whole bloody lot that he learned at his father's knee. Purity, gallantry, invincibility—that was their image. But when he told his father he was joining the Provisional IRA and entering into the long succession, "Please, no, no, Johnny darlin," the old man said, "sure that hero stuff's all just a lot of oul talk." And the stuff he learned in school—Wolfe Tone, Robert Emmet, Daniel O'Connell, Patrick Pearse, Michael Collins that was "a lot of oul talk" too when he went to see Bull Baillie, the master who taught it to him. "They're not your kind, Johnny." Maybe not, but they all filled his head with the stuff and it took the reality to get it out. Powers was the reality. Sudden rage boiled up in him. His foot was hard on the pedal. He slammed on the brakes and flung his passengers about in the car.

16   ((

"What the bloody hell's wrong w'you?" Powers yelled at him.

"I'm sorry. I was thinking." He wanted to hit Powers. Not just to hit him. He wanted to smash the big arrogant face.

"Thinkin, for Christ's sake! You were puttin your foot down. That's what a driver does when he's angry. What's up?"

"Nothing."

"Nothin my fuckin arse. I'm thinkin we'll have to take a look at you, McManus. Away on."

That was the first time any of them had given a direct indication that they had doubts about him. If they wanted to take a look at him they believed there was something to look at. He drove very carefully, his mind shut down. But his hands sweated freely and to keep his grip on the wheel he had to wipe them dry on his trousers. He knew Powers watched him do it. It made him sweat even more, wipe oftener, and feel his arms empty of substance.

He wove slowly out onto the Springfield Road and up towards the housing estate where the girl lived. He had never seen her. Her name was Mavis. The thought of her name almost brought a weak hysterical giggle to his throat—Mavis McGonigal. Holy God, what a stupid, vulgar, and ridiculous name. He set his lips and his teeth and forced his mind to its work.

"In at the next right turn," Powers said, and he pulled in to the curb. "She'll come from behind us," Powers said.

A boy of about nine years left his post at the curb and came to Powers' window. "She's gettin off the bus," he said, and walked away, waiting across the street, not to miss the sport.

"Get out, Danny," Powers said to Callaghan. He said to McManus, "When she walks past you, drive beside her."

"I've never set eyes on her."

"Kelly knows her." Powers got out and walked up the street with Callaghan.

"I wisht I did know her," Kelly said from behind. "I'd like to bite her nice wigglin arse."

McManus watched his rear-view mirror.

"She'd make a right good fuck," Kelly said. Then, resentfully, "Just think of that fuckin soldier fuckin her." He thought about that. "Jever fuck a Protestant, McManus?"

McManus could see a gaggle of girls coming up the street. One came alone, some distance behind them.

"Did'y hear me, McManus?"

"Yes."

"Well, did you?"

"Mind your work."

Kelly twisted and looked back through the rear window. "That's the bitch behind."

Powers and Callaghan were walking back now, towards the car. The chattering girls passed them. The solitary girl drew level. McManus moved the car with her. She was pretty and shapely and her bottom swiveled.

"She's askin for it," Kelly said, "look at her wigglin her arse."

Her hair was long and auburn, soft and well cared for. McManus wanted to shout to her to run for it. But where would she run? Almost every woman on the street would try to stop her. They were at their doors now, watching and waiting and smiling. Nobody had spoken to the girl for weeks, except to say "hoore" as they passed her. The children had chalked "hoore" on the walls of her parents' house, and their mothers had painted it back when the girl's father washed it off, and their fathers and brothers had beaten him when he tried to burn off the paint with a blowlamp. And the McGonigals had nowhere else to go. So they lived with silence or abuse and went a long way from the district to buy their food, where nobody knew them and could not therefore refuse to sell to them.

Powers and Callaghan blocked her way. She tried to walk around them and Callaghan moved to stop her. "Just a minute, you," he said.

"Will you leave me alone," she said and tried to pass around Powers.

"Get into the car," he said.

Then she knew. McManus looked the other way.

"You leave me alone," she said helplessly.

The women were leaving their doorsteps, grinning, moving down to the curb.

Powers reached for her and she screamed and clawed at his face. His grab for her hands came too late. She got her nails to his face and lashed at his shins with her feet. Callaghan came in behind, his arms around her. He closed his hands over her breasts and squeezed as he dragged her back. Her screams tore the street and her father came roaring from his house, a club in his hand. The women were on him from behind, and he went down on his face. A dozen of them tore at him, dragging on his club, kicking and stamping on him. "Run, run," he howled to his daughter as he scrambled to his knees and was kicked back to the ground.

But she couldn't run. The rear door of the car was open and Callaghan and Powers had her halfway in. Kelly took a handful of her hair and hauled on it.

"You won't have it long, you dirty wee hoore," he told her and yanked her through the door.

They had her across their knees when Powers got in beside McManus. "Away on," he snapped, and put his hand to his bleeding face. "The last lamp post at the end of the street."

She was no longer screaming; only sobbing in terror. The women were running up the street after the car, the father stumbling behind them washed in his own blood, beaten with his own club which had been clawed from his hands.

Everything they needed was neatly packed in a cardboard box in the boot—a gallon can of black paint and a stick to stir it, a pair of barber's scissors and a nylon clothes line. Powers and Callaghan held her and Kelly tied the girl's ankles and wrists to the lamp post. "Shift the motor into the clear and keep the engine goin'," Powers told McManus, and he moved the car forward along the street from the gathering crowd of women and children.

A twelve-year-old girl stirred the paint, singing into and under the shrieking, laughing turmoil of bodies and voices:

"Oh! see the fleet-foot hosts of men who speed with faces wan,
From farmstead and from fisher's cot upon the banks of Bann.
They come with vengeance in their eyes, too late, too late are they,
For Roddy McCorley goes to die on the Bridge of Toome today."

She might have been busy on some classroom project. She had been reared on songs of this sort, at home and in the church school she went to—her mind was filled with Ireland's wrongs, for Ireland's history, her teachers told her, "is a catalogue of wrongs," none of them Irish. The child felt nothing for the now still and silent girl at the lamp post. Mavis was suffering no wrong; she had been found wanting in loyalty and solidarity; she was engaged to a soldier; Mavis was a hoore, and that was neither Irish nor good.

A large fat woman took handfuls of Mavis's soft auburn hair in her big fist, slapped the girl's head back against the lamp post, and snipped the hair off close to the scalp. The girl's eyes were shut, her hair was tossed in the air; children fought for it as it fell.

When that work was done an angular woman with the face of a bitter man took the can of black paint from the stirring, singing child and upended it above the bound girl's head. It oozed thickly down her face and head onto her summer shoulders, blackening her pretty blue-and-white dress, draining over and between her white little breasts. Wiping out her self. She was a rag doll, slumped forward and down, her head lolling, her knees bent, without speech. She was nothing.

On the edge of the ring her father fought the furious women to

20   ((

reach his child and was battered again with his own club. They tore at his head, clawed his face, and gathered his flesh under their nails, beat him again to the ground, kicking him in the stomach, the back, the face, the groin, jumping on his feet and ankles, hooting, howling, screaming in deranged triumph. The man lay still.

The circle danced; fat women jigged around the lamp post and the girl, their skirts hauled high, big putty thighs bouncing and jiggling like sows' bellies. They jeered, sang, chanted, "The soldier's hoore, the soldier's hoore the soldier's hoore," and their children danced with them, chanting.

The father crawled on his hands and knees through the ring and they kicked him as he passed. He hauled himself to his feet and took his child in his arms to ease the pain in her wrists and ankles. His face was blackened by her painted head and he moaned, "Oh ma wee darlin ma wee darlin ma poor wee darlin . . ." and she could not look at him or speak to him for fear her eyes and her mouth would be filled with the paint.

The shotgun blasted like a cannon and some of the dancers were down, screaming, not chanting, bleeding, not drawing blood. They were on their faces in the street, their crying quick like panting, or long-drawn wails, or out-of-pitch foghorns on Belfast Lough. Their fat legs were torn, their fat backsides full of shot.

The discharge almost knocked the girl's little crippled bird-mother onto her back. She staggered backwards, her steel glasses tossed down to the tip of her nose, the stem dislodged from one ear. She knocked her glasses back onto her nose and the gun's barrels dipped, too weighty for one thin arm. She grabbed it quickly again with both hands.

Powers and Callaghan and Kelly were standing to one side. They moved together towards the woman.

"I'll take the gun, missus," Powers said in his leader voice.

"You dirty cannibal," she yelled. "Come near me and I'll kill you." The idea pressed in her mind and she screamed, *"Kill you, kill you, kill you!"* She looked around wildly at the frozen women on their feet and the moaning women on their faces and the gun swung with her look, *"Filthy, filthy, filthy muck,"* she screamed at them and swung the gun back to the three men.

"You, you dirty wee turd," she shrieked at Kelly, "you tied her. You cut her loose."

Kelly did it quickly. "Take her home, Sam," the maimed little kestrel said to her husband.

"Oh mammie, mammie," he wept and half-carried their child out of the malignant ring.

"Yis kin get up off yer fat bellies and git away from me now," the little woman said. "All but you, ye filthy dog-dirt," she said to Kelly.

Moaning and crying and bleeding and wronged the women backed and limped and bled away, and Powers and Callaghan backed with them.

"Stan in the front o'me," she shrieked at the waiting Kelly. "You're the one that tied her," she screamed, and pointed the shotgun at his legs and squeezed the trigger. But it was harder to pull than it had been before. She was frightened now and weakened by the storm, and the dragging with two fingers on the trigger lifted the barrel of the gun from Kelly's legs. She scattered his guts for yards over the paint-stained street.

The kick of the gun threw her back on her heels and she sat down in the street. Kelly lay about her, his eyes staring at the lamp post. He was eighteen. He had never had a job and had never looked for one. It had never mattered before. There was always British welfare. Now it would never matter. The little woman got up slowly and picked up the shotgun. They watched her limp awkwardly away to her house and her husband and her child.

Powers and Callaghan walked to the car. Somebody could look after what there was of Kelly. He was non-operational now. McManus drove them away.

((

"That one's a vicious oul bitch," Powers said like a man who had been wronged and could see no reason for it.

That night the McGonigals' house burned down. Mavis was in the Royal Victoria Hospital. Her father and mother had no such refuge. The army took them in. Young soldiers fed and sheltered them.

"Here, m'am, take some of this," they said, and tried to coax tea or soup or something into her.

The mother and father sat, huddled and staring but not seeing. "Oh ma poor wee darlin," the man intoned like a litany and his tears were endless. The woman sat stiffly and like a corpse and stared in tearless desolation at nothing or some secret thing.

The police came for them in the morning, big red-faced men in middle life. One of them coaxed gently, "Come on, missus, don't be afeard now. Nothin's gonta harm you. Your wee girl's gettin better."

"Do you have to part them, constable?" a young army officer asked him.

"Och, no, sur, nothin of the sort, sur," he said, "we're just gonta tuck them away where there's no harm. Poor oul souls. Och, that poor wee girl. They're a right parcela fuckin cunts, thon boys." He looked uneasily at the officer. "If you'll excuse that class of talk, sur."

McManus wrote his letter to his sister on his scraps of soiled newsprint in the dark, under the covers. It said:

1. When 2. you 3. get 4. my 5. next 6. letter 7. please 8. do 9. exactly 10. what 11. it 12. says 13. or I'm 14. dead 15. Johnny.

THREE

Botched operations have to be explained. Simple operations that are badly botched have to be explained away.

Powers stood stiffly before the kitchen table in the house in Andersonstown and cast a cold eye on the three men who sat stiffly behind it. Their voices lapped about his ears; one part of his mind listened for sudden questions; the rest of it swam in a pool of obscenities that were the only words he could find to fit his judgment of his judges.

McCann glowered up into Powers' muscle-tight face and said, "It was a plain wee job. Four trained men and the Springfield Women's Revenge Committee had to tar and feather one wee hoore five feet to the top of her skull and six-stone weight. Christ, one of youse coulda done it handcuffed. The wee girl's oul man was let get her away and her wee limpin oul mother shot the arses off half the committee and spread Kelly's guts all over the street. There'll be an accountin. . . ."

Powers stared straight back at him and thought, ". . . big-mouthed arse-hole. When was the last time you handled a gun? What are you, anyway, stickin out your poor wee chest. . . ."

There were blocks of silence in the small kitchen. They isolated words and thoughts in sharp metallic channels, enlarging them in the mind, barbing them in the air that was sour with malice and suspicion and jealousy.

McCandless was on the right behind the table. "It's a pity,

Powers, a great pity," he said in his high-toned way. "Whatever we do, however simple, even a small act of social discipline like this, has to be done properly. The Official IRA would like to see us back in their yard. You gave them a chance to laugh at us. An act of discipline botched by you and defeated by an old crippled woman. If the Catholic *community* laughs at us, let alone the Officials . . . where are we, I ask you, where are we? Done!"

Powers settled his stony face in McCandless's direction and thought, ". . . you're past it too, y'girnin oul woman . . ." but all that could be seen in his expression was the disciplined submission of a good soldier.

Clune spoke of propaganda losses, of the wee cripple who defied the power and authority of the Provisional IRA and made it a comic spectacle in the English papers. "They'll read about this in America too. Are you tryin to stop the money comin?"

Powers heard it out. He had no choice. The rules of evidence had no meaning here. There was no right to be heard. "Internment without charge or trial" was a good propaganda line in the *London Times* or the *New York Times* and in the French and West German and Swedish papers when it was made against the British, but it was a public bludgeon for the enemy; it had no relevance to these courts. They were "different." They had right on their side; they were Irish; they were the courts of the wronged and the blameless; there was neither time, nor inclination, nor reason to apply the rules of evidence here. So Powers waited for the word.

"Well?" Clune gave him the word.

"Fair enough," Powers said. "There's no word of a lie in what you're sayin." He remembered the time an innkeeper from the West Country told him the greatest asset Ireland ever had was "the Irish smile that disarmed the world and made enemies think they were safe." The three of them sittin there like the Holy bloody Trinity were ignorant has-beens but the innkeeper from the West had a word for them too: "Sure, tellin a bloody lie to an eejit is a sort of kindness." "I'm the one that's to blame," he said. "That's why I feel bad about makin a third bad report on McManus. I'm not sayin he's to blame about the girl. It's worse than that or I wouldn't be bringin it up again."

"Well, bring it up." That was Clune with the wee thin face and the hot eyes. He was born in the Markets and wanted no la-de-da's from universities and places like that in their ranks. Soft bellies and softer heads, he said.

Powers gave Clune his steady look and focused on his social envy. "He gets worse," he said. "When we blew up the Carleton Restaurant" (seven dead and forty-five mutilated) "he said it was planned by a stupid fool," (Clune planned it) "and done by a stupid savage" (Clune's brother carried it out).

He gave McCann his steady look. McCann's most recent planning exploit was the Chester Hotel (four dead, six blinded, four without arms, two with legs lost, and twenty more in the hospital). "He was screamin about that. He came here to fight soldiers, not commercial travelers and wee office girls," he said. "He said it was thought up by a cowardly barbarian."

"The girl, Powers. Get to the girl," McCandless said. Let's stick to the point at issue, McCandless always, always said, like some fuckin professor.

"Yes, sir." Powers got to the girl. "McManus was drivin," he said. "When we got her to the lamp post I told him to keep his eye on the street in the direction of the girl's house. He didn't. He went and sat in the car."

"He refused to do his job?" McCandless said.

"No, sir. He was against tarrin the wee hoore. He said he wasn't goin at first. Then he just didn't do his job. I had my hands full at the lamp post. I couldn't see through the crowd. It was his job to watch the rear. He just didn't do it. That's how the wee woman got in behind us with the shotgun." He wiped the corners of his mouth with his fingertips. "He's not with us, sir," he said to Mc-Candless, and added his solemn judgment. "He's against us. He's weak. He's a danger. One of these days he's gonta try to run and if he gets away he's gonta run straight to the army."

"You know that?" Clune said.

"Yes, sir." He gave his mouth another wipe and said. "It's his talk. When the order was made to shoot Protestants in the street to try to make the Orangemen attack the Catholic districts, he said the men assigned to it and the men that ordered it shouldn't go to Long Kesh—they should go to the gallows, he said. We should turn them in, he said, they're nothin but common murderers." That was the right fuckin line. Your father could rape half the women on the street and you could live it down, but if your great-grandfather informed, your great-grandchildren would pass the mark of it to theirs. Nothin set the nerves shiverin and the blood boilin like the fuckin thought of an informer. Questions? Proof? No fuckin questions, no fuckin proof—*they* took time and chances. Powers gave them all his steady look. "I'm askin now that you take him from me. I can't trust him. He cost us Kelly. Who'll he cost us next?"

The silence he got was the silence he wanted. He could feel the judgment in their personal spleen. He could see them translating it into justice.

Clune said through the festering air, "Away on out. We'll call you."

Powers smoked a cigarette in the street and worked out the odds, his back against the wall of the house. McManus had been nine months in this army. Powers had been in from the firing of the first shot. His loyalty was clear, his zeal unquestionable. He had four soldiers and a policeman to his credit. He was born in the Falls and had never lived outside the district.

The children playing ball games and hopscotch on the street called to him. "Hullo, Pat," they said, or "How're'y, Mr. Powers?" Wasn't he a hero in the Falls? The women on their doorsteps shouted, "Havin a smoke, Pat?" and, "Cuppa tea, Pat?" Didn't they thank God the likes of him were here to keep them safe from the Orange? And didn't the boys scare the shit outa them anyway? Who wanted it in the knees?

Mary Connors the widow paused on her way down the street and tried to look casual.

"The night, Pat?"

"I don't know yet."

"Trouble?"

"A wee bit—maybe."

"I'm fizzin—ready to be corked."

"If I can, Mary."

She walked on, under the women's attentive eyes. Anybody can give the time of day to one of the boys.

Powers didn't look after her. How the hell can she expect me to come up to her house with a hard cock and do her or me any good when I'm in this sorta trouble, he wondered impatiently, and got his mind back to McManus.

What was McManus with his la-de-da ways and his Antrim Road manners? Sure he was only a student, a middle-class Catholic brought up on the Antrim Road among middle-class Protestants. It had taken him at least three years to decide to offer his services to the IRA. That implied doubt and argued a lack of ardor or conviction. He was argumentative, talked fancy, and questioned the judgment of the leadership. He wasn't ghetto, he wasn't workin class, he wasn't safe. "Them," said Clune of Ulster's middle-class Catholics, "they're just greedy fuckin Protestants that cross themselves." Powers could depend on Clune in there. McManus finished his degree before he came to offer his services. That proved somethin. Ireland One Nation didn't matter a damn to him. First, he got himself ready to take a good job when the Border was burned off the Irish map; after that he came to help with the burnin.

When McCandless opened the door and called Powers, his balance sheet was in good order.

But it wasn't Clune who spoke. McCandless did the talking.

"The purpose of the present policy of street assassinations," he said in what to Powers was his pompous way, "is to make the Loyalists attack the Catholic districts so that we can keep the loyalty of the Catholics and tighten our grip on them. I don't need to tell you that, Powers."

"No." Then why the fuckin hell tell me, you puffed-up windbag?

"We've got to make them fight. The more chaos—civil war at the least—the more chance we have of getting the British out and the United Nations in, and the Border cleared away."

"Yes." Everybody knew that. Why the pompous bloody lecture?

"We've reached a decision. You'll carry it out."

That was better. "Yes, sir."

"You'll take Callaghan and McManus and shoot a brace of Shankill Protestants." Brace, for Jasus sake. Say two, you stupid arse.

"Yes, sir." That was all right. But what about McManus, you big windbag?

"McManus will be on the gun." McCandless smiled like a thought reader.

Holy Jasus. You do the bastard up and they give him a gun.

"And if he doesn't obey orders—if he tries to get out of them *at all in any way*—take him up the Black Mountain and don't bring him back."

Don't be eager. "Yes, sir."

"And if he does the work—report how he does it."

"Yes, sir."

That was fine. They blamed him for the Mavis McGonigal business, but they still trusted him, as far as anybody trusted anybody, and that wasn't too far.

He was to sit in judgment on McManus. What he said about him would have the power of life or death over the la-de-da bastard. He couldn't have explained why he hated McManus. La-de-da. Everythin about him. He had no business in the Falls. The looks he gave them. The way he talked. The questions he asked.

(The day after he came, "How do you get a bath around here?" for Christ's sake. In a district that hadn't a bath in it? "Y'go to the public fuckin baths like everybody that wants one." La-de-da.)

He breathed the power and went back to their house. There was nobody in it. Hadn't he told McManus to stay in the house? He began to compose the report on McManus's performance on an assassination exercise that hadn't taken place.

He found Callaghan and McManus at the postbox not far from the house. They were stuffing the box with pages from old copies of the *Irish News*.

"I thought I told ye not to leave the house? What the hell d'you think you're doin?"

Callaghan looked sheepish. "Ony for fun, Pat."

"Who thinks that's funny?"

"I do," McManus said, and felt the blast in his face. His legs were weak. He felt transparent. "We only wanted to make the postman dig through this stuff to get the letters." The best lie, their propagandists said, was closest to the truth.

"What letters?"

It sounded to McManus's guilty mind like an accusation based on certain knowledge.

"The letters in the box," he said, and tried not to look back into Powers' accusing glare. He tried harder not to evade his eye and felt evasively cross-eyed. He rolled the rest of the newspaper and slapped his treacherous thighs.

Powers snatched the paper from him and dug demonstratively for matches. He lit the paper and reached for the mouth of the postbox. "Is that all they taught you at the university? Are'y tryin to make policy now, McManus?" It was a right good line. Hadn't he just come from Clune and McCann and McCandless and what did these blirts know about what passed there?

"Och, for Jasus sake, Pat," Callaghan protested, "my oul woman put a letter in there a wee minute ago."

Powers dropped the burning paper to the ground and a child

darted in to pick it up. "Away on back to the house," he said, and tried to read McManus's face. He was, he believed, a reliable reader of faces. Leaders need to be.

He believed also that he was a shrewd manipulator of men. They walked to the new car at seven o'clock and only Powers knew where they were going, or why.

Twice, Callaghan asked him what the job was. McManus did not, and Powers turned that over in his mind.

McManus thought about it too, and decided his silence was a mistake. "If the car's loaded with gelignite, I should be thinking about a good route," he said carefully, "to wherever we're leaving it." He had never needed to say that before. It was too careful without being casual enough. Powers didn't answer him. He couldn't immediately think of anything to say but he knew that silence is a disturbing weapon.

McManus felt the warning in his silence. He was being taken to a court, he was certain. His sister would get his letter in the morning if the postman didn't lose it throwing away all that paper in the postbox, and in the evening she would read in the *Telegraph* that a man had been found in a ditch, a black hood over his head. Another IRA execution, the *Telegraph* would explain. Sickly, he walked to the car. If he ran, they would wound him from behind and have to shoot him more than once. If it was a court, it would all be over in one shot. He would probably be crying as he turned his back to wait for it. He wanted to cry now and fought it away. Everything was pointless—fear, grief, tears, regret, contempt. He tried to suffocate thought and scarcely felt the granite sidewalk under his feet and did not see the car when they came to it.

"I'll drive," Powers said. "Up wi me, Danny. In the back, Mc-Manus."

McManus was not aware of Powers' self-consciously searching

32 ((

stare. He was not aware of anything till they were passing through Castle Junction in the center of the city. It came to him slowly that if he was on his way to meet a court, they would not be here. He paid attention.

Royal Avenue, York Street, Duncairn Gardens, the Antrim Road. The whole trip was one of those malignant acts of gleeful Irish sadism. They'd already had their court and he was destined for a ditch beyond the edge of the city. Why else was Callaghan sitting sideways, watching him like a cat? They were going to drive him to the execution ground past his own home. They liked sadistic symbolism. Symbology, one of those glass-eyed American specialists in Irish affairs called it in a book in his last course at Queens.

But they turned into Cliftonville Road, into Manor Street, down Crumlin to Agnes Street, and out of Agnes onto Shankill. They went up the length of Shankill, turned on Woodvale, and came back.

"Under your seat, McManus," Powers said. "Put your hand down."

When his hand touched the gun in its sacking, he knew what it was all about and slid his hand between his thighs to hide its shaking. He heard Powers mutter something to Callaghan but couldn't tell what it was. He hadn't been listening anyway.

When he straightened up, Callaghan's jacket bulged towards him like a tent peak. The man was grinning.

"Pick yourself two Shankill Protestants, McManus. At the corner of Northumberland," Powers said, and there was gloating challenge in his voice.

It didn't take brains to work it out. He hadn't covered his thoughts well enough. They were like animals tasting the moving air, fearful always of treachery, dissent, doubt, and they dealt with them or with what they suspected with the paranoid ruthlessness of gnawing insecurity. Sidelong he watched the tent peak in Callaghan's jacket and lifted the gun to his knees.

The street was crowded. Some idle walker was about to die because men who killed with ease and without conscience wanted to examine the state of his mind. He put his hand through the hole in the canvas bag around the gun, released the safety, and curled his finger on the trigger. His back was tight in the corner of the back seat. There was no finesse in this sort of thing. The window was down. He had to press hard against the door behind him, use the gun as an extension of a pointing left arm, and squeeze for one quick burst. That, or sit under Callaghan's gun till they got him to the edge of town. Then they would kill him. They would tell him they were sorry, but it was for "Ireland One Nation, and this is no time for treachery." They were haunted by treachery.

He wanted to live. The yearning to live burned in his chest like oncoming indigestion.

"The Boyne Water," he said. His throat was rough and tight. The pub was three hundred yards ahead, on their left, and only a quick jump from the right turn that gave them a short run along Northumberland and back into the Falls. There were always lounging corner-boys on the corner of Agnes Street. There was nothing in his head.

He could see The Boyne Water a hundred yards ahead. There were half a dozen young men leaning against the building on the corner. If it had to be them or him, it would be them.

"Go," he said, and Powers whipped the car out of its line of traffic and back again, ahead of three obstructing cars. In his corner-eyed vision, McManus saw a scruffy shambling figure step out of the front door of the pub. There was a clear line of fire to the wino and the men on the corner were covered by women walkers. He lifted the gun, put his burst into the blocked doorway where the drunk stood looking foolishly about him, his limp hands dangling chest high. The gun dropped to the floor, the car seemed to lift its front end off the ground, and McManus, facing across the seat, was heaved forward on his face as Powers took it into the right-hand turn, weaving and roaring in second through the traffic into the Falls. There wasn't time for the sounds of the street to be

34

rearranged by a scream. All McManus saw was the drunk lurching backwards into the doorway as if he had been pushed. That was all. There wasn't time to see him fall. Killing was so easy.

"One bloody drunk," Powers said.

They got off the Falls Road into the little streets at a discreet speed and stopped at their front door. "Clean the gun," Powers said, and took the car away to be dumped. Clean the gun. First things first. He *was* a wino, McManus assured himself. He *looked* like a wino, he said. I *think* he looked like a wino, he told himself, and cleaned the gun while Callaghan watched him curiously.

"The fuckin street was packed and you pick one bloody drunk," Callaghan said, and spat into the range.

Killing a wino in the street—if he was a wino—wasn't a small thing, but then, neither was a shot in the back of the head. And he had after all picked the wino, if he was a wino. His line of fire was blocked to the men on the corner of Agnes Street by women and families walking. Killing them would have been better political provocation than a miserable wino, but his own life had to be lived after it was saved. He couldn't shoot them. But the drunk wasn't enough. They'd both made that clear. A kind of throw-away? A lame evasion? "One bloody drunk." Powers was away reporting. He knew that. They sent men on operations to test a suspected failure of nerve or loyalty. If it was only nerve, they sent him south to rest. If it was loyalty, they sent him to the ditch. "One bloody drunk," Powers' report would say. He was for the ditch and Callaghan was watching him like a hungry cat.

When Powers took two hours to come back and brought with him two men McManus had never seen, he knew the wino wasn't enough.

"You're movin," Powers said. "They'll take you."

In the past, after any operation in which he had been involved, he had always moved on his own. Now he was moving under what was in effect an escort, and his escort didn't speak to him. When he got to his new hiding place in the Markets, there were two other men in the house. They didn't speak to him. They didn't look at him. He felt his own stuffing turn to lard and didn't try to speak to them. They pointed to his bed.

He didn't sleep. The signs spun in his head. These four men in the Markets treated him as if they could shoot him a lot more readily than give him the time of day. That made nine people who knew he was a question mark. If nine people knew, it wouldn't be long before a lot more people knew, and who would trust him? They'd refuse to work with him or be known to him. That's what the rank and file did when they wanted a man put away. If he was distrusted he couldn't survive. A question mark who was picked up by the army or the Royal Ulster Constabulary would name names and places to save his own skin. Even though he didn't know much, it would be too much. In this violent machine there was neither time nor room nor inclination to make fine distinctions: questions were dangers; stop the questioners and remove the dangers. The rules of evidence were for bloody Englishmen trying bloody Englishmen. If you can't be certain, make certain: that was the rule here. His mind ran hopelessly over his blunders.

He was moved again on the second day, from the Markets to a house in Ardoyne. These new men talked no more than the others. There was about all of them something he hadn't noticed about his countrymen when he knew only his middle-class Catholic and Protestant neighbors and friends outside the ghettos. Even in repose, even when they were bubbling with the charm and humor that wore thin on sustained acquaintance, there was about them a disturbing atmosphere of impending eruption. He learned quickly that words and looks and attitudes which were part of the daily commerce of middle-class life could provoke in these men in the midst of laughter the most violent offense. It was as if there was in them a lurking watchful hysteria. Even the withdrawn coldness of his guards in the Markets and here in Ardoyne was like a fuse waiting for a match.

The match came the night he arrived at the house in Ardoyne. He was taken to a back room. The window was boarded up. There were two palliasses on the floor, and two kitchen chairs; nothing else. The door was locked behind him. He had not spoken a word, or been spoken to, for twenty-four hours, except to say, in the Markets, "I need to go to the water closet." In this house he would be able to say bathroom. He had seen the bathroom on his way upstairs.

About an hour after he lay down on his straw mattress they brought a boy to the room and pushed him inside. His right eyebrow was split and bleeding. His nose was bent and bleeding. He was, McManus thought, about fifteen. His crossed wrists were tied very tightly behind his back. He was sobbing.

The man who brought him stood in the doorway and looked at them both. He was rigid with cold fury. "Coupla dirty cunts," he said, and slammed and locked the door.

The boy sat down heavily in one of the chairs. The impact hurt his beating head and he cried without restraint. "I niver done it, mister," he said pathetically.

"You never did what?"

"I niver spied for the sojers."

"What did you do?"

"I ony talk t'them, y'know? They give me a few fags. M'da was a sojer. I jist like the army, y'know? But I wudn't tell on these boys."

"I know."

"They didn't bate you yet?"

"Not yet."

"What'd you do?"

"I thought."

"My hans are awful sore."

)) 37

They were purple. The cords were cutting the boy's wrists. Mc-Manus worked at them patiently in the darkened room till they were untied. "Lie down," he said, and lay down himself.

The boy's voice had a peculiar nasal tone. "I think they broke my nose," he said, and cried again. "My ma'll be outa her head. They come and got me outa the house."

"Did they beat you in front of her?"

"Aye. She was on her knees t'them and her legs is bad. When she gets down she can't get up. Y'know?"

"I know."

"Holy God." It gathered up all his terrors, for himself and his mother. "M'da's dead," he said desolately. "O, Christ Jasus, da, da, da," he wailed in lonely misery and fear.

McManus sat up and braced himself into the angle of the wall. The light went out on the landing and the room was in total darkness. The night chill settled and he folded his arms and shrank into himself for a little warmth. There was no sound in the house except an occasional shudder and a deep sob from the boy on the straw mattress. There was no blanket to cover him. The night settled. The sounds of the street died. The boy was still. McManus dozed and woke, stirred and settled and dozed.

He woke suddenly, angry from a dream of his father being beaten by Powers. His father's nose was broken. His mother was kicked when she tried to help him. His sister was thrown deep into water that was ill-defined in the dream but as dreams are, he knew it was Belfast Lough. He woke to her cries and couldn't help her.

The black was pitch. He was deeply chilled. His anger transferred itself from the abusers in his dream to his own pathetic and passive attempts at self-preservation. In the dark chill his fury grew and warmed him. He fought for his school, he fought for his university. Last year he fought for his country when they smashed America's golden gloves team and put them in order to the canvas. But he kept a self-preserving stillness and silence among these psychotic scum. His anger boiled till he sweated. He went to sleep without knowing it, still packed into the angle of the corner walls.

When the door slammed back against the wall behind it, he threw up his arms defensively. The boy did not wake. A man was standing in the light of the door, fitting a light bulb into the empty socket in the ceiling. He switched on the light. Neither light nor sound woke the boy. Two men stood on the landing, looking in.

The man in the room kicked the boy in the leg. He woke suddenly, confused, half-blind, cowering. "Sit in the chair," the man said.

"Yes, mister." The boy put his hands to the mattress for support, and made little sounds of pain. "Oh, m'wrists," he said.

"Who took the cord off?" the man said without looking at Mc-Manus.

McManus said, "I did. They were cutting him. Look at his wrists."

"Where's the cord?"

"In my pocket."

"Throw it t'me."

"No."

The man grinned, spreading it across his face like an infection. "That's the way of it, is it?"

The boy was sitting in a chair, his head hanging.

The man said to him, "What'd you tell the sojers and when you talk to me look at me."

The boy raised his head to speak and the man shot a vicious right into his mouth. The chair tilted backwards, the boy gave out a choked and terrified sound, and boy and chair-back went over onto McManus.

"Shove him back," the man said. "Come on, shove the lyin wee cunt up here."

McManus tilted the boy gently from the chair to the mattress and pushed the chair aside. He got up slowly, picked up the other mattress, and covered the boy.

"What the fuckin hell d'y think you're doin?"

McManus was bent half-over the boy. He spun and straightened his right leg as he hooked into the man's guts, low down. The face came down and forward, uttering a long weird sound, and McManus was set. He hooked left and right to the sides of the face, crouched and uppercut the nose as it swung back onto his knuckles. He felt the nose fold. The body whipped up, bent backwards, and fell, its head at the feet of the two men standing on the landing. They pulled the body away and came back to the door. They did not try to come into the room but their eyes had blazing in them the peculiar light of a high Irish dementia that is never quite concealed by its own thin surface. One of them yelled, "Liam!" and the sound broke, shrill, against the roof of his mouth.

"What?" from downstairs.

"Up here."

"Did one of youse fall off the landin?"

"Up here!"

McManus thought of the chairs, but his fighting room was too confined. He could do more damage with his feet and fists. He moved closer to the door and waited. Three of them would take a while to get through the narrow doorway.

Liam appeared on the landing. He looked at the man on the floor, his nose flattened against his face. "Christ, aye," he said. "I see what y'mean." He looked in at McManus. "Aye," he said, and charged.

McManus met him with a jab and a straight right that sent him back to the landing, his mouth mashed and bleeding. He tried to say something but his mouth wasn't working properly. He pulled out the tail of his shirt and dragged it up to his mouth. The lower buttons of the shirt flew off and tinkled on the landing. He touched the shirttail to his mouth, looked at the blood, held up three fingers at the other two, nodded, and charged again.

He had to come first, the other two behind his shoulders. He came low, going lower as he came, and McManus kicked. The lifting right foot with the left leg extended behind it from the toe would have put a rugby ball into orbit. McManus felt the impact through his foot and leg. He felt the face collapse and saw the body fall away, spun sideways into the path of the man to the left. The one to the right came on, going low, and there wasn't time to recover and kick again. He tried to ram the charging head down onto his rising knee, but the face merely dug against his thigh and the man's arms were around his waist, rushing him back against the boarded window. The other one lifted a chair, smashed it against the floor, and came at him with one of the jagged legs.

McManus was pounding at the base of the neck of the man who held him against the boards, but his head was tucked tight against McManus's side and the blows were ineffective. The man's arms slid down over his rump and fastened tight around his legs. McManus threw up his hands to protect his head from the swinging chair-leg and the wood smashed his hands away and rose again and fell, raking his neck and again, on the rise of his shoulder. His left arm dropped. He yelled in pain and rage and the man holding his legs keeled over. McManus keeled with him and the man with the chair-leg got him on the chin. He wasn't out, but he was going. He was on the ground and they were kicking. He rolled in a ball, his arms around his face and head, and took the chair-leg and the boots on his shoulders and thighs and rump and backside. And on his hands and wrists. Slowly and painfully he slipped away. The last thing he heard was the lunatic whimpering and guttural whinnying of the men who were kicking the consciousness out of him, and the screaming of the beaten boy, who was being trampled like a lumped-up rug.

FOUR

McMANUS was tied to his chair when he drifted painfully back. After an uncertain while, in the light from under the door, he dimly saw the boy tied to another chair.

"Y're there are'y, mister?" the boy said. His hair was long. His pale face shone ghostily through it; its cuts and bruises were like shadows. "They give youse an awful batterin, mister," he said plaintively.

It was old news and poor comfort. Every bone and muscle in McManus's body ached from the battering; there was half-dried blood on his face and neck; the fingers of his hacked hands stuck together behind the back of his chair and the cords sawed at his wrists. In his unconscious state his wrists had taken the weight of his slumping body.

Resolutely he tried to escape out of the pain into a hard look at his follies. Why is it only in Ireland, he wondered, that a man looks straight at you and asks you if you're there? Because we are confronted by so many welcome illusions? Because we lie first to ourselves and then to everybody else? Has lying become so deeply a part of the texture of our being that we can no longer believe ourselves? "Y're there, are'y, mister?" Peering into your face.

Maybe it wasn't lying in the ordinary sense? Maybe it was communal suction, when lie and truth and half-truth and the screeching collective emotion swamps the senses and draws you into a pool you don't want to swim in? Maybe the stronger ones stayed on the sidelines, waiting to "deplore" the losers—denounce meant something else and something more and was an impolite word—and make conciliating noises to the winners? In the North, the Catholics were always the losers; born losers. The middle-class Catholics with cold unromantic minds waited it out; but now and then there was an immature one, a less calculating, less stable one who suddenly felt the communal suction and for a while couldn't calculate his own long-term interest.

That's me, McManus thought—Holy God, I can eat my own weight in apes if you put me in a ring with eight-ounce gloves on, and I'm water in the stream when the crowd roars or the songs make my roots tremble.

He remembered walking away from Convocation at the university, his degree clutched in his hand. That walk brought him to this house and this battering, by way of his friend and former history master's study.

When the pleasantries were over he told Bull Baillie, "Now I'm going to the gun. There's nothing more to keep me." He could hear the old man's approval before his announcement died in his mouth. He needed the old man's approval. Bull Baillie had bred in him a need to walk the hills with Ossian and McMorna and Cuchullain "and walk"—his father said—"in an Irish shroud." It was Bull who roared his pleasure over the names of the political parties in the South and told his classes, "Listen to the ring of them, boys, Fianna Fail, The Warriors of Destiny. Fine Gael, The Tribe of Gaels! Roots! They have roots! No political party in Ireland that doesn't reach back to the Gael through Tone to Finn and the ancient Fianna will ever get off the ground. *The Labor Party?* Good God! *The Labor Party!* What a name! No color, no roots, no ring, no history—in Ireland, no future!"

They believed him. Didn't he read them things like Willie Fellows' letter to his darling mother before his own countrymen shot him in Mountjoy Prison in 1922 . . . ? God, he could put steam into Willie's words . . . McManus could hear him . . . he could see him in his head, as if through a plate-glass window of the mind, in the class; in his study when he went to see him after Convocation. . . .

"Welcome be the will of God, for Ireland is in His keeping despite foreign monarchs and treaties. Though unworthy of the greatest human honor that can be paid an Irishman or woman, I go to join Tone, Emmet, the Fenians, Tom Clarke, Connolly. . . ." God, that litany. "You must not grieve, Mother Darling. . . ."

And Bull Baillie . . . tweed was part of the persona he put on the day he started teaching, and untidy hair that drifted about. He smelled of sweat and tobacco in the winter and McManus had never seen him in anything but tweed. He could see him now in his study, raising his shaggy old head and plucking at a leather button on his waistcoat, his head cocked and his eyes slyly laughing. "Holy God," he said.

Not, "Good boy. Great. Grand. Lovely." Just "Holy God." In an astonished, disbelieving, ironical tone of voice. "You're coddin me, Johnny."

"I'm not codding you." He felt hollow already. He had written the scene on his way here. It wasn't working. He was disturbed and disappointed. Frightened, maybe. Bull *had* to approve.

"By Jasus, I need a drink. Will I pour you one?"

"No."

The master went to a sideboard and poured his own. "Holy Jasus. You're not pullin my leg?"

"No."

McManus watched it again through the plate-glass window with his eyes closed, his head hanging. It might all have been different if this moment had been different. If Bull had said something else. . . .

He said, "Not you, boy. Not Gentle Johnny McManus."

McManus could feel the sweat that broke on him then. He had said nothing. He felt rejection, humiliation. Yes, betrayal. This man

)) 45

helped to weave his Irish shroud and all he had to say now was, "Not you—Gentle Johnny McManus." As if he were some big tame animal in a television series. Gentle Johnny was what they called him when he was on the school boxing team because, they said, he always apologized to a fighter when he knocked him out. They laughed at him then. Bull was laughing at him now.

Bull said, "You wouldn't last a week. You're not the kind."

McManus sat, wounded and silent.

"You're offended. It's pourin out of your face."

There was more than that pouring out of his face. He hadn't merely been rejected. He was being dismissed. He wasn't the kind. What kind? Like Willie Fellows? What was he, then? Some bloody sissy?

"You're talking out of a different side of your mouth now, Mr. Baillie. I'll go."

"Sit there, for Jasus sake. Talk to me, boy."

"Don't 'boy' me." But he didn't go and he would have liked to cry. He didn't. It would prove something he was fighting not to believe about himself. Wasn't going to believe about himself. His middle-class Catholic friends could wait on the sidelines. He wasn't going to and he wasn't sure why.

And he wasn't coming here to tell Bull Baillie he was going to the gun, and then weakly sneak off to look for a job just because this old man said he wasn't the kind. He had more self-esteem than that, by God.

"You talked plenty in class," he said.

"All oul talk. Just oul talk. I regret every word of it. The guns weren't out in those days. It was great talk, like reading Gaelic poetry when you had four pints in you. You weren't meant to *do*. . . ." He was going on. Something was dawning on him as he talked. Or had dawned on him in the sound of the demolition by day and by night. He was confronted by it now in the person and intention of one of his old pupils. The unlikeliest one. "What makes you think any wrong we suffered was big enough to justify

46 ((

the killing of women and babies in furniture shops?" His anger was a confusion; it was against McManus and himself and the bombers and the Irish shroud.

"Christ, I'm guilty," he said miserably, and sat down and forgot his drink.

"You pumped it into us about the raw deal we get in Ulster and now you're telling me we've suffered no wrongs?" McManus said, rebuilding his assurance.

"Oh Christ, boy, don't give me that stupid street-corner rhetoric —of course we suffered wrongs, but put today's nearly six hundred deaths against the fact that some Catholics can't get work in the Civil Service having stood up and said we want to destroy the state. Is it human to kill six hundred people for that? Is there no sense of proportion in us? Does mutilating babies equal gettin prestige jobs in a state we said we'd destroy? Ulster was *not* a Nazi state and there was no excuse for this wanton killin."

"And no jobs in the shipyards and no houses for Catholics who need them?" McManus said.

"A fact and a lie. All right, the shipyards are a Protestant preserve, but the houses—that's a civil rights lie and the IRA deeply influenced the civil rights movement. There's been no discrimination in housing since 1964—five years before the trouble started, and everybody who wants to know the truth knows it. The truth was established by Coleraine University in an inquiry led by an American and staffed by a group of Catholic scholars. During the sixties, Ulster was puttin up more housin than any other country in Western Europe. We're lyin and we're killin and you believe every bloody lie you're told because people like me got at you in Separate schools and filled you full of patriotic bullshit that gave us a lot of satisfaction and you a lot of illusions. By God, our priests and schoolteachers have a lot to answer for— first off, six hundred dead. We made people like you ready for the IRA not because we wanted you to kill but because we're emotional, self-indulgent bastards who never expect to have to answer for our self-indulgence and never expected you would do anythin but talk. *You* weren't ghetto Catholics. We could pour the stuff out on you without startin a fire. But there's damned little difference between the fools who *got* you ready and the IRA psychopaths who put you to work with a gun or a bomb *when* you're ready."

Baillie remembered his drink and gulped it down. "Johnny," he said. "It's none of these things, boy. There's cause for anger and there's need for change. But it's the killin, Johnny. They're *wanton* killers. They *like* killin. And you're not a killer. They won't put up with you, Johnny. They'll kill you."

That was ridiculous, of course. The silly old fool had never meant a word he said. All his life he'd been a boy among boys, a posturing Irish literary kind of figure—a Dublin poet-figure who talked away his poetry in pubs because it might turn out to be rotten if he wrote it down. McManus had heard about them.

He looked at his old master with bitter resentment. The man wasn't what he let on he was; the man was a coward. . . . "Why don't you say these things in public?" he said, scoring a point.

"That's easy, Johnny. Who'd hear me? Who'd let me? And best of all, boy—I'm afraid to."

That was it? He thought of his former middle-class Protestant friends who had quickly found him less than welcome where before the riots and the shooting started, he had been welcome. When the Protestant ghettos erupted in violence, he was still welcome but so was his silence. When the Catholic ghettos rioted, he suddenly was seen to be a Catholic and one with the ghettos, and not to be trusted. Sucked into and pushed into his communal prison, his anger grew and his myths enclosed him. The solution to his frustration grew in his mind. And the man who gave him his mythology laughed at his solution.

"Look, Johnny," Baillie said to his silence. "Look at me." The old man got up, ran to the far end of his room, and held out his palms defensively. *"Shoot* me, Johnny. Go on, *shoot* me—that's what it's all about now. *Killin,* boy. *Kill* me!"

Christ! There'ye are, are you, Baillie? Yes, by God, there he was. He was disgusting. A cowardly old playactor too. The man wasn't real. McManus picked up his rolled parchment in its little cylinder and got up.

"Christ!" he said, and made for the door.

"You're not the kind, Johnny. You're not the kind . . ." the old man shouted pathetically.

He slammed the door on the treacherous old fool . . . he wasn't *real.* . . .

"They'll eat you, Johnny, head and all," the old man shouted through the door. "They're the kind. . . ."

"The kind" were coming upstairs. They were not last night's lot. A woman led two men in. She was carrying a tray and on it two dishes of porridge, two spoons, and a miniature jug of milk. She was about thirty, black-haired, square-bodied, and big-bosomed with her bulky breasts tied down against her rib cage as if they were testimonies to crushed lust.

"There y'are," she said. "Did y'sleep well?" She set the dishes on their laps, put the spoons in them, poured a thimbleful of milk into each dish, and said, "There's yer breakfast. Ate up now."

Then the three of them leaned against the wall, their hands behind their rumps, and watched.

"I can't get at it, missus," the boy said with innocence. "My hands is tied."

"What did ye tell the sojers, McCartin?" the woman said.

"I niver told them nothin, missus. Honest to God. They just give me fags. M'da was a sojer. . . ."

"What'd they give you the fags for?"

"T'smoke," he said without guile.

"What did ye tell the sojers, ye dirty wee boy?"

"Nothin, missus. It's the God's honest truth, missus. I niver done it."

"What did ye tell the sojers, McCartin?"

She opened the boy's trousers and fumbled for his penis.

"Oh, please, missus." Shame and terror mingled.

She took it out. "I could cut it off ye," she said.

"Missus. . . ."

"Gimme a knife." One of them handed her a knife. She laid it against his small organ. "What did ye tell the sojers, McCartin?"

McCartin was crying. "Nothin, nothin, nothin," he whimpered, "Before God and the Holy Virgin, nothin, missus. . . ."

"Give him a spoonfula porridge," she said to the man beside her and handed him the knife.

The man took a spoonful of porridge and shot it into the boy's face. It hit him between the eyes and stuck, a little heap of surplus sliding down on either side of and over his flattened nose. He bent his head and some of the porridge plopped off his face into his lap.

"What did ye tell the sojers, McCartin?" the woman said again in her toneless voice.

"I niver told them nothin, missus. Please, missus, I told them nothin."

She stood beside him curling some strands of his long hair in her fingers. "Yer hair's durty," she said, and jerked it out by the roots.

The child squealed helplessly, "Oh, Jasus, missus. Please, missus." He didn't know how to appeal to her or plead his innocence.

She took a heavy handful of his hair, secured her grip, and jerked it viciously. McCartin yelled but the hair did not come away. She jammed one foot against his chair, swung her thick body, and hauled the second time. The hair came out. The wide bald patch on the boy's head seeped blood. She threw the hair on the floor. Its tiny white roots blinked under the naked light in the ceiling. Backhanded she struck the boy across his wounded face. He fell sideways and boy and chair lay helplessly imprisoning one another on their sides. He was crying desperately. She kicked him in the chest with the sensible shoes on her broad feet.

"If ye want any porridge, McManus, y'ony have t'ask fer it" she said, and they took the bulb from its socket, left and locked the door.

"They're gonta kill us," McCartin whimpered from the floor.

"Yes," McManus said.

"What for?" It was a desperate little cry.

"It would take me all day to tell you."

"I was afeared she was gonta cut my thing off," he said. "Thons a terrible woman." Then he said pathetically, "I'm starvin."

They starved for two more days, in two more houses and with eight more men. The boy's head was covered with bald patches from some of which the scalp also had been torn. The next day they were taken back to the Markets. McManus had been beaten every day. McCartin's face was pulp. The child no longer cried. He seemed to McManus to have stolen away into a voluntary coma. Sometimes he started in his semiconscious stupor and mumbled something. Twice McManus heard, "Ma . . . Ma . . . mammy," and just before they were moved for the last time, "I wisht I was dead." So did McManus.

Back in the Markets the regimen was eased. But when they arrived and were taken upstairs the faces of cold and lurking hysteria were even more explicit. Three men came upstairs behind them. It was a slow climb. McManus had to shoulder the boy to the top. The men behind watched his struggle in satisfied silence.

They were met on the landing by a small lean youth who in his middle-class mind McManus would formerly have called a corner-boy—a hanger-about at street corners. In the face the hysteria was hot, and silently screeching. He let McCartin pass, stood aside a little for McManus and said, "Stop where y'are."

"That'll do, Shamus," one of the men on the stairs said stiffly.

"It was my brother's face you kicked in, y'traitor cunt," the small man said. It came out like air escaping from a tire.

McManus was standing sideways to him, weak and light-headedly alert. He knew from the man's stance what he was going to do, and when he swung at his belly, McManus shifted slightly and the knuckles grazed his stomach but the uncontrolled savagery of the swing took the man with it. He teetered on the top step, and dangled.

)) 51

McManus was past restraint. He kicked the suspended and slowly moving stomach and the man went out, spread, and fell on the stairs on his back. McManus jumped, both feet high and together, and landed on the extended belly below him. With his hands tied behind his back he could do nothing to save himself and went crashing forward onto the two men immediately below. The man behind them took the burden of bodies and crashed backwards. They were heaped at the bottom of the stairs, McManus on top.

Yet there was no more violence. They unscrambled, lifted the man from the stairs, and over his screams one of them said to McManus, "You broke his fuckin back."

"I hope so." He went up to the bedroom alone while they attended to their comrade who was taken away. Then the men brought food and untied them. When McManus had eaten, a man they had not seen before cleansed their cut faces and bathed their bleeding wrists. The man who did this was well dressed, he had pale long hands and knew what he was doing. He had to feed McCartin. He went away when he had finished with them. He didn't speak all the time he was with them. But he didn't at any time betray shock or offense at their condition. The other three men treated him with deference.

The day that followed was a healing day. Their food was good. McCartin escaped into almost constant sleep. McManus announced that he had diarrhea and was allowed to go to the water closet when he said he needed to.

He had a soft lead pencil. What he needed was paper and he couldn't ask for it. Toilet paper was his only alternative and there was none in the water closet. There was a box nailed to the wall with cut-up squares of the *Irish News* in it. On this, during frequent visits to the water closet, he printed his letter to his sister, got it into its stamped envelope, and stowed it in his sock.

His passivity was gone. He had made up his mind to run or die—maybe both. If he was going to die, he told himself, the initiative would be his, not theirs. Forgiveness, he decided, was a

Christian but not an Irish virtue. With festering magnanimity he presented a modestly friendly front to his guards. They kept their silence and their distance.

He wasted his time. On the third day back in the Markets, when his strength had increased and McCartin ceased to be a battered zombie and was once again a terrified child, Powers and Callaghan appeared.

"You're movin," Powers said, full of command, and took him back to the Falls.

The man with the good suit and the long pale hands came to see him twice in the next two days. He drew pus from cuts on his face, stitched some wounds, put medicinal tape on the ones that needed it, and came and went in silence.

"You're a doctor," McManus said to him. Perhaps the man did not hear him.

At nine on the second night, Powers said, "Bed. We're workin the morrow. Up at six."

The time was now. McManus didn't care what it was, or what they were going to make him do, so long as it got him outside. However slender the chance, he was going to take it. He slept. They had something in store for him. He was to be a patsy of some kind. It didn't matter. One good crack at it in the open air was the most he could expect. He had to be ready for it. He slept soundly, resigned and ready. His composure surprised and pleased him.

In the morning, Powers issued gray step-in overalls and gray peaked caps. On the breast pocket of the overalls a red circle had been embroidered and in the circle, a large M. The badges on the caps were the same. They were the uniforms of the vanmen from Marsh's biscuit and cake factory on the Springfield Road.

At eight they walked to the Falls Road and up it to three houses set back behind small railed gardens in the middle of a block of shops. Powers and McManus walked together, Callaghan behind. The third of these houses was the home of Dr. Brendan

McDermott. His car was parked in the street. The keys were in the ignition. Callaghan got into the back seat. Powers held open the front passenger door for McManus and said, "Slide over and drive."

The doctor watched from behind his curtains as his car was stolen. Then he went back to bed. "I'll report it at ten," he said to his wife, "that'll give them enough time."

"Want some coffee?" she said, and went to get it. The doctor propped his pillows and opened his paperback. Surgery at ten. Plenty of time. After coffee he might have the wife; last night he'd been too tired, but this morning he felt like it in an indifferent sort of way.

If she'd let him. If she did, she'd lie there suffering like a stone nun. The thought put him off her; he'd go elsewhere for it this afternoon; the car and his wife were put out of his mind.

McManus drove where he was told to drive; slowly, against the traffic going into the city.

"Up the Springfield," Powers said.

Then he said, "Turn and park beyond Marsh's factory." It was a quarter to nine when they settled to watch the factory gates.

"What is it this time, Powers?" McManus asked.

"We're makin a delivery."

"Where?"

"Off the Loughside Motorway. To the worker's canteen kitchen. The chemicals factory."

"When's it timed for?"

"Half-ten."

"That's close. Who delivers it?"

"You and me."

"What's Callaghan doing?"

"He'll bring this car for the switch when we leave."

A delivery van pulled out of the factory gates at exactly nine o'clock. "Thon's Wee Jimmy," Callaghan said.

"Get in behind him and just follow him," Powers said.

McManus tucked it behind the delivery van. It led them down the Springfield Road, around a bend that hid them from the factory, then turned left off the road and headed through the housing estates back the way it had come. It picked up speed, left the outskirts of the city, and took a lane towards, then a bumpy track across the lower slopes of the Black Mountain. They stopped in a dip that hid them from the houses in the lower distance and the road far to their right.

The driver of the van got out and came grinning back to the car. His puck-face was creased by the lines of the irrepressible witling. He leaned on the door and spoke as a familiar to Powers. It was easy for him to lean on the door. His head at full stretch didn't reach the top of the window frame. He was indeed, Wee Jimmy.

"Pat," he said. His grin was engagingly harmless.

"Jimmy," Powers said. It might have been a casual meeting on a highway.

"Who's yer man?" Jimmy said, and nodded at McManus.

"McManus."

"You drivin?"

McManus said, "Yes."

"Take her to the third door on the loadin ramp. The man ye want is Tommy Davison. All ye do is tell him I'm sick. They'll give youse a trolley and ye take the case to the kitchen. Then ye come out and drive away. That's all." He grinned encouragement. "Tie me up, boys. An make me comfortable, for Jasus sake. I'm gonta be here for bloody hours." He handed over his delivery book. The possibility of major hardship occurred to him. He glanced up at scattered white clouds moving sedately across the sky. "If it rains, I'll get my deatha cold." He winked at McManus. He was a witling all right. This was a great lark. He was here, remote on the Black Mountain. The half-shift at the chemical plant, down in the canteen for the tea break, was far away on the edge of the Lough. Out of sight. Out of mind. No connection between Loughside and Black Mountain. Not in Wee Jimmy's mind. He could deliver at the Chemicals tomorrow, survey the ruin and the bloodstains and say to the survivors, "Holy Jasus. That's fuckin awful."

"Ireland One Fuckin Nation," Wee Jimmy said with glee before Powers put the tape over his mouth and propped him up behind a drystone wall.

"See you the morrow, Jimmy," Powers said, and patted his head. Jimmy nodded vigorously, his eyes glittering with amusement. "Away on," Powers said, and shoved McManus towards the van.

Wee Jimmy sat behind the wheel of his van on two thick hard cushions. McManus shoved them away to prevent his head pushing through the roof.

"Joy Street," Powers said, "like shit."

When they came out of Joy Street again the packing case, all properly marked like a case of Marsh's products, was behind them in the van. It was a quarter to ten. Callaghan picked them up in the doctor's car when they came through Divis Street and McManus watched him follow and watched him peel off for the Shore Road when he took the van into Duncrue Street and onto the Loughside Motorway.

It was the widest—ten lane—and the shortest—two miles—high-speed motorway in Europe, built on stilts to serve a growing complex of industrial plants located close to the docks. The chemical plant was less than a mile down the motorway, on the left. McManus put his foot down. The skin of his neck was beginning to tingle. It was a quarter past ten when he turned down the ramp into the plant yard and pulled up the van at the loading platform. Then he saw a strange thing in the side mirror: Callaghan, in the doctor's car, pulling up beyond the yard entrance. Callaghan was supposed to wait a mile beyond this point, on the Shore Road just off the Greencastle Interchange, where the van would be abandoned and the switch made. It was ten-twenty. He swung the van rear-on to the ramp and ran round to open the doors. A middle-aged man came forward with a long-tongued trolley.

"Where's Wee Jimmy the day?"

"He's sick. Are you Tommy Davison?"

"Aye."

"Here's your delivery note."

"What did somebody do to your gub?"

"You can see."

The packing case was on the tongue. It weighed, McManus was sure, more than a hundred pounds and there were likely to be at least a hundred people in the cafeteria and a dozen in the kitchen when the case blew up—in about seven minutes.

Powers was beside him. "Hurry it up," he said, and jumped down from the platform.

McManus took the shafts of the trolley and ran the case through the platform door. He was out of sight of Powers, in a shipping shed. Davison was just behind him. McManus grabbed him and pushed him to the wall.

"There's a hundred-pound bomb in that case," he said. "For Christ's sake, clear this shed and the canteen before half-ten. Run, man."

It was ten-twenty-five. He stood around the frame of the shed door and watched the doctor's car roaring across the plant yard. Behind him he could hear men shouting, a herd running. He dashed across the platform and jumped down behind Powers as the doctor's car stopped. When the door opened he rammed Powers through it and climbed in on top of him. The car swung in the yard and went tire-screaming around the plant to the Shore Road. Nobody spoke. Powers was breathing hard, working something out.

"Tell me, Powers. How was I supposed to get out of there?" McManus said.

"You're out, aren't you?"

"That's right." But that was all and it wasn't enough. "You weren't waiting for me, you bastard."

They were passing the railway station at the end of York Street when the bomb went off. People stopped in the street, looking into the sky to watch for the smoke that told them where it was this time. When the cloud rose, black and billowing, they moved again, like figures in a movie that has been stopped for a moment, and quickly started. The car turned up Duncairn Gardens, crossed the Antrim Road into Cliftonville, and parked in the front yard of the Royal Academy. They left it there and walked out to the street into a car parked and waiting by the curb. In ten minutes they were back in Joy Street and the car that picked them up was on its way to be dumped.

It had to be now, before they went into the house again. He had to get rid of his Marsh's overalls. In these, on foot down in the city, he would be caught in minutes. Here, he could be shot in seconds.

He stopped by the door of the house. "Powers," he said, "I bloody nearly got trapped in that factory."

"You were as slow as an oul woman."

"Like bloody hell I was slow. But I'm still shaking and whether you like it or not, I'm going down to Machin's shop for a packet of cigarettes. If you don't like it you can shoot me in the back, you black bastard." It was more than a month since he had been so angrily defiant. It might earn him a few yards' start.

He turned and walked back down the street. Mrs. Machin's huckster's shop was about fifty feet from the bus route.

Powers stood watching him. McManus wasn't supposed to be here at all. He was supposed to be among the dead in the kitchen at the Chemicals. Powers was still working it out as he watched him turn into Mrs. Machin's. Something wasn't right: about the timing; about the way McManus came off that loading platform. It should take him, Wee Jimmy told them when they planned it, a long five minutes to get the stuff to the kitchen. It should take him another couple of minutes to get out of the kitchen when the stuff was stacked. He hadn't been away for more than . . . how long? Two, three minutes altogether? He put his hand into his overall blouse, moved a few yards closer, and waited for McManus to come out of Mrs. Machin's wee shop.

"Johnny, how are ye?" Mrs. Machin said to McManus and laughed all through her bosomy bulk.

McManus stripped down the overalls. "A packet of Players, Mrs. Machin," he said, and hauled the overalls over his shoes.

"Where're we gonta do it, Johnny? On the counter?" Perhaps Powers heard her laughter.

He pulled the letter from his sock. "Mrs. Machin, for the love of Christ, post it for me. Please." He pushed it across the counter and it fell to the floor behind it.

She picked it up. "That's yer fancy wee sister, isn't it, Johnny?"

"It is. *Please,* Mrs. Machin."

"Yer down, are ye?"

"Yes."

"They bate ye."

"Yes. Please, Mrs. Machin."

"You've not been informin, have ye, Johnny?"

"Before God, no."

"Away on," she said, and stuffed the letter between her huge breasts.

"I'll have to go running. Powers is outside."

"That big cock. God help ye, chile, an give ye strong legs."

McManus opened the door and came back to the counter. He was trembling. In seconds he might be very still. He left the little shop in full stride, weaving for the bus route. He heard Powers' shots and his pounding boots, but he didn't look round. The road and the corner and the crowds were a few strides away and a handgun was an unreliable weapon. Maybe it was useless (except in the movies) in the hand of a moving gunman trying to hit a moving target. He turned the corner at full belt and hit an old man chest on and went over him, rolling. He rose rolling and galloped into the traffic. Where Powers was he didn't know till he heard him yelling, *Stop him! Stop him!* Nobody tried. People on the street don't try to stop big charging young men. How can it be done without getting hurt? A double-decker bus passed him and he jumped for the rail and swung onto the platform. Powers was in the middle of the road, looking after the bus. He turned and ran again, to Mrs. Machin's little shop.

FIVE

MRS. MACHIN was leaving the shop when Powers reached the door.

He rammed a harsh fist into one of her immense soft breasts and said, "G'on back in, missus."

She backed in, her hands against her bosoms, her mouth hanging open.

"What'd he want?"

"Players, Mr. Powers." She wheezed it, hardly able to breathe. Her eyes were wide.

"What'd he want, you fat bitch?"

"Players, Mr. Powers."

"Where's his overalls?"

"Under the counter."

"Get them out."

She gave them to him. There was nothing in the breast pocket. He threw them back behind the counter.

"What the hell did you think he was doin when he took them off?"

"I didn't think. He went out that fast."

"What'd he tell you?"

"Nothin, Mr. Powers." Her hands were tight against the cleavage of her breasts.

Powers reached for the neck of her dress and dragged on it. It held. "What've you got in there?"

"Nothin, Mr. Powers."

" 'Nothin, Mr. Powers.' " He gripped the cloth with both hands and wrenched. It ripped and two great pale breasts and McManus's letter spilled out. She stood with her breasts naked, her nipples like the rear lights of a car at night, and stared at her guilt on the floor. She was suffocating in fat and fear.

"Pick it up," Powers said.

She picked it up and as she rose, her breasts dangling, he swung and hit them with the hard flat of his hand. "Holy Mary . . ." she began desperately, and he hit them again. "You fat oul hoore," he yelled at her and snatched the letter. "His sister, now. And you were gonta post it for him."

"I'm sorry, Mr. Powers." Her mind was frozen.

"You're sorry. *Jasus Christ!*" The hysteria screeched in his throat and his thick knuckles beat her breasts, and her arms when she tried to cover them. He hit her again, in the face, and something broke in her. Like a bear on its hind legs, feet apart, arms out and fingers clawing, she howled and charged and in his surprise reached his face. Her nails dug and she drew them down, lifting skin to the line of his jaw, and closed her grip on his jawbone. Then he hooked her and the big woman went down, hanging on for a moment, dragging his head down and his mouth wide open. But her senses faded, her grip loosened, her legs collapsed, and her immense body crumbled. She did not get up.

He was blind now, insane with rage. He smashed the eggs on her counter, swept her bottled sweeties to the floor and kicked the bottles to bits, tore down the shelving and wrecked the little shop. He pawed like a dog scratching for a bone in the drawers behind the counter and found the white-fluid pen with which she advertised her bargains on her poor shop window. Out in the street he printed on the window,

INFORMER

ran inside for the Marsh's overalls, and had to jump over the inert

mass of compassionate blubber on the floor. Then he set out snort-
ing like a frightened horse to find Clune.

"You opened it," Clune said gently. "That wasn't your first mistake. You made a balls of the Mavis McGonigal operation and
lost a man to a limpin wee woman with a shotgun that kicked
her onto her arse. You let the same oul woman fill the arses of
half the women on the estate w'shot. Your job this time was to
execute a man we can't trust and while you were doin it, you
were to get as many Protestant Vanguard and Ulster Volunteers
as a hundred pounds of gelignite could kill. The fuckin Chemicals
is fulla them. All you got was a despatch shed—y'didn't even
make sure the bloody bomb was planted right. And you didn't
execute McManus. He's out where he can talk, about men and
houses and bomb factories, and you couldn't even hit him on the
street. Then you bate the hell outa this Machin woman on your
own initiative and branded her without authority as an informer.
We make them decisions! She's shown her big black and blue
diddies t'every woman on the street and every time you walk down
it, they see what she did t'your face. She's makin it sound as if
she bate the shit outa you and the whole bloody street gave her
the money to fix her shop that every week they give t'us for the
cause. *And then you opened McManus's letter without authority."*
Clune was silent for a moment. The strain of restraint was telling
on him. His hands opened and closed. His middle-tone voice was
high and tight when he spoke again. *"If we had many like you
we'd fuckin-well be off the streets in a week!"*

To the three men standing sternly behind Powers, he said,
"Take'm down to the Markets and keep'm there till we want to
see him—if we want to see him."

"Sir," Powers began.

"Shut your gub!"

The prisoner was taken away, stubbornly erect. The court ad-
journed and its members relaxed their formal and official posture.

They got a bottle of John Jameson from under the kitchen sink. All three preferred Scotch or Bushmills, but in one another's company, and certainly on a security matter, it was imperative that they drink John J. It was made in the Republic of Ireland, its purchase offered no support to the economy of the occupied and oppressed North, and there was in any case the importance of symbolic gestures, even when they were made in secret. In public they were important as propaganda, in secret they were a part of a program of autosuggestion.

Over their glasses of John J. they drew conclusions from McManus's instructions in his letter to his sister. He wanted the family car. It was to be left at a specified point on the Limestone Road. It would be found by her in the car park at the Muckamore Abbey Hospital, just outside Antrim town. He wanted the £200 savings his father kept for him. Since Aldergrove Airport was out Antrim way, that was where he was headed. It was the fastest and shortest way out of the country. McManus was for England.

But he wanted also the old clothes he used when he painted the garage, and his walking boots, and his camping gear with the pup tent. The stuff was to be in the trunk of the car. That didn't necessarily mean England. It looked more like the hills of Ireland.

Or youth hostels in Scotland or the English Lakes? Fly from Aldergrove to Prestwick? Then he could go north or south, to the Scottish highlands or the English Lake District. Hostels, with a tent? Well, you couldn't always get into a hostel and he'd have to sleep in the open. That's why he wants the tent.

Clune listened to the talk. What the hell does it matter where he thinks he's going? He's going to the Abbey Hospital—that's the one thing that looks certain.

So the letter to his sister is printed in pencil on bum-paper; print the address on a new envelope, in pencil, post it, and wait for him at Muckamore Abbey Hospital.

A watch on his house and his sister? Jasus, yes. Wherever she goes, whomever she sees—she's got to be under the eyes of watchers till her light goes out at night. Watch the car too, once it gets to the Limestone. Wee boys from the junior IRA would be the best during the day and women at night, with a couple of wee boys or wee girls as runners.

Where would McManus go while he was waiting for his sister to act on his instructions?

What the fuckin hell did it matter where he went or was? Clune sometimes lost patience with his comrades. None of them was of his level of intelligence. He often wondered how they would succeed at anything if he wasn't there. Your man's goin to Mucka-more, isn't he? They'd wait for him there, and if there was any change the watchers would know it and report and the treacherous bastard couldn't get far.

The bottle was three-quarters down. They had everything clear. McManus was dependin on his sister. He didn't know they knew that. They had the eyes. That's one thing Powers did right. There wasn't much they missed. It was McManus who was runnin blind —and frightened. Set the watch. Send the letter. Wait and search at the same time. Get done with him. Wee boys and women and girls could do it, all but the killin. Meanwhile, there was a war on and it had to be got on with.

McManus knew where he was going. He sat where he could see through the platform of the bus and watched the traffic coming behind. If they'd drummed up a car there'd be more than one man in it and they'd be watching the bus as other drivers and passengers never did. But the cars he could see from his perch on the back seat had only the drivers in them.

A frightening thought occurred to him—that they might somehow have gone ahead of him, and were waiting where he intended to leave the bus, at Castle Junction. He jumped from the platform between stops and walked and ran and trotted all the way to the Salvation Army hostel.

For half an hour he watched the street from a doorway opposite and saw nothing that suggested the hostel had ever entered their minds. It was Protestant. It was strange. Only the poor had knowledge of or dealings with the Salvation Army. They would give a lot of thought to where he would go. They would take his background into account. The Salvation Army was not part of it. They would surely conclude that he would hide among his old Protestant friends in some middle-class district. He bolted nonetheless for the front door of the Sally Ann and was confused that the woman at the desk was young and pretty with the sort of tranquility in her face he expected only in the faces of good nuns.

He was twenty-two, running for his life from men he had joined in a spasm of ardor and anger and had learned to despise and had not betrayed, and she smiled as if there was nothing odd or desperate or dangerous about him and as if there were no plasters on his battered face.

She said, "Hullo. It's nice to see you. Can I be of any help?"

He didn't know what to call her. Sister? It was better not to call her anything. Suddenly, for no reason that he could account for and at the instant didn't try to, he was aware that he was supposed to be dead now and out of the way, and was alive. He was staring hard at the woman.

"Is there something wrong? Can I help you?"

"Could I have a room here?" he said. "Miss."

He saw the way her head seemed to dip and her face came forward a little, then lifted up towards him as she smiled and said, "A bed?" It was a shy sort of movement and also a kindly modification of his expectations.

"Anything," he said. "I. . . ." It isn't easy for young middle-class Ulstermen to do what North Americans of the same sort do with the ease and acceptance of Egyptian bazaar hagglers or Billingsgate fishwives. "I . . . have hardly any money." It was difficult to say.

"Neither have I," she said. "Maybe we're both lucky."

66 ((

"Yes," he said, and watched her open a big book. "Would you sign the register?" She turned it round to him and held out a pen.

He took it, scrambling in his head for a name. Tommy Davison was the first one that came and he stopped it. It seemed to block the exits from his mind. He leaned down over the book, turning the pen in his fingers, roving, over books, records, athletes . . . records? Somebody sent him once a recording of the Bethlehem Bach Choir, conductor, Ivor Jones. He wrote Ivor Jones. He had an American cousin who said he knew him. "Ivor Jones," he said, and turned the book back to her and laid down the pen.

She read it and put a number after his name and said with a rising inflection, "You've been in an accident." She was looking at his hands, not at his face, but she was thinking of his face, he was sure, not of the cuts and bruises the chair-leg made on his hands. He said nothing. "Come. I'll show you." He followed her upstairs.

It was a large dormitory, with twenty-four narrow iron-framed beds. "That's yours in the far left-hand corner. Number one. Is that all right?"

"Yes, thank you."

"The place fills up," she said, and gave him a key and turned to leave him. "That's for your locker. It's under the bed."

He walked up the long floor between the beds thinking, "Clean. Who else comes here? Derelicts? Drunk sailors who miss their ships?" When a woman's voice said, "Mr. Jones," he walked on. Then she was at his elbow. "Mr. Jones?" That was him. He couldn't hide his surprise. "Are you hungry?" she said.

He hadn't had time to think about that sort of thing. Now that he took time, she watched him asking himself, and said, "I could get you something." She really was pretty, and restful like a good nun.

"Yes," he said, "I am hungry. If it wouldn't be any bother. . . ."

"No bother at all. Put your things in your locker under your. . . . Oh, did you leave them somewhere?"

Hadn't she noticed before that he came empty-handed? "Miss?" he said awkwardly.

"Yes?"

"All I have is twenty-five pence."

She took a little change purse from her pocket and looked in it. "We have fifty pence between us," she said. "Come on down to the office."

He hadn't noticed the little chapel when he came to the dormitory. Going back, he looked right into it. Impulse took him in. He crossed himself, kneeled behind a chair, and offered thanks for deliverance, crossed himself again and came out to the corridor. She was waiting.

"Eat, now?"

"Thank you, miss."

"We'll go into the office."

It was a little glass room beside the front desk. She told him to sit down. He watched the entrance hall with growing uneasiness. If any of them came in here, searching, he was trapped in this glass house. The only way in or out of it was the door into the hall and onto their guns. They could do it here. They would do it here.

She unwrapped a brown-paper package of sandwiches and did not appear to watch him. He watched the front door, his imagination flying high. "I keep these to nibble on," she said, and gave him one. Ham. He wasn't hungry now. Coming here was a mistake. Into a trap. He ought to have kept going. Phoned his sister from a call box. No. Now that he'd run for it, they'd have somebody watching her. Yes, and God Almighty, he hadn't thought of that. They'd watch every move his parents and his sister made and when they brought the car to the Limestone, Powers would know it. They would come after him with tireless malice. Wasn't the last murder arising out of the Civil War committed in 1969—almost fifty years after? Was it a son avenging a father he'd never seen? They were like that, down the generations.

"Eat," she said, looking the other way.

He bit the sandwich. It was tasteless. He chewed at it and swallowed and choked.

"If I can be of any help," she said, looking directly into his face. "Sometimes there's something. . . ."

He bit again on the sandwich. It took time and prevented talk. It was as much of a trap up in that dormitory as it was in this glass box.

She said, "I'm not prying. You're a Catholic, aren't you?"

"Why would you say that?"

"Protestants don't cross themselves in chapel."

"Am I not allowed in?"

"Religion is no qualification here. Only need."

He chewed dully on the sandwich, watching the hall.

"I was in South Africa when the blacks rioted in Port Elizabeth and ate the two nuns," she said.

He looked at her, puzzled. Why did she say a strange thing like that? She looked a lot younger than she was. So did the good nuns. He could see, now. She was a lot older. He remembered reading about the two nuns the blacks ate. He remembered it because his political science professor had pointed out that the two nuns were among the best friends of the Africans who ate them. "Either the blacks were pagans who believed they could digest the nuns' virtue—or it's unwise to make friends of the blacks," the professor said. He remembered it also because Catholic martyrs weren't eaten anymore, their priest had pointed out: killed, jailed, hanged, tortured, crucified in one place or another, but not eaten. What am I supposed to say to her? he wondered.

"I remember the next day sitting waiting for them to come for us. We were their good friends. So were the nuns. We became former friends. They ate their former friends."

He didn't expect talk like that from the Sally Anns. They thumped tambourines, blew trombones and trumpets, and sang on street corners. He didn't know what to say. He didn't care at the moment whom the blacks ate in Port Elizabeth.

"I felt the way you look," she said quietly.

"What? I beg your pardon?"

"I'm not prying," she said.

"No." What am I supposed to say now? he wondered. He was leaving here, by God. But where was he going?

"You're a Catholic, you've been very badly beaten, you haven't a thing, not even a razor, you're very frightened, and you're hiding with no money in what a lot of people think of as a Protestant doss house. Would you like some tea?"

"No. No. No thank you." Her little catalogue was dinning in his ears.

"So you're not running from Protestants."

He set eyes on the woman half an hour ago and she had it worked out. If he was that easy to spot he hadn't long to live.

"You're not the first to come here," she said in her gently persistent way. "Some of them accepted help. Three of them didn't. We read about them—black hoods. . . ."

"Jesus Christ." He put the half-eaten sandwich on the desk. He thought he was going to throw up what he'd eaten. He could see them and hear them. He could feel their lurking cold hysteria and their righteous savagery.

"You poor boy. If we can help. . . ."

Help. What could these people do? Did they train, carry guns, make careful plans, shoot with ease and without scruple? "What could *you* do?" he said almost too softly to be heard. It wasn't really a question. It was a whisper of desperation, or despair. They'd trained him to use a gun. He would use one if he had to fight for his life. He didn't have one to fight with.

It would be a dog's death.

"How do I know," she said, "till I know what you need?"

"They might come here," he said.

"They have come here," she said. "Slept here, searching."

"You knew that and didn't turn them in?"

"And have gunfights in the hostel? And have them blow the place up? Then whom could we help?"

"They'll come here," he said. His stomach was vapor.

"Do you want help?"

"Oh, Jesus, yes, yes, yes."

"Then come with me." She pressed a button on the desk and led him away.

He followed her weakly, looking over his shoulder. They climbed the stairs, past the chapel and the dormitory, up a flight of back stairs to a small attic landing, and into a little apartment at the back of the building. "This is our home," she said, and at the expression on his face, "my husband and I live here. He's a Major. . . ."

"Major. . . ." Yes. They had ranks. Everything scared him now. He had wounded a major in the shoulder, up the Falls. What would she do if she knew that?

It was a very simple place, uncomfortable in the overcrowded fashion of what he called the upper working class. The armchair she pointed him to was hard-packed; its arms and back were not quite in the right places, or at quite the right angles, and the cover on the round table in the middle of the room was sateen with a picture of the Holy City printed on it, and tassels hanging from its edges all the way round.

"All right?" she said, looking shy and smiling.

Was she asking for his approval? He remembered a Scotsman he'd taken through the Stranmillis Museum and who said "Very nice" to everything he saw. "Very nice," he said, "thank you."

"You'll take that cup of tea now, won't you?"

"Thank you very much." He had no idea what to say to this woman. Not: Can you get me a gun? Not: Sometimes I feel like a motherless child. Not: I went among wolves like a romantic little boy and now I'm just a terrified big boy.

"You're not like some of them I've seen," the woman said, putting things on a small lacquered tray.

"Oh?"

"No. You look . . . how? Studenty?"

"Oh. Do you think I could have something to eat now? Down there, near the door . . . I was too scared. . . ."

"I know that. Ham again?"

"Anything. I'm sorry, Mrs. . . ."

"Beddoes. Now," she sat down to wait for the kettle, "what do you need?"

"My sister . . . the phone. . . ."

"You want to see her?"

"No! She's at work now. She works in an insurance office in Donegal Square."

"You'd like to call her there?"

"No. You never can tell who . . . no. Would you . . . ?"

"You'd have to tell me her name."

"Oh, yes." The woman didn't know his name; only that Ivor Jones wasn't his name. He must be very easy to read, disasterously easy, vulnerable. "Her name's Maureen McManus."

She got the phone book, the name of the insurance company, and the number, and said, "Now?"

"It's very important what you say. You can't mention this place, or my name. But I want her to know who wants her. She's to phone me here. She's not to go home early from the office. Just, you know, go home at the usual time. So I have to give her a time to call me—one time, no other. You see?"

"I see. Of course." She looked mockingly reproving. "Lectures weren't this complicated?"

"No. Just say she had a letter a while ago on scraps of paper. The writer wants to speak to her. Will she phone this number. At seven tonight. No. Six. Six. She couldn't wait till seven. Neither can I."

Mrs. Beddoes called the number, got the girl, and gave her the message. The girl was cold, precise. "Yes, madam," she said formally after each point was made. "Yes, madam. I'll just make a note of the number." Then, "And he is well, madam?"

"Safe and well."

The sister, Mrs. Beddoes thought, was tougher than her brother. "Make yourself comfortable here," she said. "Sleep if you need to. I have to go back to the desk."

He was weary. He was a little farther along a rocky road. He slept. It was one way to escape the leaden burden of passing time. She called as the hands of the mantelshelf clock touched six.

She did not use his name. "I love you," she said. "Tell me what to do."

"You'll get a letter tomorrow. Ignore it. I need the car. I need money. I need old clothes, the ones I wore when I painted the garage, my walking boots and my camping gear. Are you ready?"

"Go ahead."

"Dad has my £200 savings. I need it."

"He'll have to get it from the bank."

"All right. I'm safe till then. Tomorrow night?"

"Yes."

"Can you still visit Elsie Parker? Take the car? Tomorrow night?"

"Yes."

"Wear a big floppy brimmed hat and leave it in the car. Back the car into her drive. Got that?"

"Yes."

"Don't report the car stolen till after midnight. Can you stay there that long?"

"Anything I have to."

"I'll leave it at a place called Corrymeela outside Ballycastle. It's an old YMCA camp Ray Davey uses as a conference center now. Got that?"

"Yes."

"Just leave the money in the pocket, and, Maureen. . . ."

"Yes."

"Dad has a gun in the top left-hand drawer of his dressing table. There's a box of shells. Put it all in the pocket."

"Do you think . . . is it best . . . ?" She wanted to argue and didn't want to leave him defenseless.

"Yes. It's best. I'm not a dog."

"No. All right."

"They'll be watching you. Just do everything normal tomorrow."

"I'll try."

"Do everything normal every day, after. . . . Go out with Jack the same as always . . . you know. . . ."

"Yes."

"Kiss Dad and Mum."

"Yes."

"I'll be all right."

'We'll all pray for you. We love you."

"I love you all." It was a sheepfold phrase, gathering a million inexpressible thoughts and associations and now, longings, into an affectionate and inadequate commonplace. "I'll be all right. And Maureen. . . ."

"Yes."

"Put ten pounds of my money in an envelope and send it to Major Beddoes of the Salvation Army—B-e-d-d-o-e-s."

"I see. Yes. Be careful. Don't forget to say thanks."

"No. I love you." He put the phone down to stop the talk and the tears that threatened. What are you at twenty-two? A little boy with a gun, behind a barricade? A little boy, without a gun, being hunted for his life, hiding behind women and soon, alone, behind bushes and hills? To want to cry and not want to—that's what little boys are made of. He had to reach England. But not yet. Not till they stopped watching the ferries and the airports and began to comb the country for him. Then he'd get to England. And if they got his direction and found the car first they'd hunt for him a while in the North. He went into the tiny bathroom of the flat and cried anyway, and washed his face.

When he came out the Major was there. He was a small tubby man with a Pickwick sort of face. It was all he could do to reach an arm around McManus's shoulder. "All set?" he said, and patted.

"Tomorrow night, sir. On the Malone Road."

"We'll get you there in our van." The cherubic little man chuckled. "I don't know whether God approves of people like us mixing in this sort of thing, Johnny, my boy. I'll take it up with Him once you're away." He sat down and picked up his Bible. "By the way." There was some small thing he'd forgotten to mention. "There's a fellow in the hostel who's looking for his friend—they got separated in a brawl in a pub, he said." All the time, peering into his Bible. "His friend was badly beaten about the face and hands. About six feet, the friend is, about twenty-two years old. His friend's name is Johnny McManus, but he might not be using that name."

It was insulting. McManus knew he ought not to ask. He couldn't help himself. "What did you say, sir?"

"I lied." He turned the page of his Bible.

"Thank you, sir."

The Major said, "We'll keep the door of the flat locked at all times."

"Yes, sir."

"The man has a bed for the night. He said he'd stay in case his friend showed up. There'll be others around. There always are on these occasions."

On these occasions. McManus looked at the door. Locked or unlocked, it was a fragile thing. Chance was a fragile thing: he looked afraid and studenty and out of place in a Sally Ann hostel and Mrs. Beddoes saw it and he was up here instead of down there in the dormitory with his "friend." The Major was a fragile thing, plump and cheerful and gentle and soft. His wife was a fragile thing, sweet, good, and young-looking, waiting passively in a state of grace at the Salvation Army in Port Elizabeth for the blacks who ate the nuns to come and eat her.

McManus sank down in his uncomfortable chair. He was fragile too.

The news that night on the telly in the little flat was painful. A fifteen-year-old boy whose name was not being disclosed had been found unconscious in the gutter on the Falls Road. Around his neck was a placard which said only,

RAPIST

His face was beaten to a pulp. All his hair had been pulled out by the roots.

That night, McManus began to cough.

SIX

THE children of Ireland are wondrously beautiful, like wild flowers on a dungheap.

They played hopscotch in front of one of the good houses that cut off sight of the golf course from the Antrim Road. The eighteen-year-old twin brothers of one of the children sat in a car in the lane that joined the Antrim Road to the Shore Road, along the western edge of the golf course. They were giving all their attention to the golfers.

A speedy boy came tearing round the corner into the lane. "She's away into the gareege," he said.

"Away on home the lot of ye," the twin behind the wheel said, and pulled out into the traffic on the Antrim Road.

They stopped to give the hopscotch players a bag of sweeties and enough money to get them back to the Falls on a bus, with something over. The beautiful children ran laughing to the bus stop.

Maureen McManus stopped to let them pass across the driveway exit and stayed for a gap in the traffic and came carefully out into the stream.

"Fancy-lookin bitch," the driver said, "I'd like to have a good go at her."

His twin said, "I'll tell ye whether I'd like a go at her when I see her other end."

That was enough for a while. They followed her into the city center and through it past the university to number 542 Malone Road. She watched the car that followed her all the way, backed into Elsie Parker's drive, and called the number Mrs. Beddoes had given her. "Tell him not to come," she said when Mrs. Beddoes came to the phone. "They followed me. They're waiting for him."

"We'll have a conference," Mrs. Beddoes said. "Give me your number."

The twins settled a hundred feet from the house. "Gon back t'that phone booth an tell them," the driver told his brother.

An army of monitors listened to phone calls from and to specified areas of the city. The twin called a phone box on the Falls. *"Malone,"* he said. "Is *Malone* there?"

"Can I give *Malone* a message?"

"Aye. Tell'm the winnin sweep number is *542*."

"Aye. *Five-four-two?* That's for *Malone?* Did he win anythin?"

"The fuckin lot."

"Aye."

The twin went back to the car. They waited and watched. In time a car stopped at the intersection a hundred yards in front of them to the right. It stayed there, just off the Malone. In five minutes another car came down the Malone and parked across from the intersection and a little beyond it. There were three men in these cars. They waited and did not seem to talk.

The twins talked.

"She backed it in," the driver said, "he's in there with her sure as hell. That's where he hid, by Jasus. He'll come out like fuck."

At eight o'clock the driver said, "He's takin his time."

"Look. The front upstairs window. That's her, watchin." Maureen McManus disappeared from the window. "We'll go round the street and come back. Park further back this time."

When they turned the corner around the parked car the man in the back shouted, "Keep yer station." An old navy man.

"She spotted us. We're gonta sit further back."

"Hurry up."

This time they settled two hundred feet back, behind another car. They would be a bit harder to see.

Nine o'clock. The driver said, "He's gonta wait till it's dark."

"A hell of a lota good that'll do'm. He's boxed."

Ten o'clock. "Anytime now," the driver said. "It'll be dark in half an hour. I wisht I had a gun. All we can do is get in his bloody road."

Ten-thirty.

Major Beddoes came into the flat "They're still there," his wife told him, "but further back. He says he's going anyway."

"Just how good a driver are you, my boy?"

"They thought I was good, sir. I think so too. If I can get out of that driveway I can lose them."

"If they don't hit you first. And if you lose them, where will you go?"

McManus looked steadily at him. "England, sir," he said.

The Major nodded thoughtfully. "Yes. The English are a hospitable people. Not everybody here agrees. If the Germans were dealing with your friends, or the B Specials, they'd all have been dead or in Cork years ago." He was nervous. "We'll go down the back stairs. The van's open at the door. Step straight into it and close the door."

"Yes, sir."

"You'll need money. . . ."

"There's money in the car. Thank you. . . ."

Mrs. Beddoes said, "Your cough's so much worse, Johnny. Why don't you wait?"

"It'll go away. It's nerves."

"Have you any pain?"

"Not much. Mrs. Beddoes, I've got to go."

They went down the back stairs, out a back door into a yard with a row of garbage cans on either side of the door. Mrs.

Beddoes got in beside the Major. The van doors were wide open. McManus stepped straight in and closed them.

They were moving. "You're sure you can pick the house from the street behind it?" the Major said.

"I know it very well, sir."

"Well, we'll go in behind Malone from the Stranmillis Road. When I give the word, you'll have to come forward and tell me which house."

"It's two houses down from the corner where Stranmillis runs into Malone, sir."

"All right, my boy."

The Major was a good driver. He swung his little Salvation Army van in and out of the traffic like a getaway man on a devious course. In twenty minutes he called McManus forward. "I'm about to turn off Stranmillis into the street behind Malone. Second house?"

"Yes, sir. I'll go through the garden into Parker's garden."

"Which way will you drive?"

"Back into the city."

"They're facing away from the city. Does that mean they expected you to go the other way?"

"No, sir. It means they have a car up the Malone facing the other way. Maybe two."

"Then why go? You can't get away. They'll have guns."

"Yes, sir. I didn't want to tell you, Major. There's a gun in my sister's car. It's my father's, sir."

The Major shut off the noisy engine. "I think we should think, my boy. They're watching for you here. If you use your sister's car there'll be shooting in the street. If you're not killed, some innocent person may be. Come back with us and tomorrow I'll drive you to Aldergrove."

"They'll be there, Major."

"The Heysham boat?"

"Everywhere like that, sir. They'll be there."

"Johnny," the Major said severely, "that cough's a lot worse."

"I have to go, sir."

"You'll be killed, child," Mrs. Beddoes said.

"But not like a dog, Mrs. Beddoes."

"Oh, us poor Irish," she said.

"Johnny," the Major said cautiously, walking on eggs, "let me drive you to the police? Give yourself up. You'll be safer. They'll hide you."

"The *police?*"

"Or the army. Why not?"

"I'd have to talk, sir, or they wouldn't hide me."

"Well?"

"Inform, sir? *Me?"*

"Why not? They're going to kill you, Johnny."

"Inform? Oh God, no. You don't understand."

"Other people are going to be killed on the street when they shoot at you. Think of them, Johnny."

"Inform? Oh God, no. No no no. Not that."

"Oh, us poor Irish," the Major said. "God pity us."

"I couldn't, sir. I *couldn't."*

"Johnny, the Provos have killed the prospect of a united Ireland for a hundred years."

"It isn't that, sir. You're a Protestant. You don't understand."

"I suppose not. God bless you, anyway. I know He'll forgive you."

Mrs. Beddoes kissed him quickly. "God guide you better now than He did before," she said heretically. "You dear poor boy."

"Thank you," he said. "Thank you."

McManus closed the rear doors and walked across to the gate of the house behind the Parker's. He did not think again of the Salvation Army Major and his wife. He thought only that now he was alive and in two minutes he could be dead. Or crippled and dying. He was shivering now. He sweated, then he shivered. It would pass. They trained him for this, to hit and elude policemen and soldiers, and he was alive and not crippled. Now he would see. He was not confident. Neither was he terrified. All he felt was a sort of stony fatalism. It was a matter now of good luck or bad luck. The Americans would have said, "The breaks."

He did not know that instead of driving on down the street the Major backed his van into Stranmillis and turned the corner into the Malone Road. McManus stepped onto the grass. There were people in the house; lights were blazing; there were three cars in the drive. Guests. Noise. He passed the house and hoisted himself onto the stone wall dividing this yard from the Parker's.

When he dropped to the grass on the other side of the wall, his nerves struck. The car was there, beside the house. The back door of the house opened. Maureen was there. Oh, no, God no. He didn't need any emotional strain. He walked to her and she took him in her arms.

"They're still there. Mr. Parker says he'll hide you, Johnny. Come into the house."

He held her hard. "You'd have to drive out in that case," he said, not wanting his mind on anything but what it was set to do. "You can't drive well enough. They'd riddle you before you were turned into the road. Go back into the house and don't watch."

"Dad loaded the gun," she said, knowing him. She had tried. "Will we hear from you?"

"After a while. Maybe a long while. Go on in now."

"God curse Ireland," she said. "Kiss me for Mummy and Dad."

He kissed her and the door closed behind her. He walked to the car. It was now. He was no longer shivering. He was trembling. He stood, taming his nerves. He opened the door and got in. The floppy hat was on the seat. He put it on. The gun was in the pocket with the ammunition. He checked it, started the engine, and tried the gun in his hand, tried his hand on the wheel with the gun in it, adjusted it to make it more comfortable, took off the safety, and settled himself. The tank was full. The engine sounded as if it had been tuned. It was now. He slipped down the driveway almost to the open gates, very slowly. If some pedestrian or a passing car crossed in front of the drive in the next second or two, the deaths would not be political. He put down the front windows, sank low in the seat, and put his foot down. It was now.

He did not hear the bleating horn of Major Beddoes' van as the car leaped at the street and spun, skidding, into the road. The rear end spun left and, as his foot dug, spun right, swinging the car across the road and back. Then it shot forward.

He sank lower in the seat, peering through the wheel. He heard the sputtering shots and the roaring of engines and the screeching of tires as his back window and windshield shattered. Glass flew about him, fell in his lap, struck his back and head. A car swung out from the curb to block his road. He waited, whipped his car right, felt the sideswipe through his spine, rode up the sidewalk and, hauling desperately at the wheel, back into the road.

He was clear. His rear-view mirror was whole. The Salvation Army van was side-on across the street, a car backing away from it, with a bashed bonnet. Another car with its bonnet sprung open was backing off the sidewalk away from a lamp post. A man got out and rushed to struggle with the open bonnet. A police siren sounded; off to his left, he thought. A plump, uniformed man climbed out of the van and handed a woman graciously down. Major Beddoes and his wife had done what they could. It had been enough. He gave his mind to the street and the traffic. His hands were wet and slipping on the wheel, his face was pouring sweat, his neck was bleeding behind from a smarting cut. He swung on two wheels into Elmwood and down the Lisburn Road; left into Dublin Avenue. There was nobody close to him behind. They were probably running now from the police siren. He wove through the little, empty streets, heading for the Antrim Road, and unaware of any irony, turned down the lane past his father's house and the golf course and came out to the Shore Road.

He was clear, and cautious till he passed through Carrickfergus.

Then he opened up. Larne. The empty Antrim Coast Road. Flat out. Free. Away.

The air off the sea poured through his shattered windshield as sweet as a fresh clutch at a not very old but a damaged and vulnerable life.

He sucked the air in like a man with a dry thirst and laughed; but from hysteria winding down much more than from mirth.

In Carnlough he stopped at a phone booth and called the Parkers'.

"Mr. Parker? I'm away, sir."

"The shooting on the street, Johnny? They didn't touch you?"

"Just a bit of glass. Will you tell them I'm away, sir? And thank you."

"Thank some fat wee Salvation Army man that completely buggered them up. We saw it."

"I know." He had said all there was to say.

"You're away now?"

"I'm away, sir."

"Away on, boy—like the hammers of bloody hell."

"I'm away now. You'll tell them?"

"I'll tell them. Away on." The big moments are hard to talk about.

The moon was high and the sky clear when he turned up the narrow approach lane to Corrymeela. The camp sat on the top of the cliff, its whitewashed hutments like shining apparitions in the moon's light.

He parked the car at the rear of the main building, behind the kitchens. There were cars parked against the east wall, by the side entrance. Not one of those, he thought, and put his father's gun and shells in his pocket. Everything he had asked for was in the trunk, expertly packed in his rucksack with the pup tent tied on top. His sister had remembered even his walking stick. There were sandwiches and cheese in the side pockets of the sack. His walking boots were loose in the trunk with a pair of heavy walking socks stuffed inside them. He changed into his walking boots and tied his shoes to the pack.

It was half-past one. He felt marvelously safe in the northeastern night. What he must do now was reach the border, and reach it long before daylight. It was not possible on foot. A stolen car had its dangerous risks, but there was no way to avoid them. It was forbidden now to park cars in towns of any size and roadblocks on the outskirts sifted traffic through them. He didn't want to pass through towns, but that was where the cars were to be found. He walked to the road and down the hill towards Ballycastle. He would take the risks that had to be taken.

At the foot of the hill three roads joined. One turned right into Ballycastle, another hard left up over the hills. He was on the third. The roadblock was at the junction of the three.

He climbed the stile in the wall of the old churchyard where Sorley Boy Mac Donnell is buried and walked through it to the golf course. There was no point in getting himself caught trying to sneak into the town. Even if he managed it, he couldn't sneak out again with a car. It was wiser to cross the golf course, walk around the town, and steal what he saw outside some house or country shop on the road beyond.

But things were going well tonight. The clubhouse was not in total darkness. There were five cars in the car park. Drinking hours were long past, but there were many ways to sustain a serious pastime so long as they didn't involve drinking in the bar. The only question was how much farther into the night they would drink and talk.

He rejected the Mercedes. How could a young man cumbered with camping gear explain a Mercedes? The four-cylinder Vauxhall was more like the thing. He lifted the bonnet and started the engine. The night was quiet, only the sound of the sea came across the links. The car was well tuned and no louder than the sound of the sea. He drove it across the links, through a wall gate onto the high road, and let the little car out.

Main roads were no good to him. Secondary roads were not much better. Tertiary roads were often rough riding. But it wasn't his car. It was his life. He took the rough roads and went west with his foot down.

How long do drinking men drink at their golf clubs when they stay until the small hours for serious business? He was around and beyond Garvagh when the question began to worry him. There were hundreds of four-cylinder Vauxhalls on the road, but not at this time of night. By now—two hours on the third-class roads—the car had been reported missing. It hadn't passed through any road-blocks going in any direction. For that reason the army and the police would be keeping an eye open for it. Why would a car avoid roadblocks in the middle of the night? A stolen car? The army would be keeping more than one eye open.

He saw nothing to ease his anxiety on these roads until he reached Sixmilecross, where he exchanged the car for an Austin parked outside a crossroads shop and came at Clady through a complex of narrow lanes. In a field against the Border and close to a small farmhouse he left the Austin. It was snug behind a high hedge.

It was almost five. The sky was lightening and in an hour it would be broad daylight. He took off his suit, cleared the pockets, packed the clothes into a water ditch, and put on the old clothes from his sack. They were paint-stained and baggy—right for a man of the roads.

This was raiding country. The IRA sneaked over here to murder a Northern Senator and burn his house to the ground, and again to kill a policeman and leap back across the border into Donegal. They had helpers in the towns and farmhouses on the Ulster side.

McManus had once been moved to admiring excitement by the misty ease with which acts of violence were committed and men dissolved into the faithful and covering Catholic crowd. His first disenchantment came with his first sight of how this universal loyalty was achieved. He had seen pregnant Mrs. Nolan beaten on the belly, and her husband's shop wrecked, because he refused to pay the imposed weekly levy for Ireland One Nation. The whole street understood the word when it went out: Don't buy from Nolan. So Nolan went bankrupt, and because he was self-employed he couldn't draw the dole and had to go on relief. It was a lesson often repeated, and executed by little men who now ran a protection racket where formerly they had been despised petty thieves in the districts. The small-time criminals had become the enforcers of patriotic unity. Even here in the western Border backwoods, small Catholic farmers with cattle to be poisoned or children to be maimed, kept check on the movements of Protestant neighbors to be shot or burned out.

So McManus went cautiously through the copse against the Border at the end of the field, out of the North and into the Republic, into the safe haven and lair of his former friends and present enemies. He went haunted, by eyes he could not see and that might not be there, but Mrs. Beddoes and the nuns of Port Elizabeth were in his mind. In Ireland friends and enemies had a way of looking alike.

It was broad daylight when he took the road along the Finn to Stranorlar and Ballybofey. His boots were wet with the heavy dew, the smell of burning peat was rich on the hills, and the soft morning air had a sweet taste. He was well away.

He strode into Stranorlar at ten in the morning on the strength of two long lifts, swinging his stick in time with his striding confidence. What was he, after all? Anybody could see by his clothes. He was a man of the roads. They thought so at Kee's Hotel and with some reasonable reluctance gave him a room, to be paid in advance. He had been up all night, walked most of the morning, and he would sleep away what was left of the day and walk through the night. From then, it was the tent in the day, and sleep, and the road after dark, till he got where he was going.

I'm away, he thought as he waited for sleep in a good bed and wished he dared send a wire to his sister. But who would read it in the post office, here in Stranorlar or in Belfast? God, what a land of mistrust and skulking suspicion Ireland was. Who in Christ's name could you trust? Not the ones you could see— not the ones you couldn't see. For the first time in his life he thought he hated the place. The place? No, never that. But the people, some of the people? That was a damn sight easier.

They'd be watching his sister. A telegram boy at the house would tell them he was clear. What Mavis McGonigal got would be only the beginning of what his sister got, if they thought she knew where he was. They would think she knew where he was. They had to hunt him. They would hunt him with the terrible Irish appetite for revenge. He remembered reading about "Pa" Murray who died in 1968 and once was sent to New York to execute an informer who escaped there. New York Irish policemen found the man for him. Murray killed him, for an offense committed in 1922.

His last conscious thought before sleep was that they wouldn't find him. No wire, he decided, and the odd thought drifted into his peripheral consciousness that almost all Irishmen loved Ireland and despised the Irish.

Then merciful sleep took him over.

SEVEN

P O W E R S' confidence declined and his rage mounted.

Was he goin to spend the rest of his fuckin life standin in front of some bloody kitchen table in the Falls listenin to that Holy Trinity of flappin bacon-mouths, Clune, McCann, and McCandless?

They were on about Mavis McGonigal again, about losin Kelly the useless wee bastard that never held a job in his life and never looked for one; and about the Chemicals and McManus. And Clune was sittin there with an eye patch over his left eye, tryin to look like that Jew-soldier from Israel! He tried to make a bomb last night, for Christ's sake, and it blew up on him and only made a wee poop that burned one of his eyes—singed his eyebrow, very likely, but he wants that patch for the telly—the wounded fuckin hero— "We wanted McManus found dead in there," Clune was goin on ". . . middle-class Catholic joinin the Catholic workers in their fight for a free Ireland . . . all Catholics united in the Historic Struggle . . . *you* lost him. . . ."

Powers' narrow, urbanized peasant mind saw them all vaguely, but it still listened with one ear for the quick question that would put the black hood over his head and leave him in the gutter. . . . Big Willy Devlin, all of twenty-two years old, came home on leave from the British army in Germany the day before yesterday and they ordered him shot, Catholic or no Catholic; he could be an Irish spy in the pay of the English. And the Devlins howled and wailed and two hundred fat bitches marched to Clune and

McCann and McCandless and said it was cold-blooded bloody murder killin a Catholic and if it happened again they'd take their families out of the Falls and let the army clean out the IRA. . . . They'd be blamin him for that too in a minute. . . .

"You lost McManus." That was what was comin out of Clune's thin wee face now. "You fuckin-well find him, and when you find him, you fuckin-well kill him. . . . Start on the sister and do anythin you have to . . . that fancy wee biddy knows where he's goin . . . take Callaghan and away on . . . the word's out on him all over the thirty-two counties and we don't want to see aither of youse till he's dead. . . ."

He didn't talk like that when the cameras for the telly came around. It was always Clune or McCann or McCandless on the telly and they didn't say fuckin-well to the cameras. It was all fancy and la-de-da then. They were like bloody Englishmen then. The cameras'd hear it different from me. . . . These three didn't plant bombs, or kill soldiers or policemen. . . . Staff work, by Jasus. That was right soft work. . . . All Clune got when he tried makin a bomb was an eye patch and a singed eyebrow!

There she was up ahead by a hundred yards going through Larne, drivin in her young man's car with a big picnic basket in the back seat. *She* knew where her brother was, by Jasus. She was right easy in her mind about him, to be goin on a picnic on a day when it was goin to come down in sheets.

"It's a queer bloody day for a picnic," Powers said to Callaghan. "Look at it. It's gonta pour."

"Och, the picnic's ony a blind for her oul woman. He's takin her to some hotel for a good knock at her. They'll ate all that grub when he's had all he wants."

"Maybe."

Powers kept her a hundred yards ahead. The Holy Trinity of the kitchen table were out of sight. McManus was out of sight and out of reach. He concentrated his fury on Maureen McManus.

Already in his mind he had disposed of her young man. Not by any specific act. The thought that he would kill him didn't consciously enter his head. He had already killed him without a thought. Somewhere back on their journey from Belfast behind the car ahead, he had cleared the ground. That fellow was a nuisance. He wouldn't be free to deal with the girl with him around and alive. The young man died in his own vague dismissal from Powers' mind.

Powers didn't think about life and death, apart from his own. He had no sense of time-future. Acts were acts that ended without future effect in him. They arose out of the intensity of his emotions. They died with the emotions. When McManus asked him once whether he ever thought about "the fact of someone dying when you sight in from an upstairs window on a soldier," Powers said, "I'm a baker." McManus didn't know what he meant. Neither did Powers. The question was abstract. The baker's trade was not. Another man's death was abstract; his own was not.

His own death was something to be thought about. He rolled names about in his head—Wolf Tone, Robert Emmet, Patrick Pearse—a long string of them. Their names were on monuments and on the lips of schoolchildren. He didn't know much about them except that they were rebels and fought the English and died "for Ireland," and there were songs about them. Children learned the songs in the Separate schools. And there was a pub in Dublin where Robert Emmet used to go and the old men who drank there every day talked about him every day. That was what Powers wanted for himself.

McManus said to him one night when Powers was talking about them, "They were hanged," and Powers winced. That was no way to die; a disagreeable way to die. He said nothing, but the alternative, the only alternative he could face, was to die fearlessly with a gun in his hand, storming the enemy or being stormed by the enemy, in some action with the makings of a song in it.

He understood what Clune and McCann and McCandless were at when the decision was made to lure civilians onto time bombs and kill Protestant children at play on the streets. Sooner or later it would bring civil war for sooner or later the Protestants would throw off English restraint and come storming into the Catholic districts. Then the great actions the song-makers could make songs of would take place and Pat Powers would be sung about, like Tone, and Emmet, and Pearse. . . . But hanging; that was the way a bloody rabbit died, in a snare.

And Clune sent him chasing this girl, like a ferret down a rabbit hole. Why did he keep thinking about rabbits? If you're used like a ferret you'll think like a ferret, and for that he blamed Clune. But the girl was there, a hundred yards ahead, and one thing was enough, sometimes too much, at one time. His rage burned at her like a blow-lamp.

"I don't like being this far from the Falls, Pat," Callaghan said.

"You're coddin."

"I'm not. I mean, you leave a bomb in a car and walk away and there's another car down the street to whip you back into the Falls or Ardoyne or somewhere. But Jasus—where d'ye run to here?"

"Are you thinkin of runnin from thon wee girl?"

"Y'know what I mean."

"Aye. Y'mean you've got the wind up. Jasus, Michael Collins run rings round them all over Ireland. . . ."

"He got killed in an ambush. . . ."

"Och, shut your gub."

"That's all right, but I'm no Michael Collins."

Powers wanted to say, "Well, I am," but Callaghan was an ignorant wee bugger. He's the kind who wouldn't know you were just talkin the God's honest truth if you said you were another Michael Collins; he'd think you had a swelled head. He wasn't goin to explain himself to bloody Callaghan.

The car ahead stopped outside an ice-cream shop in Carnlough and Powers parked behind it. The girl and her young man went into the shop.

92 ((

"You're a wee bit near them," Callaghan said.

"You watch this. Come on in."

They went into the ice-cream shop. It was a tiny place and four adults crowded it. Maureen McManus ordered a vanilla cone with a Cadbury's Milk Flake bar stuck in the ice cream. The young man ordered the same. Powers turned his back to the girl and ran the palm of his hand quickly over her hips. She jumped and spun. Powers turned to her and said mournfully, "I beg your pardon, miss. There's not much room in this wee place." To her young man he said, "It's a grand day for a spin round the coast."

"Yes." He was slender and not made for angry reprisals.

Powers tried the Irish smile. "Are youse goin all the way round?"

"No." It was curtly dismissive of a working-class intrusion on a middle-class right to privacy.

Callaghan ordered the same for Powers and himself and while they waited they watched Maureen and her friend get their raincoats from their car, juggle the cones while they put on the coats, and cross the road to sit on the seawall.

In the car again, Powers sucked his cone and munched on his Milk Flake and said like a greedy boy, "Jasus, this is nice." Then, waving his cone towards the shop, and grinning like a naughty boy, "Did you see what I did in there?"

"No. What?"

"She has a nice soft arse. I had a wee feel at it."

Michael Collins could have done that. When Powers did it, he felt like Michael Collins standing by his bicycle on the edge of a Dublin crowd that watched the police searching the house from which Collins had just escaped. Powers' Irish history was learned in the streets, in the songs, and in the paperback editions of Irish exploits like Dan Breen's *"My* Fight for Irish Freedom" or Bernadette Devlin's "The Price of *My* Soul," though he didn't understand much of what Bernadette wrote in that one. A month ago when Powers was talking about these books McManus said the best book by an Irish hero was *"My* Big Ego in the Fight for Ireland's

Freedom." Powers felt there was something wrong with that, but he didn't know what it was. He said that if he could write a book he would call it *"My* Fight for Ireland One Nation."

Callaghan liked the joke about Maureen's bottom. "Maybe that fella'll give her another wee feel up the Glen," he said.

"A wee feel up the what?" That was another good joke. So good that Maureen's young man looked quickly from the wall to locate the laughter, looked quickly out to sea, said something, and hurried the girl back to his car.

Powers and Callaghan went after them, a hundred yards behind. The road was serpentine. As often as not their prey was out of sight. That didn't matter. In less than half a minute they were in sight again around the bend the same hundred yards ahead. So Powers brooded on a dull drive.

The road wound. The rain threatened but did not fall. The rising wind blew off the gray dreach sea shaking the car. The expression on the face of Maureen McManus's young man as he hurried her to his car had suddenly fixed itself in Powers' brooding mind. His hands were tight on the wheel, his foot heavy on the pedal. He came round bends and found himself within twenty-five yards of the car in front. "Stupid shit. Can't drive. Can't keep the same speed. . . ."

"It's you, Pat. You keep puttin your foot down. . . ."

"What the fuckin hell d'ya mean, it's me?" A screeching anger sawed in his head. He held the wheel hard to keep himself from backhanding Callaghan's face. "You saw his face when he shoved her into the car. You'da thought he was gonta vomit, lookin at me . . . lookin down his fuckin nose at me. . . . By Jasus, he'll learn. . . ."

"Slow down or you'll climb up his back!"

"Shut your fuckin gub!"

Callaghan sat hard against the car door making his small frame smaller, telling himself not to speak not to speak not to speak. He had seen Powers leap from morose silence to almost hysterical geniality to screeching rage. Sometimes he thought he had a sorta

94 ((

softenin of the brain. Sometimes, though, he was very stiff, very soldierly, very stern, the oul head up and the shoulders back and the chest out. Secretly, Callaghan thought sometimes that Powers would have liked to be in the Paratroop Brigade and worn their berets and their mottled camouflaged uniforms and their military boots, but he was careful never to say so. Secretly, he thought sometimes that Powers would have liked to be the Major he shot a couple of months ago leading a sweep through the Falls. He'd said afterwards, when they talked about the ambush: Now if he'd done this and this and this and come up here and went down there he coulda . . . and there were things you had to be careful about, with Powers. Callaghan looked out to sea to keep from looking at Powers, and remembered the night in one of the pubs in Dublin when they were down there for a rest—it was a long narrow pub where the musicians came to play—and Powers sat back on his stool, blocking the narrow aisle and keeping it blocked till every man who tried to push past him read the smile on his face and said, "Excuse me, please," in a nice voice. And then the well-dressed business-lookin fellow came down the aisle and wouldn't say it. He said, "Sit forward a bit and let people pass." "Och, just stay there for a while. I'll be leavin myself in another hour," Powers said, and the man shoved him. It was funny. He was in great form after he smashed the fellow's face in . . . laughin, jokin. . . . He hadn't realized the memory made him laugh.

"What're ya laughin at?" said Powers.

"I was thinkin about the night in Dublin thon fella wouldn't say please."

"Aye. I'll bet you his oul mother still doesn't know him."

They came round Garron Point into the long sweep of Red Bay and the road was empty. No car. No girl. No girl's young man. *"Jasus Christ!"* Powers lifted the car and went round the bay and through Waterfoot flat out, screeching the tires on the cold summer road at the sharp right turn out of the village. But the road was still empty when they reached Cushendall and Powers was sure they hadn't traveled at his speed: they were up Glenariff. He went back, still roaring over the road, and turned up the Glen. And his anger was different anger now. It was cold, level, and malignant. "He tried t'make an arse-hole outa me," he said. "He musta went like buggery t'get to the Glen Road before I turned Garron Point. *Right y'are! Right y'are! Right y'are!*"

The young couple's car was parked across the road from the official entrance to the Glen. Powers turned in the lay-by and went back a quarter of a mile. He parked his car hard against the bank.

Glenariff is a beautiful wooded fairy-gorge through which the Glenariff River tumbles and twists to the open fields below. Its rough descent to the sea has been tamed by a complex of rustic stairs and bridges and rails that confine the public to a narrow path. The sun, when it shines, is filtered through the foliage, and there is a magic about the place that is compounded by the sound of little waterfalls and the chatter of the stream. The sound makes talk impossible. Roger Casement used to walk here because the sound shut out the voices of men and left him free to brood on their iniquities, or to weave fantasies of his own.

Powers and Callaghan came into the Glen down the steep bank of trees and bushes and ferns above the stream. They found a rock ledge above a noisy little waterfall. The path down to the next level was a series of twisting steps that passed directly below the ledge. They sat down to wait, unable to see or hear the approach of their prey. They watched, instead, the rustic steps immediately below them. Maureen and her young man would simply appear there. Presently Powers stood up. He had decided how to handle this thing. The drop below was, he thought, about twelve feet, and he weighed more than twelve stone, bone and muscle.

The couple stepped suddenly into sight, hand in hand. The young man was carrying the picnic basket. Powers stepped out from the ledge and pushed off. He landed with both feet on the young man's shoulders, his heels striking on either side of the base of his neck, and rode down, well balanced on the falling body. He shoved

Maureen with his left hand as he passed her, sending her sprawling on her face. He took the rail with his right hand as the body hit ground. He did not fall but stepped off the body onto the stairs, like a circus performer. He scarcely heard the girl's screams above the sound of the water and Callaghan was down and had her pinned to the ground. He was sitting astride her with her head pulled back and her mouth covered firmly with both his hands. The picnic basket was intact by her head.

The young man did not move. Powers turned him over. His eyes were wide open. His neck was broken. He was dead. Powers picked him up and heaved his body through the sheet of water across the rail. It disappeared from sight except for its lower right leg and the foot that hit and stayed on a polished brown rock. The rest of the body was under and behind the waterfall. Powers considered going over the rail to lower the foot into the water. He looked at his boots. No: he'd get his feet wet. "Up the bank," he yelled, and they dragged Maureen McManus to her feet.

She tried to fight and was slapped savagely across the face. Powers rammed the muzzle of his .38 police revolver against her screaming mouth and it froze open, and silent. He pointed up the steep, bushy bank. Callaghan dragged on one of her arms, Powers put away his gun, rammed his open right hand under her hips and shoved, his big blunt fingers probing. He had the picnic basket in his left hand.

The road was empty. Callaghan sat beside her in the back of the car, his gun against her belly. Powers turned the car again and drove up towards the high and desolate land.

"I'm hungry," he said, "tell the wee girl t'givus a piece."

Terrified, Maureen gave them sandwiches. "Jasus, they're nice," Powers said. He looked back at her. "You're nice too." He was grinning.

"You killed him," she said.

"Who?"

"Him." She couldn't say his name. Somewhere in the back of her mind there was a pathetic instinct still to protect him. She knew he was dead and disposed of and she had not yet absorbed his death.

"Aye," Powers said, and left the unfenced road. He drove across the tufted grass, around the base of Evish Hill and up its west side. They were out of sight of the road here. The tires spun on the polished grass and he gunned the car forward, swinging it about to avoid big stones. They went over the rim of a wide hollow. Evish Lake was below them, a tiny body of water with a bare hut on its shore.

"Away on in w'her," Powers said, and Callaghan pulled her from the car, waving his gun.

The hut was little more than a shelter. It had a window at each end covered with plastic. There was straw in one corner and a three-legged stool lying on its side in the middle of the dead-grass floor. The door closed when it was pushed hard. It had to be lifted a little. Hill farmers sheltered here when the weather was bad and they came with their dogs to gather their sheep. There were three hill farms. They were far away. So were the sheep.

"Y'can sit on the stool," Powers said to her, and set the stool on its legs. The ground was uneven and the stool teetered. She steadied it and sat down. The high wind whistled around and through the hut.

"Take off your Burberry," Powers said.

She clutched her hands together in her lap. "I'm cold," she said. He was dead. It was beginning to sink in. This man killed him. She was trembling.

"Where's Johnny?"

"I don't know."

Powers was very quiet. There was a terrible gentleness about him. His big peasant face was soft.

"I'm not gonta sit here all night listenin t'lies," he said. "Y'gave him your car. Where was it found?"

What was the harm? If Johnny drove the car north it was because he wasn't going to stay in the North. "Ballycastle," she said.

"Then where did he go?"

"I don't know."

He could scarcely hear her above the wind. "Where did he go?"

"I don't know. I don't know." The stool tottered. She had to scramble to stay upright. Her knees opened. Powers eyes opened with them.

"He sent you word he was well away. Where from?"

"There was no word. Honest to God, mister, there was no word. We don't know where he is. He never said. . . ." She was rattling on and he listened.

"I'm ony gonta ask you one other time," he said softly. "Where'll we find him?"

"Mister, God be my witness, we don't know. He never told us. Please, mister, we never had word from him."

"Callaghan," Powers said. His voice was low and gentle. "Away up the hill and see. Walk all round the lip and then walk round it another time. Don't come back till I call you." He did not look at Callaghan. He was looking straight into the girl's face. "Away on."

"Right y'are." Callaghan went out. The wind whipped into the hut. The girl pulled her coat about her. Callaghan closed the door, looking at her till the door shut her from sight. His look was gluttonous.

"I'll give you one more chance, miss," Powers said. "Where'll we find Johnny?"

"In the name of God, believe me, mister. I don't know."

"Y'know somethin."

"I know nothing."

Powers took off his jacket and threw it on the floor. "Your time's done," he said. "Take off your Burberry."

"No."

He unbuckled his belt. "Take it off."

"No." She stood up suddenly, the stool in her hand. She gripped one leg in both hands. "I'll brain you if you try to beat me with that belt."

"I wouldn't use a belt on you. You're a nice wee thing. Take off the coat."

She backed to the wall and raised the stool. Powers didn't take off his belt. He opened his fly. "Look, that's what I'm gonta beat you with. Take off the coat." He dropped his trousers around his ankles and she charged and swung with the stool. It was a vicious swing. All her frantic strength was in it. It was too strong. He bent under it and yanked an ankle from under her. She went forward and her head hit the door. She was stunned but not out. Her struggles were weak and to weaken them more he rapped his knuckles against her jaw and ripped at her clothes. It was difficult, for she fought as she could, half conscious; and his anger rose with every difficulty. Clothes wouldn't tear. He thought of a knife and couldn't reach his pocket, in case she reached the door. He dragged and tore and threw her about. Her cries were met by the wind and thrown back at her. She had to be naked. It roared in his head. The whiteness of her maddened him. When everything she had on was shredded and scattered about the hut, he threw her on the straw.

By the time he got his boots off because his trousers prevented him in his frenzy from getting at the laces, she had staggered to the door and had it half open. He brought her down with a rugby tackle and rolled her back on the straw, driving his knee at her clamped thighs. She was still stronger than he had imagined, and his nails drew blood from her thighs as he tore them open and pinned her down.

"Fight, you wee white bitch. Go'n—fight me. Gimme a fightin fuck. . . ." He closed his hands around her throat. Her body was stiff and hard. All she could do was spit and he slammed his mouth onto hers. She tried to bite and he tightened his grip on her throat. He took his time and told the hut and the hills and the girl of his pleasure.

Then he rose off her and put on his trousers. He sat on the stool to tie his laces. She lay curled in a ball on the ground, moaning and wailing. He put on his jacket.

100   ((

"Thank you very much, miss," he said gratefully. "That was good." He gathered up the shreds of her clothes and wrapped her shoes in them. Then he opened the door of the hut and waved Callaghan back from the rim of the hollow.

"Away on in," he said. "I'll get rid of these."

He spent an hour on the hill, gathering stones and building a cairn on the heap of torn clothes and the shoes. Somewhere up here, he didn't know quite where Ossian was supposed to be buried. Ossian, Cuchullain, Diarmud, Goll McMorna, Finn—Jasus, if there was any truth in the oul stories, they were the boys that could put a woman down. And *what* women! Big, strong, the stories said. The Champions of the old time musta had many's a fightin fuck they remembered all their lives. The storytellers remembered some of them. The old Gaelic days must've been bloody great. He was sorry he knew no Gaelic—Irish they called it now, because it was a sort of invented language. But he'd built a cairn to a good fightin fuck like the oul ones got. When he went back to the hut, Callaghan was tying his shoes outside the closed door.

"She gave me a wee bit of a wrasel the first time," he said, and tried to light a cigarette in the wind. "The second time she never bothered." He asked Powers curiously, "D'you think they get t'like it that way?"

"I never gave it a second thought."

"How're we gonta do it?"

Powers didn't tell him. He went into the hut and closed the door. "Where's your brother, miss? It's your last chance."

She was curled in a corner, silent, half conscious. Her white body was covered with bleeding scratches and discoloring bruises. She didn't take her last chance. He knelt over her and took her by the throat. There was no struggle.

They threw her into Evish Lake.

"There'll be roadblocks," Callaghan said when they were close to Ballymoney.

))   101

"We'll dump this car and take a bus."

They rode the bus to the Belfast depot and walked to the Falls. The streets were empty. The streets were never empty on a summer evening, unless there was an ambush. The stillness was not the stillness of an early Sunday morning before first Mass. It was a deserted stillness. There were no soldiers.

It had been raining in Belfast. The street surface was dark and wet. The air was heavy. From somewhere, but from what direction it was hard to say, the sound of a voice brushed against the stillness. Shouting? Not shouting, but loud and far away; or muffled by the little houses, half drowned by the heavy air. A man's voice. And not shouting. But persistent. Making a speech? That was it; making a speech. They stood in the street, listening.

Then a massive sound rolled over the stillness, a familiar sound but different; a higher pitch than the familiar sound, a collective roar, like a football crowd, but filtered by women's voices, a roar that whirred and shrilled.

"Celtic Park," Callaghan said. "What's on there?"

"A meetin?"

"What meetin?"

Powers walked to the end of the street and looked down the intersection. The same deserted stillness. Con Casey's was on the corner. He walked into the pub. Casey picked up a handful of clean glasses and put them in his sink. Head down, he washed them. "Pat," he said.

"What's up, Con?"

"Nothin up w'me, Pat."

"The Park, Con. What's on at the football field?"

"A meetin."

"What meetin? Just get it out, Con, from start to finish. What's up?"

"All right." Casey looked at him as if he had reserves of courage and was ready to draw on them. "The night, on the telly. The Protestants put up barricades for a no-go area. . . ."

"Och! And the army tore them down?"

102 ((

"Aye. But you shoulda seen it, Pat. Christ, them men. They were a fuckin army, Pat. An army. You shoulda seem them march. They're trained, Pat—they're a fuckin army. . . ."

"Maybe we're not?"

"There's thirty thousand a them. Holy God, y'shoulda seen them, Pat."

"D'you think we're gonta run from them?"

"No." Casey seemed about to say more, and decided not to.

"What's this meetin, Con?"

"The women saw the Protestant army on the telly. The priests saw it too. The word went round like forked lightnin, then people were headin for the Park when your boys opened up on an army patrol Two wee girls an their mother was killed . . . twins, five years old. The father's dead. The whola the Falls is at Celtic Park, Pat."

"The army killed the wee girls?"

"No." Casey had said enough. Then he said too much. He said again, "No."

"Who?"

"Your boys." He almost raised his head.

"The army killed them, Con. Did ya hear that?"

"The army killed them, Pat."

"Y'heard that?"

"I heard it, Pat." He looked into his sink. "But nobody believes it. They're goin outa their minds."

"Up you." Powers stormed out, trailing Callaghan like a small shadow. They trotted all the way to Celtic Park.

The Falls was in Celtic Park, men, women, and children. The great host filled the playing field. The priests were in Celtic Park. They were there from the Falls, Ardoyne, Andersonstown, and Springfield districts. They packed the stands. The telephone monitors must have had a busy time. They must have heard and reported a lot of what the phoning priests said to one another. Whatever it was, it justified the army being pulled back to let them at it.

They were at it. They had gathered together loudspeakers and a microphone. Father Murphy had its stem by the throat and was speaking quietly. "Two babies," he said. "Two babies and their widow mother, shot down in their own street by their own people. Shot dead in their own street. Shot to bits and not a soldier anywhere near them.

"What were they shot for? To protect you. To protect us. To protect us from the British army. To protect us from our Protestant neighbors." His preacher's voice teased their ears. "The people that protect us all shoot us dead in our own defense . . . I saw this one happen," he said, "and there wasn't a soldier within a hundred feet of that wee widow and her babies. Are they goin t'tell us our protectors can't shoot better than that? Are they goin t'tell us the British army did it? The soldiers hadn't fired a shot. What *are* they goin t'tell us?" He paused and his voice growled harshly. "That while Catholics are dyin we need them to protect us, even if they have to kill Catholic widow-women and their babies to convince us? An end of it! That's what I say to you. In the name of Almighty God, an end of it. There are better ways. In all the centuries these men never won anythin for us. They always lost for us when there were other ways to win. They are in our hands. We're not in their hands. Who covered and protected them? We did. Whose children kept the soldiers from takin them? Yours did. They're in our hands. Without us they can't go on—so in the name of the Son of God and his Blessed Mother, make an end of it.

"We love our Protestant neighbors. Give them a chance to love us. Put away the guns. . . ."

He was heard in silence. When he had finished the silence remained, scratched by the small voices of children crying and laughing and calling to one another. There was no football roar for Father Murphy, but the set faces and the stillness of a great crowd had its own sense of dread. They were waiting for something else. The priests were helping it to the microphone.

It was Mrs. Machin of the little shop.

Powers and Callaghan were almost at the front now, walking around the edge of the crowd. "The Church was never for us," Powers said to Callaghan with an air of angry exposition. "It was always for England." He had heard a man say that at a meeting.

Nervously, Callaghan, who had heard this often, said, "I've heard that."

"I'm *tellin* you."

Callaghan wasn't sure that Powers knew much more about these high things than he did himself, but he knew the high and exalted look on his comrade's face, and kept his silence.

Mrs. Machin was ready, a priest at each elbow in case her balance failed her. Powers was directly in front of her now, standing beside Clune in the front rank of the crowd. "There'll have to be punishments for this," he said strongly to Clune.

"Keep your mouth shut here."

Powers' lighted face darkened. He turned it from Clune, whose one visible eye was fastened bitterly on Mrs. Machin.

"Priests can talk about lovin their Protestant neighbors," she said, and a rustle that might have been quiet laughter went over the crowd like a light wind over barley.

"I don't love my Protestant neighbors. I never had any. I live in the Falls and there's none here." They laughed at that, more openly but with restraint in the presence of danger and death. "But from what I know about them from livin in Ulster and the Falls all my life . . . *I hate the dirty bastards!"* The priests looked stonily forward.

The football roar went up. And down, quickly. But that was not what was on their minds or in their fears.

She spoke what was on their minds. "Did'ye see the telly the night? Did'ye see the lovin Protestant neighbors on the telly?" The silence in the field was dead. "They're ready!" she screamed. *"Did y'see them?* Thons a real army. Thon boys isn't English. When they start, there's gonta be no English MP's to tell them not to be too rough w'the poor bloody Papishes. An' whose gonta fight thon boys?"

She had seen Powers beside Clune in the front rank. All her rough eloquence and her instinct for drama and her fear leaped on him.

She raised a big fat arm and pointed. *"You,* Patsy Powers? Are *you* gonta fight them? That's the one that tried to tear the tits off me for wantin to post a letter for a wee boy—an luk at his face! Me, an oul fat woman near tore the face off him. Is that what's gonta fight the Protestant army? *That!"* She screamed it. "And you, Mr. Clune down there, you one-eyed bloody wonder, are you gonta lead your brave boys into the fight? Them that shoots at sojers and hits widow-women and their babies a hundred feet away? You heard the Father himself tellin you . . *. a hundred feet away!*

"Well, thon army's not gonta fight Provos or Officials. They're gonta come in here and burn us to the groun . . . the Falls'll be in flames and they won't give a damn who burns. Them that can get out'll walk to the Border and they'll niver be back. . . ."

They knew it. They received it in silence. There was nothing to roar about. It was a time for tears and fears.

But suddenly there was scattered dissent and Mrs. Machin, who had been tasting her eloquence and its effect on more people than she had spoken to in all her fifty years, responded to it with fury.

"Thon lot isn't coddin," she shrieked. "They're sick of IRA bombs and IRA bullets and they're sick of us hidin them and they're ready to give it back. An they'll give it to *us*—you and me. We're gonta get massacreed and they won't want what's left of us in the bloody Irish Republic."

Her instinct drove her to the point as the dissent grew louder. "There's women walkin among youse w'papers to sign—a petition for peace afore there's none of us left. Put your name to it . . . the night. . . ."

The word was out, the sources the press relied on had got to the phones, the reporters were arriving, and a BBC mobile television van. . . . With her own version of the Irish Smile, and the native instinct for the paying word, Mrs. Machin yelled for the reporters and the camera, "We love our Protestant neighbors . . . sign the papers for peace . . ." and the camera caught her raised arms and distorted face, the shotgun microphone caught her declaration of love, the fugitive scraps of paper on which verbatim reports appeared to be written, were being covered with Pitmans on peace.

The football roar went up for Mrs. Machin. The scattered dissent turned into scattered fighting. *"Sign for peace!"* Mrs. Machin roared.

"Let me go up there," Powers shouted to Clune.

"What for? I'm goin up."

"Here's Clune to tell you the shootin's not done yet," Mrs. Machin jeered. "D'ye want to hear the wee man? D'ye want to hear wee Patch Clune?"

The roar was not a word, but it was "No," and the fighting about the field spread. Women moved about to avoid it. Petition papers were torn and thrown in the air, and women blocked Clune's passage to the microphone. "We don't need you, Clune," Mrs. Machin yelled at him, and the roar supported her. The women drove Clune back.

"I'll go up," Powers said.

"Och, for fuck's sake shut your big mouth," Clune said savagely. "There's gonta be punishments. The shootin'll not stop for a bunch a scared bloody woman. There'll be punishments for this."

Petition-paper carriers were already being roughly handled and their handlers were being attacked by women. The Park was empty- ing. The press had the message: the Provinces and England would have it on the late news, the papers would enlarge on it, and the whole world would have it tomorrow. The Catholics plead for peace: Will the Protestants let them have it?

"Away on back," Clune said to Powers.

"What house?"

"Joy Street." Clune pushed away with his chosen after him. Powers followed. Clune saw him. "Not a fuckin crowd," he said, and waved him away.

Sullenly, and scalded in his self-esteem, Powers took Callaghan and walked to Joy Street.

Clune was there, and McCann and McCandless and a dozen more —the Belfast Brigade staff—and three English journalists, from the *Sunday Times,* the *Observer,* and the *Guardian.* "The pipelines," Clune called them contemptuously. "They're so fuckin eager to be nice they'll believe any bloody thing y'tell them."

He was telling them. His voice was tight and harsh and high, and he spoke quickly, on the brink of eruption. He was angry, and afraid. The Catholics were slipping out of their hands.

"The war goes on," Clune said urgently. "We want peace but not at any price. There'll be no peace till there's justice and there'll be no justice till the British gunmen take their guns and their armored cars outa here and back to England. . . ."

"Can there be justice till the shooting stops?" the *Guardian* man asked like an associate professor of political science.

"Thas all," Clune said with a homicidal one-eyed glare. "Away on."

Nervously, the journalists left. They would be brave in the papers. "Joseph Clune, interviewed in an IRA house in the Falls. . . ." Daniels in the lion's den. They left as they were bidden.

The Belfast Brigade got down to work.

"Powers," Clune said from behind the kitchen table. "Did'ye get the girl?"

"Yes, sir. She wouldn't talk. She's dead."

"McManus left her car at Ballycastle."

"She said that."

Screaming, *"I thought she wouldn't talk?"*

"That's all she said."

"He stole a car at the golf course. He left it at Sixmilecross. He left the one he took there in Francis Healy's field at Clady." He pulled a pile of clothing from behind him. "Is them his?"

"Yes."

"He crossed the Border at Clady." Clune waved an impatient hand at a man in the circle. "Give them fifty pounds. Find him, Powers, and bring back the change. Away on, the two of youse, and don't come back till you kill'm."

They went up the street to their bare house, and made some tea, and sat at the kitchen table in silence.

Powers was black in the mind. Clune lay in his head like a solid lump, obstructing thought. He was murdering Clune with every throb of his raging nerves.

"Pat," Callaghan said tentatively, "thon wee girl was a nice piece."

Powers nodded and heard only the sound.

"I never fucked one like than afore. She was all white."

The head nodded, full of Clune. It was nodding at Clune.

"Pat?"

Powers raised his head, looked and saw after a while. "What?"

"What'y like best—fuckin or killin?"

"Och." He stood up. "One's as good as the other."

He went up to bed.

EIGHT

GOD be merciful to the young and clever. McManus knew exactly what to do and how to do it.

He awoke in the evening at nine and, in his middle-class way, went along the hall for a bath. At ten he went down to the small lobby and asked for a pack lunch to be prepared. It would be ready for him at breakfast time, the young man on the desk said.

"No. I want it tonight."

"It'll be stale by the morning."

"It'll be eaten by the morning." McManus offered no explanation and the desk clerk looked at him with doubt and annoyance.

"I'll have to make it myself," he said. "People don't work in the kitchen all night. And you'll have to pay for it now." Why would a man sleep all day and want a pack lunch before he went back to bed at night? He didn't ask. His look asked for him, and fixed McManus in his memory.

At midnight, his pack on his back, McManus came quietly downstairs to let himself out. The small hotel seemed asleep. The young man was still behind the desk, staring at the pages of a paperback book. He did not look up but he was not reading. McManus watched his reflection in the glass porch and saw him raise his head to stare. He turned in the street to see the clerk standing on the steps, still staring, like a man reading a trail.

No matter: he was away again. He passed the church, paused on the bridge to look at the stars in the waters of the Finn. The night was cool. He crossed the bridge into Ballybofey and walked out of the town into the dark country where there were no lamps, only hedges and stone walls and, as he climbed towards the Barnesmore Gap, earthen banks bound by grass, and higher up, the rising moor on his right and the dropping moor on his left. And the moon, coming and going in a sky that clouded with every step; and presently the drizzling rain. He took his plastic poncho from his pack and went on. He had walked this road since his school days and had never been on it on a dry day, or night.

But the rain made no difference. He was away. He walked steadily, stopping for ten minutes' rest in every hour. Once he heard footsteps approaching and slowed his pace. A man came out of the dark, crossed to the other side of the road to pass him, and did not speak. McManus stopped to listen for retreating footsteps and did not hear them. He moved, and stopped, and heard them, running. Men are afraid of what they meet in the dark. This passing stranger's fears revived his own. He walked faster, took fewer rests, and in the false dawn climbed down under a bridge over a stream to wash his feet, dry them, and rub them with metholated spirits. He changed his socks, rinsed the old ones in the stream, and pinned them to his pack. Half an hour later the light was in the sky and Donegal town was below him.

With ten good miles behind and before him a sleeping town that would soon be crowded, he climbed the hill and made camp out of sight of the road. The pack lunch was still untouched. Chicken sandwiches, a solid lump of smoked cheese, a piece of heavy fruitcake, a bottle of Harp Lager, and a plastic knife. They had given him what the tourists get, in spite of his clothes. He wasn't hungry but it was time to eat. He ate in his sleeping bag, the poncho on the wet grass under it, his damp trousers hanging from a loop on the tent peak. He was hot again, sweating again, and sleep would not come. The day came up, the sun came out, the wind rose, and he was still awake. He took the poncho to a rise on the hill and lay on it, watching the road.

112 ((

The sleepless waiting in the day worried him. Ten miles in a night wasn't enough. The way he had chosen to do it wasn't the best way though it looked good when he first thought of it. He was well away, but not far enough away. His thinking was nervous. When this pack lunch was eaten he had to find more food to carry. That meant shops and cafés in towns, or nights in hotels. It meant people. What people? That was always the question. The word would be out on him, over the thirty-two counties of Ireland. Here and there some men wouldn't bother to look for him, but some would sniff the air, look in every face, watch the roads and the hills and the main routes through towns.

Down on the road cars passed occasionally now, going west down to Donegal town or east to Ballybofey and Stranorlar, or maybe up to Letterkenny, or maybe over the Border to Derry.

The wind died, the sun warmed. He went back to his tent. Should he see a doctor? He felt desperately tired now, light-headed. What doctor, where? His socks were dry and his trousers. He slept till noon, lying on his sleeping bag, then went back to watch the road. Busses passed, going east and west.

The coach tours were up and about. They passed up the road through the Gap, going counterclockwise round Donegal, carrying their quota of American tourists doing a circuit of the Republic. The English had stopped coming to Ireland since the British Embassy in Dublin was burned down. Not so many Americans came either. They didn't know the difference between the North and the South, even when they were Irish-Americans full of wind and passion against the English.

They were no better than the English; just busier, but it was the English who brought the cash and spent it. The Americans brought the pink slips of their package tours and spent very little hard cash. Still, they came.

Another coach passed. Three since this morning. They probably went up the Foyle Estuary and down the west coast to Bundoran, maybe back as far as Sligo. He lay thinking about that. An old man came up the slope across the road and stood by the roadside. He seemed to stand without purpose, looking at nothing. A bus came over the Gap and the old man waved it down. There was no bus stop. Another coach came up from Donegal town and went over the Gap. He thought for a long time about buses and coaches half-full of American tourists. He packed up, went down to the road, and waited for a bus to come. There was an easy solution to his problem, if he could make it work.

The bus came and he slept most of the way to Sligo. I'm well away, he told himself till it bored him. There was a way to lose himself. He bought a cheap tweed suit in a shop in Sligo and stuffed his old paint-plastered clothes in his pack. At Sligo's Great Southern Hotel there were no questions, no doubts. He had the look of a young gentleman with his pack on his back, tired of the wind and the rain's way, wanting a soft bed for a night and a shave with hot water, and a bath.

He came down to the bar and bought the barman a drink. The two days' growth was still on his face. It was thin, unimpressive, and untidy, and it made him look immature. "Do you put up American coach parties?" he asked the barman.

The man was small, plump, and busy. He ran his professional eye over McManus. "What else these days?" he said. "The English took their bats home."

"What are the chances of joining an American coach tour here?"

The barman poured drinks, filled his tray, went out to the lounge to serve his customers, and said when he came back, "You were askin me, sir?"

"Could I join an American coach tour here?"

"Tired walkin?"

"I'm tired of sleeping out and walking."

"That's a bad cough you've got."

"I want rid of the cough. What are my chances of a seat?"

"It depends." The bartender priced the tweed suit. New and cheap. "Some drivers are a bit pricey."

"That's not a problem." McManus pushed a pound note across

the bar. The man ignored it. He pushed another one after it. "You know the drivers?"

"The lot. There's always empty seats these days, but it's against the law—pickin up, y'know. Where d'you want to go?"

"Bantry."

"Charley Murphy's your man. He's not greedy. He's due in an hour." He pocketed the two pounds without acknowledgment. "I'll see what I can do. What's your room?"

McManus told him and went upstairs. He lay down, got up, tried the radio and found it irritating, paced the room and found it too small. He lay down again.

There was no reason to be nervous now, but he was shaking and sweating heavily and suddenly aware of loneliness and isolation. He was a fugitive, and sick. He was twenty-two and a badly trained gunman (three days in a camp in Donegal) and a little boy who needed his father and mother; six feet tall and very small, with pains in his chest. It was all well and good to decide to run to the southwest. It was empty and lonely. But when he got to the southwest? He hadn't given that a thought; all he had done was run.

Father, father, father. The image was in his closed eyes; his father's pale gentle face. When he was a child and they had walked past corner-boys on Belfast's streets and he was afraid of them, the quiet voice said, "Don't worry, Johnny. I'll take care of them."

They shouted "oul four-eyes" at his father because he wore eye-glasses, and "bible feet" at his mother because she turned out her toes when she walked, and "bacon mouth" at his father because his lips were heavy. Then what in God's name made him go among them when he was grown? He didn't know; some Irish illusion; he couldn't think.

The phone was at his elbow.

He could risk using it now. He needed desperately to use it, just to hear a voice he could trust. They couldn't watch a phone call reach the house the way they could watch a telegram arriving. He asked for his father's number. It brought a momentary sense of sweet easement that crept through him and went quickly stale. He waited impatiently through cracklings and clickings that sounded conspiratorial, hostile obstructions between him and the comfort of his father's voice.

A voice he didn't know said, "Yes? Who is speaking, please?"

"Who is that?"

"Who is speaking, please?" It was a heavy voice, careful, repulsing, unyielding.

"Have I got the right number? McManus?"

"Yes, sir. Who is speaking?"

"Will you stop that and get my father, please."

"You are John McManus?"

"Yes. Who are you? Will you get my father, please?"

"Will you hold on, please?"

He heard the voices in the background, a woman and several men talking, and a kind of wailing. Then the receiver banged on its little table.

"Johnny? Johnny? Oh, Johnny, my darlin boy . . ." and his father sobbing.

"Daddy!" It came out of him as if he were still a frightened child. "What's up, Daddy? What's up?"

"Maureen . . . oh, Maureen. . . . They killed my wee Maureen . . . Johnny, Johnny, Johnny, run my darlin boy, run, run, run. . . ."

"Daddy! Daddy!" But the phone was taken from his father.

There were more voices, more confusion, and his mother spoke. The strong one. "It's true, Johnny. They murdered her. Your daddy's goin out of his head. Go away, Johnny. Don't come back, my baby. I'll take care of him, Johnny. You run. Don't let them catch you. . . ." She was breaking too.

"Mammy!"

The man who answered the phone said, "Hullo? They can't go on, Johnny. I'm sorry, son. I'm sorry."

McManus could hear only his father's desolate wailing somewhere in the house.

116 ((

"Johnny? Are you there?"

"Yes." It was only a sound.

"Who did it?"

"Powers. Callaghan, Clune. Anybody. Who're you?"

"Police. Inspector Macmillan."

"Joy Street. . . ." He rhymed them off without thinking about them. Streets, numbers, names. Bomb factories. Transit houses.

"Wait a minute. Give me that again. . . ."

"She's dead?" he said.

"Yes."

That was only a fact. How? Questions were almost asked and drifted uselessly away. She was dead, that was the fact that mattered. "The Chemicals' bomb," he said.

"Yes?"

"I drove the van. Wee Jimmy, the Marsh's driver, was in on it. We didn't steal Dr. McDermott's car. He left it for us, with the key in it." It was all spilling out without thought. "She's dead?"

"Yes."

"Tell my mother and father I love them."

"Yes, Johnny."

McManus put the phone on its cradle slowly, as if it didn't matter. And as if putting it back would cut his links with life and death. So it fell very slowly into place, held up by doubt, or air, or irresolution.

Maureen was dead. The full impact came slowly, then it erupted suddenly. He wrapped his face in his pillow and let it come. It tore him, turned to brief rage and revenge, and degenerated into fear and despair.

The barman's knocking turned to banging, and McManus came out of the pillowcase and opened the door. The man's homely-charm smile died.

"There somethin wrong, sir?" Any fool knows a face wracked by weeping. Who knows what to say to it?

"What do you want?"

"I got a seat for you, sir. Is there somethin I can do for you, sir?" It was not part of his barroom performance.

"My sister. I just phoned home. She's dead." McManus shut his teeth to cut off anguished chatter.

After a silent while, "You'll not want the seat then. You'll be goin home?"

"I want it."

That was the queer thing, now. Your sister dies. You swamp your face cryin but you don't go home? "It's entirely up to you, sir. He says he'll carry you by the day for a couple of pounds a day—you buy your own food and beds. O'course—I don't need to tell you, a wee bit of front money would make the man feel nice. . . ."

"How much?"

"Och—three quid, say." Two for me, one for him, you might say but won't. "Remember the name now—Charley Murphy. They're leavin at nine in the mornin."

McManus paid him.

"Can I get you somethin now, sir? Before I go off duty? You're sweatin awful hard. There's a doctor on call, sir. That's the fearful cough you have, now. Anythin I can. . . ."

"No." Go away now.

"I'm sorry about your sister, sir." He went away, mourning.

McManus didn't want to eat, but he drank a bottle of wine, and ordered a second, and a third, and slept a drunken and unrestful sleep, and wailed in it, lamenting his guilt.

He got the back seat in the coach. Nobody wanted to sit there. He crouched numb in his seat waiting out the miles, nursing his guilt. Maureen's death was his fault. He joined the Provos in spite of Bull Baillie's warning. He led his sister to her death and his parents to their heartbreak.

He did not see the landscape. He did not see the American girl with the long brown legs who came and sat beside him and spoke to him. He did not hear her and she went back to her seat, only a little discouraged.

They spent the night in Limerick and he went through the mo tions of getting a room in a fog of sunken indifference.

The next morning he took his place and was alive enough to notice the curious stares and the tentative smiles. The old American couples were cover. That was all he wanted. The American girl came again and spoke to him.

"I don't want to disturb your thoughts, but you're Irish, I know. I heard your voice when you spoke to the driver. Are you a writer?" It was an important question. In her English classes at Boston University they'd done the Irish writers: Yeats, Gregory, O'Casey, Joyce—very difficult, but there were good notes you could buy—and Behan.

McManus said, "Good morning," and ignored her and felt miserably ill. At Bantry, he would find a doctor. A bottle of something would fix his cough, and the sweating, and the shivering, and the pains in his chest.

The girl came down the bus and said, "Sometime can we talk?" He said, "Sometime," and wasn't really aware of her. When she went back to her place, old ladies whispered to her and jerked their heads at the back of the bus, and glanced around quickly, looking concerned. He was staring out the window and didn't see them. He didn't see anything.

In the afternoon McManus decided not to crouch in his place in the bus during a stop at a point chosen, the driver said, ". . . for its scenic beauty and its proximity to modern plumbing." God, that smiling-voiced courier Murphy—is that what the tours called them?—making his jokes, rhyming off his pat spiel on the loud-speaker as pious as a priest . . . was there one Irishman who wouldn't make a commercial traveler? He went for a walk.

The young American girl with the brown gangling legs went after him. She did it in spite of counsel from the driver and the old ladies that he was much too strange and she was much too young and alone and far from home. She wanted to speak to this withdrawn and almost bearded creature. She seized her chance while the old ladies eased their bladders and bowels in the immobile washroom of an afternoon tea shop, and while the driver put fresh strain on his, in the bar.

McManus was sitting on the shore. All his life he had walked the Irish landscape, and looked on it with a strange intoxication. It was a personal landscape, as everything in Ireland was personal. Like a woman? He knew nothing about women. He had never had one; he was afraid of women. That didn't stifle thought; indeed, it intensified thought. Yes, like a woman. Like a mistress.

He had not looked at her on this journey. Fields were green and distant hills were blue. The sea was gray. So? He sweated and shivered and huddled, and his mistress went by in a blur, not as a lost mistress but as a blur. So he sat on the shore and did not see the sea; he heard it not as a familiar sound but as a harsh distraction. It annoyed him.

"Hello," the American girl said shyly. "May I stay?"

He turned his head indifferently. "It's not my shore."

She was traveling for the mind. Not to be put off. His face was pale and gaunt, bearded or unshaven—he wasn't sure which—and he was a brooder. She had watched him since he got on the coach. He was a writer, she was certain without asking herself why; an Irish writer. She had seen American writers who came as exhibits to their English classes. They looked like counter salesmen. McManus was the real thing. He looked the real thing. He was, she was sure, in the agony of some creative spasm. He was what she was looking for. She didn't know his name. Neither did the driver. That in itself was significant; it meant something. He was incognito and she was twenty and had been a year late getting out of high school. Somewhere—was it in *Ireland of the Welcome?* she had read that in Ireland you could rent a poet. Maybe it said only that you could meet a poet if you wrote beforehand? "I think you're an Irish writer," she said.

He was weak, with an odd feeling of instability in his arms and legs. Gentle but alarming little tremors like giggles ran through his stomach. They frightened him and forced nervous and involuntary smiles to his lips. He wanted to lie down. He had walked too far —Christ, only about a quarter of a mile—just to feel the wind off the sea on his hot face. Go away, he thought.

He said, "Isn't every Irishman who's sober enough to sit up and hold a pen?" It was more than he expected to say. He wasn't sure he'd said it.

"I think you're a real one. We did Irish writers this past year."

He made a weary sound.

She translated it and pushed on. "Yes. Lady Gregory. W. B. Yeats . . . you know . . . their marvelous fight for Irish freedom. . . ."

"Christ . . . debased currency," he said. An irrational excitement stirred in his belly. He wanted to shout something and had nothing to shout. It came from his belly, he knew that: not from his head.

"What did you say?"

He fell back in the sand, laughing, his head propped up on a tump of salt grass. Laughing at nothing. No, not at nothing. Laughing at their marvelous fight for Irish freedom. His hair was wet with sweat. Sweat poured down his temples, making them itch, and down his forehead into his eyes, making them sting. He brushed the wet away, laughing in little spasms, full of a sensation of frivolous delight.

"About 'debased currency'? What did you say?"

He didn't care what he said or would say. He felt disassociated. That was what the look and the feel of Ireland did to Irishmen. It made you feel disassociated—from any kind of responsibility, from anything tangible, from the rest of the world. The world was so very far away from Ireland—at a great distance over the hills and through the mists and far far away. It was far off in the present. That's why God's important to us, he thought, and tried to dig his head into the tumped grass; and laughed a good fat laugh. God is an Irish mist, he thought: now you see it, now you don't. God is great—except when He is inconvenient. "Old bitch," he said, and listened to himself.

"Who? Lady Gregory?"

"Lady Gregory? How did she get in here? What's your name?"

"Brendine."

"What?" What sort of name was that? Some Irish-American concoction?

"Brendine Healy. I'm from Boston."

He felt bold, he didn't give a damn, he was too weak to give a damn; he was phantasmagorical. That was a good word! He said it aloud. What was there to care about or be afraid of? "Are you a virgin, Brendine Healy of Boston?" He hadn't said anything so funny or so daring for nine months.

"What?"

He stretched his legs and drifted into a shallow doze.

"What was that about Lady Gregory and Yeats?" He opened his eyes. The sun was a sheet of light off the sea. He could see nothing but a sheet of light.

"Yes. I was talking about Lady Gregory, Yeats, and their marvelous fight for Irish freedom." As if she'd learned the form of words from a favorite professor.

"Were you, by God."

He was struggling to sit up and face the girl. "Their marvelous fight for Irish freedom, is it?" He struggled harder to stand up. His sight was like the sight of a man just awakened into the glare of a bright light. "Have you ever heard of the quarter-acre clause?"

"No. What's that?"

"That," he said, swaying on his feet, "was a clause in the relief law of 1847 which said that before a starving farmer and his family could draw relief he had to divest himself of all tenant holdings over one-quarter of an acre." He wasn't sure the voice he heard was his own.

"Oh?" It wasn't the sort of thing she cared about, but if she had to for the moment, she would.

"It was called the Gregory clause. Do you know who Gregory was?"

"No."

"He was Lady Gregory's old husband. Do you know what she thought of her husband's legal gimmick for getting the farmers' land back into the hands of the landlord?"

"No."

"She thought it was a bloody good idea. How's that?"

"I don't know."

He couldn't see at all now. Where the hell was she? "You're a virgin, did you say? Where are you, girl?"

"I'm here."

"Where?" He was falling. The pains were back in his chest. She had him under the armpits, trying to hold him up, her feet braced apart. He liked the falling feeling. For . . . ward. He landed lightly, going down by stages, talking, cushioned.

"W. B. Yeats," he mumbled. "Bloody old windbag. . . ."

She folded backwards into the sand, McManus between her legs, and couldn't raise his dead weight.

The driver and two old men from the tour came over the top of the sand and pulled him off the girl.

"Dirty bastard," the driver shouted, and drew back a vengeful and heavy arm.

"Don't!" the girl yelled. "He's sick. He fell. I was trying to keep him from falling. He's sick!"

"Like hell he's sick. He had you on your back. He was between. . . ." He seemed to enjoy putting it that way.

"You dirty bastard," she said surprisingly, and stung the old men to her defense.

"Look at him," one of them said. "He's sick. Sweating like a sow."

They humped him to the coach and laid him out on the back

seat. "He needs a doctor," one of the old men said. Brendine sat on the edge of the seat, holding him on, all the way to Killarney. She got him a room in the tour hotel, saw that his pack was taken to it, and got a porter to call a doctor. Two of the old women came with the doctor to McManus's room and found Brendine trying to undress him.

"Oh, no no no dear, not you. We'll do that." They were gentle, resolute, and unsuccessful.

"You can help me do it. I didn't know stripping a man was so difficult."

The doctor who might have been mistaken for a retired farmer said, "You're the right age to find out," and gave her a prescription for McManus and the name of a chemist's shop where she could get it filled. Brendine felt immensely useful and mature.

"We can't leave him naked," one of the old ladies said. They were kindly old women. No doubt they had sons.

"I'll find something." Brendine went through his pack and found something. She pulled out his pajamas and said nothing about his gun. But when the porter brought his medicine from the chemist's shop and they had fed McManus some soup and bathed his face and their husbands had come to take them to dinner, firmly they took Brendine with them and left the room key on Mc-Manus's dressing table where she couldn't get at it again, and saw her to her room after dinner and set up a patrol to see that if she did not stay there at least she did not go back to the sick man's room. She outwaited them till age outwitted them and they went to sleep.

Through it all, McManus was vaguely present, affected more by a tingling inertia than by any awareness of a dangerous collapse. He accepted their help drowsily and gratefully. He was buried in their midst; shielded by their protective coloring. The American shield, he thought. He would leave it at Bantry, tomorrow. Then he must do something about this flu. When they left he went quickly to sleep. He was awake again and feeling better when Brendine knocked on his door. His watch said midnight.

She closed the door quickly and took charge. "Back to bed," she ordered, and perched on the end of it. They watched one another with shy curiosity.

She's playing mother, he decided. And she's nice looking, with an erongenous face. He'd looked the word up once because somebody used it to describe a married woman they knew, and liked the idea that it really meant a face that made you think of sex. Her brown legs were showing up to the hips. They made him think of sex too.

"That was a funny turn you had today," she said.

"I haven't been feeling well. Thank you for your help." It was very formal, and careful.

"You *are* a writer, aren't you?" It was almost an appeal, as if she'd be disappointed if he said no.

He didn't care about her disappointment. He considered her uses and couldn't think of any. Tomorrow they'd be in Bantry and he'd leave them. What's the harm? "Yes," he said.

"I knew it. The driver thought you were trying to rape me."

He'd heard how frank these American girls could be, as if words had no value and less effect. Then they slapped your face. "I just fell," he said. "I was dizzy. Thank you for your help."

"You said that."

"Oh. I'm sorry."

"You're shy, aren't you?" she said.

"I suppose so. With girls. I am, yes. I don't know many. Girls, I mean."

"Where are you going?"

"I don't know. West. Down near Mizen Head, maybe. Somewhere very quiet."

"To camp?"

"I was going to, but not now. I'll have to get rid of this flu."

"Are you going there to write?"

He'd heard how they asked questions, as if another person was just an information bank. "Yes."

"What do you write?"

What did he write? He answered on the run, half-enjoying her curiosity. She sounded and looked very young. Her voice was very young. "How old are you?" He expected an evasion.

"Twenty. What do you write?"

He'd heard of their persistence.

"Poetry."

"Have you any with you?"

"Only in my head."

"Recite me a poem." Like a little girl.

He ought to have foreseen that one. Did they read James Stephens in America? He'd heard they preferred Frank O'Connor's translations from the Gaelic, so Stephens was safer. Which one? "The Coolin"? Very well known. "The Canal Bank"? Not well known.

Shyly he tried "The Canal Bank" on her. He said,

> *"I know a girl*
> *And a girl knows me,*
> *And the owl says, what!*
> *And the owl says, who?*

> *"But what we know*
> *We both agree*
> *That nobody else*
> *Shall hear or see;*

> *"It's all between herself and me:*
> *To wit, said the owl,*
> *To woo, said I,*
> *To-what! To-wit! To-woo!"*

He surprised himself and delighted her. *"Marvelous! Wonderful!"* She clapped her hands with extravagant enthusiasm. And then, quietly, "If you're not camping, where will you live?"

"Oh. There are some cottages for rent in the summer down there. The English usually rent them but they're not coming any more. There'll be plenty of places."

"I have to spend all summer over here."

"In Ireland?"

"In Europe. My parents think it's good for me."

"Is it?"

"Yes. It's going to be."

"Oh? In what way?" Well, it was a harmless way to spend an hour.

"Why do you carry a gun in your pack?"

It caught him completely off guard. Deliberately or not? Not deliberately, he decided. She had no guile. She simply asked what she wanted to know. He composed his mind carefully. "It's my father's," he said. "Years ago when I was walking . . . sleeping in barns, you know . . . ? a tramp attacked me with a knife . . . I always bring it now. . . ." It was true and far enough from the truth. But it didn't seem important to her.

"I know. A lot of people do that . . . take guns with them, I mean . . . in the States. I was wondering. . . ."

He was relieved and he waited to hear what she was wondering.

"I was wondering . . ." she said shyly, ". . . I don't want to travel anymore with these old people. . . ."

"They are a bit old for you."

"Could I travel with you?" It came out quickly, as if to ensure that it came out at all.

"Travel with me?" That was what she said. That was what he proposed the first time he tried to have sex with a girl. They'd been necking in a meadow and her enthusiasm seemed to promise all sorts of things. "Why don't we go hiking next weekend and camp out?" he asked her, and she liked that too. So he decided to make a bid for it on the spot.

She bled his nose. "You dirty-minded wee guttersnipe," she said, and he never ventured again. In a sense his sister became his girl. It was safer; free from possible humiliation and rejection. He was always afraid of rejection. What did this one mean?

"Was that awful?" she said.

"No. No." He didn't know what it was but he was thinking hard.

"I mean, young people nowadays . . . you know . . . ? travel together . . . you know the sort of thing? I can cook too. . . . You're really not well, are you? I have nothing better to do . . . I don't mean that the way it sounds . . . nothing *else* to do. . . . These tours I go on . . . you don't really learn anything with old people, do you . . . ?"

"But your people? What about . . . ?" They stumbled forward together.

"They're in Maine, at the cottage there. I'm supposed to be improving myself . . . I could put my bags in the hotel at Bantry . . . I could buy a sleeping bag . . . I can pay my way, you know . . . I wouldn't keep you from your work and any time you wanted to talk I'd be around . . . you know?"

A young couple in a cottage? Looking very normal? All people cared about was, Can you pay in advance? They could look married; there were always at least two bedrooms? Who'd pay them any heed, and when he felt it was time to make a run for England, she'd be cover. "If you feel all right about it . . . ?"

"Oh, yes. I'd love it."

"All right. I'd certainly like to have your company."

"We'll leave the tour at Bantry, is that it?"

"That's what I planned."

"I'm glad we met."

She put out his light. "We can plan in the morning, on the coach. It'll be fun."

In the corridor she thought: I forgot to ask his name, but I handled it very nicely. She wondered what he had in mind. "Are you a virgin, Brendine Healy of Boston?"

Would they? With a poet?

"Whee!" she said aloud, and startled a priest walking too carefully to his room.

He felt even better in the morning, almost cheerful, not alone, not bereft. There was company, free from taint or ill intent. They had breakfast together and he felt the censure in the eyes of the old ladies who watched over Brendine, passed the table, asked her how well she had slept, and did not ask him how well he felt. They'd been on foreign tours before. They'd seen foreign smart-boys after the maidenheads of young American girls before. This one had new tricks and she was falling for them.

"Isolationists," Brendine said, and sat with him on the coach.

In the hard light of day and the bumping back seat of the coach, McManus sickened and there was no relief in the thought that the girl would be useful to him. He was ill, he was hunted, and he had to lose himself in the southwest, and he had to get to a country doctor who would think no more of him than a vet would think of a sick cow.

When they stopped in Bantry and Brendine went to buy her pack and sleeping bag, McManus said he would wait for her, and rest. He watched her walk down the hill from the tour hotel towards Wolfe Tone Square and the shops, with St. Brendan the Navigator reaching his arms towards the bay. She was taking her hop-skip and giving him the thumbs up. She was nice, fresh, open, and a tremendous relief from the flowering shrews he knew in Ulster, but he couldn't think about her, couldn't be burdened by her; hadn't the energy to be burdened with her.

"I want my stuff," he told the driver, and hauled it out of the baggage hold, and hoisted it with difficulty on his back, and took his blackthorn stick and walked, as fast and as steadily as he could, out of the town and into the West.

He was sick. The pains were back and the coughing, and the chills, and the sweat. And the fears and the overbearing guilt.

For three days McManus walked his lacerated body and spirit in the West; to Sheep's Head on the Atlantic where he hadn't thought of going and didn't know he was. He knew very little of what he was doing. He scrambled and fell and scrambled and did not break his bones. The wind burned him, the squalls from the ocean washed him. He slept on small beaches and behind dry-stone walls, sometimes on and sometimes under his unerected tent, sometimes in and sometimes on his sleeping bag: coughing, sweating, chilled to the marrow and wandering in his mind and aware now and then with a frightening but helpless clarity that he was very ill.

Asleep and awake Maureen was in his mind, drifting free and beyond reach or tormented and terrified and beyond his power to control; his father wailed and lamented, his mother comforted and accused; and his demented guilt built within him till his screaming woke him and he saw a farmer and his wife bent over his pack, going through its contents. The man had the gun in his hand. He dropped it and ran, shoving his frightened wife before him. McManus repacked with the police in his fears and shambled away.

There was nothing in his mind now but the guilt of his sister's death and his parents' anguish. With fearful imaginings and fevered distortions, the long sequence of events rehearsed themselves in his mind, from the day he went to the Falls until he heard his father's demented wail and his mother's desperate strength on the phone. He was talking to his mother, begging her forgiveness, when he walked into the half-door of a cottage and fell across it. His pack shifted sideways and he hung over the door, too weak to get up.

He heard the distant voice, "Merciful God, you're dying, child," and felt the arms drawing his floating body through the air; he was lying now on a soft warm cloud, a warm wet cloud, and there was a drifting face above him, muttering, with glasses and monstrous eyes that grew like starfish and shrank; enormous hands reached at his face and blotted out the day, trying to smother him and he couldn't wrench his head from them or move his hot, wet, leaden body. "Maureen, Maureen," boomed in his head and all things ended and returned. Two faces now, moving and merging, and a voice that writhed in the air like a flying whip, "Pour it into him," and there was no strength for his defense and no more will. Poor Maureen. Maureen. She was at the Parkers' back door; she was sprawling on the street red and riddled; she was calling him to help her. He ran, and flew and floated and was always out of reach, too far to help her. He gave himself up. . . . What right had he to live . . . ? It was his blame and guilt that Maureen died. . . . He consented to his own death, gratefully, and sank away gently, into the cold, wet, enveloping mass.

NINE

POWERS went up to bed, but not to sleep. He needed something pleasant in his mind to keep Clune out of it. When he sank into a half-sleep he could not control the things that crawled, crept, and leapt into his head; half-dreams and terrors, and all with Clune in them: Clune with that menacing eye patch, snarling at him from behind a kitchen table, Clune orating in a roomful of men, and the words in his mouth like long tangles of seaweed which he used as whips to beat Powers' face. Powers firing at Clune and all that came out of his gun was a thin water-spray, Clune firing at Powers and all that came out of his gun were leaping frogs that clung slimily round Powers' neck and filled him with clawing, horrified disgust. And people laughing, in a strange way, a coming-and-going sound like an ebb tide over pebbles.

He tossed himself up out of it, half-rising, wide awake. Callaghan was standing by his own cot, in his shirt and shorts and socks, staring down at him. "What's up w'you?" he said.

"Nothin. Put out the light."

And for Christ's sake, thinka somethin pleasant. Like Maureen McManus? She'll do.

He spent a lot of waiting and waking time on women-fantasies. Now that he looked back on it, Maureen wasn't all that much. As a matter of fact, she was a bit of a bloody nuisance. He'd have got a lot more out of it if he hadn't had to waste so much time and energy keeping her down and getting into her. Getting at her was awkward.

Still, he got in and he could feel it. It wasn't bad. No picture in the head of Maureen white in the water, her long hair floating away; only Maureen spread, her face distorted, her teeth bared, and her fists clenched, as he rolled off her. Not much hair on it, either. He liked hair. Next?

Yes. It was a pity about the one from the Malone Road he met in the Europa Bar the night before they blew it up. Middle-aged, plain, expensive clothes. Alone and willing to talk; husband on a business trip across the water in England, she said: *Can I drop you anywhere?* she said. Up Divis, for God's sake, on the green grass was where she dropped him. He went over the details—this was better than Clune—re-enacting them. The way she laughed when he put her on the grass and *no no no-ed* when he was pulling off her knickers. *Don't,* laughing and pushing weakly: *I'm a married woman.* She couldn't have stopped him with a bulldozer, the state he was in. *I'm cross with you,* she said laughing, *don't put it in* and whoof! Who fucked who? Jasus! And after, her cryin and saying *that was rape that was rape that was rape* and *I suppose now that you've raped me once, you'll do it again? You wild animal.* The things she called him as if she liked the sound and feel of them: *You stallion, you bloody timber wolf, you big bull.* . . . And, *I'm afraid to go into the empty house. The least you can do is see me safe inside* and then, with a bottle, pouring: *I suppose now that you're in you'll tear every stitch off me and rape me on the bed.* Six in the mornin, when he was tryin to leave, in the porch, without a stitch on her: *If you're going to rape me again before you run off have the decency to do it on the couch, not on the porch floor* . . . Jasus!

It was a pity. He could have done with more of that one. *Get out of my house,* she said, *get out, get out, I suppose you're in the Europa often?* I'll be there the morrow night, he said. That was a laugh! So was she, with her head under a big hunk of ceilin. She smelled nice too.

Still, she was gone. Did her husband ever wonder what the hell she was doin dead in the Europa Bar? He got up quietly and took his clothes downstairs. The key was in his pocket and Mary Connors was in number twenty-five. It was one o'clock. He'd be back for Callaghan at six to get the bus for Strabane and the Border. Mary had an oul alarm clock that never failed.

She was asleep. The light didn't wake her. Her room smelled of paint. White paint. She'd done the job herself and the window was closed. He opened it. That smell would make you sick and he didn't come here to be sick. White was better than the dark brown and piss-house green in all the other houses around here, but those colored pictures of the country she'd cut out of magazines and stuck on pasteboard backs—what'd she want them for? Dropping his boots didn't wake her. When he was naked he pulled down the bedclothes. That didn't wake her. No nightie. She slept with her mouth open. So did Callaghan, breathing a kind of haugh-haugh-shhhooo-phhhooo sound. Mary's head was on its side, a wet patch on the pillow by her mouth, where she dribbled. Great diddies. Great rump. Good strong thighs she knew how to use. So she should; who taught her after her man died? Not as white as Maureen; thicker; more muscle than the woman from Malone. That one's thighs flapped about a bit. He flicked a pubic hair out of Mary Connors. She jerked, opened her eyes, and whooping whipped her strong legs over the edge of the bed and round his. He fell on her. Maureen and the woman from Malone were destroyed altogether and their remains beaten through the bed.

When he was off her he lay on his back, his arm stretched tightly over his head, his legs reaching and his belly drawn in.

"Aaawwww . . ." he said with gargantuan satisfaction and a huge grin. "That's the stuff, that's the stuff . . . by Jasus. . . ."

"Great, just great," she said, still on her back, still rutting, handling her splendid breasts. "There's plenty more when you're ready. . . ." Maybe this was her time? She watched him sidelong, wallowing in his immense gratification, and decided it was. "Know somethin, Pat?"

"By Jasus, I do! By Jasus you're great!"

"Somethin else."

"What?"

"It's about six months' time that you stopped comin out."

He felt his satisfaction fade a little. She was a barren woman, for God's sake. Her man couldn't give her anythin. If he'd thought there was a chance, he'da been down to the chemists. So why lose half the good of it when she can't catch? Or was she tellin him somethin? He ran a hand over her belly. It felt the way it always did. "Are you tellin me somethin?"

Should she? Smiling, she turned and ran her hand over him. He looked a bit doubtful. Her instinct told her it would be wiser to wait. "Aye," she said, "I like it better every time."

"There's nothin?"

"Aye, there's somethin. I want more."

There was nothin wrong. There was plenty right. "You came to the right quarter," he said, and relief roared in his groin. "Here it comes."

She was whimpering when he tried to wrench himself from the strong grip of her arms and the vice of her thighs held him in. "No, no. Don't, Pat. I'm startin. . . ."

"Shut your gub." He was on his knees, listening.

"What's up, Pat?"

"Listen, for Christ's sake."

"Ferrets," she said.

"Get the light off."

They crouched on the floor by the window and listened. "Bugger them," she whispered. "I was just startin the biggest one you ever gave me."

"Shut your gub."

The big engine of the armored car throbbed down the street. It went slowly past the house with its hatches closed, its machine gun swinging.

"Just one," he said.

Two. The second one was coming. It stopped before it reached the house. The first one stopped well beyond the house.

"Put your nightie on. Go and see what they're after. Hurry up."

He heard the front door open. "Inside," said a voice on an amplifier. "Inside, please. Close your door and stay inside."

"Pat," she said at the top of the stairs. "It's you they're after. There're at seventy-five."

"Put your clothes on. Gimme mine."

"Yes, Pat."

They scrambled into their clothes in the dark. "Where's my boots?"

"Here, Pat." He'd be hard to live with sometimes, if he lived at all. But he was a good baker and there'd be plenty of work after this was all over, and she had to get him. But she had to do it right. She was a month gone anyway. The way he felt her belly, he wouldn't believe her if she told him now. He'd think she was tryin to trap him. She couldn't tell him till she could show him her belly and it a bit more swole up.

The amplifier crackled and a clipped English voice said politely, "Number seventy-five. You are being given thirty seconds to come out. Come out with your hands out in front, your fingers wide open. Any attempt to carry or reach a gun—the slightest quick movement—and you'll be shot. Your thirty seconds start—NOW. The clock is running . . . twenty-eight . . . make yourselves heard . . . twenty-six . . . and when the time runs out . . . twenty-three . . . there'll be no warning . . . twenty-one . . . we'll blow out the door and the windows . . . eighteen. . . "

There was nothing left to hear but the throb of the two engines. Powers counted the seconds . . . the people in the houses were almost visible. No lights went on but men and woman were sitting up in bed, sitting on the edges of beds, hurrying children into little back rooms, pulling on trousers and knickers and shoes and shirts...

The machine gun raked the door; the lock, and up the inside edge, blasting off its hinges. The door fell inwards, pieces flying. Glass from the windows was still falling and tinkling on the street, coming down from the air, after the coughing echo of the gun in the narrow street passed between the houses, dying.

"Out," the amplifier said. "Left and center in the street. Move on."

Callaghan passed the window, his hands on his head. He did not look at number twenty-five. He was wearing his boots, and his shorts and his shirt. His trousers dangled over his shoulder. "I'll see that till the day I die," Powers whispered, and destroyed a laugh. The armored cars turned out of the street.

Doors opened along the street. The people poured out, shouting, jeering, screaming obscenities at the departing sound. Boys and girls, young men and women filled the street, throwing stones at nothing but the empty air the cars had displaced for a moment.

"They come right to the door," Powers said. "They knew."

"Who was it, Pat?"

"McManus. Go on outa the house. Leave the door wide open. If you see me, don't speak to me."

From the window he watched her come into the street and went down himself. The crowds were beyond the house, following the cars, throwing futile stones and futile insults. Peace movement, by Jasus? It made him laugh. When hate's as good as a good fuck, who's for peace? Across the district somewhere an explosion filled the night. He stepped out into the street. Michael Collins woulda done it like this. He put his hands in his pockets and walked slowly, up the street to number seventy-five. Just like the Big Fellow. About the same size too.

The place was a shambles. They'd put men in to cream the

fuckin place. The guns had been taken. He was useless; no gun. He found his little canvas bag and put a shirt, socks, and underwear in it, his razor and toothbrush, hairbrush and comb . . . the motor bike came up through the crowd and stopped outside. Powers grabbed the poker from the range and waited in the dark. He had no gun. What was a man with no gun?

A youth stopped in the doorway. "Pat?"

"Conal."

"What hit you, Pat?"

"I couldn't sleep so I went for a wee walk. The army got Callaghan. I just come in."

"Jasus, you were lucky."

"They got the guns."

"There's a meetin on. Get on the bike."

"What's up?"

"You're sent for. Come on."

They planed and keeled up and round the little streets and at the end of the journey maneuvered the motor bike into the house with them.

Christ! Clune! And I went for a good fuck w'Mary Connors to get that man outa my head. There were twenty young men packed into the little house, spilling from the back kitchen into the tiny parlor and the motor bike taking space. Some of them were no more than eighteen. All of them were excited verging on outbreak, grinning expectantly. There was blackout cloth over the front window. The meeting was under way.

Clune interrupted it. "Powers. Report."

He told his tale. "When I got in there was no guns."

"Great. Fuckin great! *You're* great!"

Powers big face colored and sweated. In fronta everybody, by Jasus; the wee shit made a mockery outa me in fronta twenty wee boys; the blood pounded in his head.

Clune pointed to a man at the front. "Get'm a gun." Clune

looked about him like a cornered ferret. "Twenty men and Dr. McDermott took the night. Arms, explosives, ammunition by the bloody ton. And they blew up one factory tryin to get in. Three of our's killed inside. One of their's at the door. And the Officials done it to us. They're behind this fuckin peace move. They're tryin to look pure and isolate us, cut us down and out and when it's all done they'll be the ones t'take over. They spotted for the fuckin British army. They sold us. They *informed* on us." He paused, shaking with rage not quite under control. "There's a list," he said. "It'll be done the night. You'll do it and you'll do it now. Knock on doors," he said, barely breathing. "Knock on fuckin doors. They'll learn the night, by Christ." He waved an impatient arm at McCann, "Give them their slips."

History and habit kept the streets in line. Fear added a rich insurance. They were free, uninhibited, protected killers who liked their work. Their faces said so. The Official IRA were against *them*. The Officials couldn't therefore be right. The Officials were like anybody else who was against *them*—police, Orangemen, Loyalists, IRA Officials. All these were wrong. All these were enemies. The wrong were those who opposed or disagreed, or doubted.

They took their slips of paper eagerly, impatient to knock doors and squeeze triggers. Eagerness flew in their faces, like banners of criminal righteousness.

"Scatter," Clune said. At intervals, two by two, they went out to pick up guns, and cars, burn their slips, and kill and run. And sleep, satisfied.

"Powers." He didn't have his slip. Clune signaled him to come. He was a stupid big clod, in Clune's book. But at this sort of work he was good. "Here's your slip."

Powers read it slowly and slowly tore it up. "I'm goin on young Conal's motor bike? No motor car?"

"We couldn't get enough in time."

That was deliberate. Maybe there weren't enough cars, but there were cars and other people got them. He got a bloody wee boy and the back of his motor bike. Clune did that on purpose on purpose on purpose. Things ran on in Powers' head when he was upset, or angry.

"You gave me Danny O'Connell," he said. "You're killin the big ones. Why did y'give me the Officials' number one man in Belfast?"

"I gave the biggest to the best." Clune would have liked to smile. He was careful not to. "You've got the address. There's two of them with him. You can do it and get the first bus t'Strabane after McManus."

The Big Fellow. He would do it. "Och, aye." He was mighty in his head, full of his own power and of his loathing for this little man.

"Pick up your gun and away on."

"Aye. Away on, Conal."

The minstrel boy to the war has gone,
His wild harp slu-ung bee-ee-hind him. . . .

Conal's face was septic with greedy pride. He would ride his fine steed in the night, see the enemy cut down, no matter who the enemy might be, and ride out again with glory. There was a shrill jubilant soundless sound in his throat. He was at school with Danny O'Connell's son. In the same class. Played on the same street. He told Powers so as they wheeled out the bike. Jasus Christ, the power of it!

"The wee streets, Conal. And slow. We'll roar comin back."

"Yes, Pat."

"Quiet, right up to the house. Park the bike right in front of the window where you can see in. Stay on the bike, ready to go. You'll see the kitchen door. If you see anybody there, just say how many—like one, or two, and say it quiet. You see?"

"Yes, Pat."

He knew the geography of the houses. They were all exactly alike. A man inside with a gun could cover the front door from the kitchen door, or up the stairs. The man behind the door was easy and the man upstairs was easy from the door. But the man at the kitchen door had to be got at from the parlor window. He might only get two of them. He'd have to see where they were. It was a short ride and a quiet one. He knocked gently but persistently on the front door, his gun waist high against it. The stairs were bare even of lino. He heard men coming down them. How many? Two, anyway. One behind the door. One on the stairs, one in the open kitchen door?

"Who is it?"

"Danny?"

"Who is it?"

"Danny, it's Pat Powers. Let me in."

"No. What're y'after, Pat?"

"Danny, it's Clune. He's goan soft in the head."

"That's your worry, Pat. What about it?"

"The army took twenty men of ours the night. Clune says your boys spotted them. Look after yourselves."

"We always do."

"Two," Conal said softly.

"Right then, Danny. For Jasus sake, don't say I warned you."

"You needn't worry."

"Good night then, Danny."

"Night, Pat."

They weren't too worried or they'd have covered the stairs. Two in the kitchen door. They were more curious than scared or ready. Powers stepped back from the door, moved across the window, his automatic rifle down his leg, turned quickly, and poured his fire straight through the window into the kitchen doorway. There was no reply.

But there was a reply from the front door. O'Connell was firing

142 ((

through it. He blew Conal off his bike. It fell on top of him in the gutter.

Powers, now between the window and the door, pressed tight against the wall. He waited for the sound of movement inside. Boots clattered on the bare stairs and he jumped out and raked the line of the stairs as if he were watering a garden. The body fell heavily and rolled.

He shot the simple lock away, dragged Conal's body into the house, put O'Connell's gun in his hands, took one of the guns from the gut-shot and dying men blocking the kitchen doorway, finished them, and rode the bike back, roaring. He parked it two streets away and walked on the sky to Mary Connor's. Mighty. Euphonious little tunes played in his throat. His eyes felt a kind of sweetness behind them. Three Officials including the top man in the North; with a gun for interest. There was young Conal shot, but he got his bike back. The Big Fellow.

The street was sleeping again. Mary was still up and still dressed, drinking tea in the kitchen.

"Where in God's name were you, Pat?"

"Workin."

"What?"

He shouldn't tell her. His head was floating, reliving a neat, efficient action. The Big Fellow. She wouldn't open her gub about him. He had this one all tied-up. "There was a meetin. Clune says the Officials spotted us. Twenty men, about, and McDermott, they took. There were punishments." He put the guns in a cupboard under the kitchen sink and poured himself some tea. He'd keep one in there for himself. Not report it. "Keep your mouth shut now."

"Jasus, you know I wouldn't, Pat."

"I got Danny O'Connell and two men with him." He had forgotten Conal.

"But you said it was McManus, Pat."

)) 143

"Aye. It was. Clune's a bloody fool."

"But, Pat, why didn't y'tell him you know it was McManus?"

Bitterly, "He woulda told me t'shut my gub and leave the thinkin to them." And I lost McManus, he thought. Why would I make it worse for me? Jasus, for the loss of twenty men they'd crucify *me*.

"But, Pat, for Christ's sake! Shootin Officials! This'll start it! They'll make a lista Provisionals."

"Let them. I'm away over the Border after McManus. I'm leaving first bus in the mornin. C'mon up the stairs." He stretched and slapped his stomach. "I feel like a stallion." Or a timber wolf. Or a bull.

Jasus, she wailed to herself moments later, you'd think he was ridin me in a steeplechase. But he was roarin and a pregnant widow-woman has t'play her cards, so she worked at it, and sounded off, and when nature failed to compel joyful and involuntary sounds, she mocked them up.

He rolled off her. "Get up an put the light out," he said, and went to sleep.

She was weary and still awake, still shuffling what cards she thought she had, when the old alarm clock rattled him back to earth. The tin box under the bed had in it a card she could play. She fumbled in the box while he dressed, and said, "Did they give you enough money, Pat?"

"You're coddin." Did they ever give you enough? Fifty pounds between him and Callaghan and bring back the change. Still, Callaghan wouldn't need his now.

"Here." She dealt the card. "There's twenty pound."

"Right." He put it in his pocket, thinking of his timetable. Not a worda thanks, she thought. But that was the way with them. Who ever saw an Irishman wheelin a pram or doin the dishes?

"Why don't you drop a day's pay and come on the bust to Strabane?" She'd be useful if the bus was checked on the road: "We're gonta see the wife's sick mother in Strabane, soldier." And

144 ((

he was stayin at the hotel till three the morrow mornin. He could do w'some more of her before he walked across the Border. She never let you down. Always up and ready. He wouldn't be gettin it across the Border, on the move.

Mary Connors drew conclusions. He didn't want to leave her. He must be very near ready to take the hook; "I'll put my good clothes on," she said.

He slapped her bare behind. "Put on them wee fancy knickers I gave you," he said. "The ones y'can see through."

Their room at the Strabane Hotel—Mr. and Mrs. Connors—was above the kitchen. The floor creaked. The old brass bed creaked and shook. Kitchen staff stood listening below.

"He's changed his beat this time," the cook said, shaking his head.

The second waitress, who was a mature seventeen with the warm glow of expectation in her eyes, said to the senior waitress, who was sixty and deformed by arthritis and kept more pills than knives and forks in her serving drawer, "D'the men always want it that much, Mrs. McLaren?"

"Mine got it once a month on a Saturday," she said sourly, and seemed offended by her own excess. And when Powers and Mary Connors came down to eat, Mrs. McLaren said, "Are y'feelin all right, missus?"

Mary cocked an insolent eye and said, "Jealous?" and to herself, "It's not me she's worried about, it's the oul bed breakin."

But Powers was actin as if he was daft about her. It wasn't one of the words she thought in, but it came to her mind: when he's gettin me up for the next go, she thought, he's *tender*. The way he nibbled at her nipples, and the things he did and the way he did them, as if she was sweet Scotch shortbread and he wanted to make a meal of her. It was nice. None of this on, up, and out stuff. But God, when he was at it, he was wild. She was sore and weary. Sleep, fiddle, and fuck, she thought. Dinner time. Eat. Upstairs again. He slept. She'd brought the old alarm. Midnight. He was very tender.

"It's the best time I ever had, Mary," he said, his mouth full of nipple.

"Me too," she said.

"I could put up w'this for bloody years."

A bell as loud as Big Ben boomed in her breast under his teeth. In her mind, carefully she undid the hook from its cork. He was ready. "What'd you like this time?" she said, and the soreness of excess seemed a small price to pay for a man of your own, legal and churched, instead of years of any oul bugger you could get, up the back of the Black Mountain. She waited for her right moment.

Two o'clock in the morning. He'd have to go in a minute. He'd had a month's worth in half a day and half a night. That'd hold him till he came back. Jasus, she was great. He squeezed her breasts and kissed her. "Jasus, Mary girl, that's the best fuckin you and me ever had."

"Great. You could put up with it for years, could you, Pat?"

"Bloody years."

"Pat?"

"No more time now. Anyway, I'm sore. Are you?"

"Aye. It wasn't that."

"What?"

She stilled her nerves and said, "Pat, I'm pregnant."

The street lamp outside their window seemed to dip. His kneading fingers were still on her breast. The knee pressed against her groin lifted. The silence was turbulent. She could feel the hook go home in his tender underlip, and she shuddered.

"Pat?"

"You said you were a barren woman."

"The doctor said I was."

"Did he, by Jasus." Hands and lips and legs away. He was out of bed. "He did, did he, by Christ?"

"Honest t'God, Pat." Hooked. In the wrong place. In the lip. Bleedin like a butchered boar. Mad ragin like a bull. "Pat."

"Fuck you," he said, attacking his clothes. The rage in him grated in his mouth, burned his eyes, closed his throat. "You ony wanted your fuckin hooks in me, didn't ye?"

"No, Pat, no. He couldn't make me pregnant and I believed the doctor. As sure as God, Pat." It was done. It was undone. Hopelessness knelt on her chest. What was the use? She'd picked the wrong time. If there was a right time. But he said he could stand fuckin her for bloody years. How was she t'know?

"Y'know what y'are?" He was leaning over her, the light on, his face almost purple with the fury in him, "You're a fuckin hoore, that's what y'are."

"Don't you say that!" Up on her knees like a wrestler balanced to spring, her own rage erupting, she yelled at him, *"Don't you call me a hoore!"* What was there to lose? It was lost already. All he wanted was a private hoore-house with no other customers and no charge. All she wanted was a man of her own, with legal rights. It hit her again. She was thirty—five years older than Powers —and she just wanted to do it right, in bed, with one man, not up Divis or the Black Mountain, with every horny oul man with a cock on him, pokin away at her. Slowly she got off the bed. "I'm sorry, Pat. I just loved you, that's all." She felt ill. She halfmeant what she said. She half-hoped. . . .

"You loved my fuckin cock," he yelled. The bedroom ruptured in screaming abuse, like a back street in Belfast.

On either side of it, awakened sleepers knocked on the walls and shouted. The manager came from his bed and screamed through the door. Mary Connors sank back into defeated silence. Powers roared his obscenities at her and she sat naked on the bed, only

)) 147

half-hearing, thinking of what would come to pass. The child. The street. The mothers to their daughters: "Don't go near that wee hoore, d'you hear me now?" The fathers to their sons, "Keep away from that one, I'm tellin you." The fathers to Mary: "How're you doin, Mary? How'd you like a wee walk up Divis?"

He was ready to go. "Pat," she said, standing naked in the middle of the room. "Pat, what'm I gonta do?"

"Put your hooks in some wee boy that doesn't know you."

"I've no money. I gave you all my spare money."

He rummaged in his pocket and threw fifty new pence on the bed. "You gave me twenty pound for the best fuckin y'ever got. There's your change." Then he rummaged in his mind for another humiliation to throw at her. None came. He opened the door.

"Pat," she said, "are you just gonta walk out and leave me here without a penny t'my name?"

"I just gave you fifty," he said, and opened the door.

"Y'made a hoore outa me, Pat."

"Y'were born a hoore." He closed the door.

She stood where she was, numb and desolate. The bill for the room, and the food, and the bus back to Belfast; she had none of them. The front door of the hotel slammed shut and the bedroom door opened as if it had been waiting to hear the front door slam.

The manager was standing there in his pajamas. She was aware of him in a distant way that drowned under her desolation.

"Did he bate you, missus?" the manager said.

She shrugged and said, "No," and shook her head without looking at him.

"He was callin you dirty names." His eyes chewed deliciously on every inch of her.

She turned and got into bed and pulled the covers up to her chin. "Aye."

"Did he catch you with a man? The things he was sayin."

She became fully conscious of him slowly, and looked at him carefully. "He took all the money. I can't pay you."

148 ((

"Oh?" He shook his head mournfully and looked sorrowful. "Poor wee soul." He sat on the edge of the bed. "You look like a very nice woman. Did he catch you w'somebody?"

Her mind picked at him shrewdly and her eyes glanced quickly at his pajama trousers. Oh aye. Too bloody right. "Aye," she said, "with a bit of a wee boy. Once. I ony did it the once."

"Aye." He was patting the covers, just out of range. He'll get there, she thought. "And how'm I gonta get home?"

"Never worry about the bill," he said. "Don't go to sleep and we'll have a wee crack. I'll just run down and lock the front door." Aye, do that. He might come back and catch me payin for my breakfast.

"Where's he goin?" he asked when he came back. He closed the door and turned the key and walked very upright to the bed. Fat belly in a bit.

"Over the Border."

"Where d'you live?"

"Belfast. I haven't got my fare home. Could you give me the loan of it? I'll pay you back."

"Sure. Sure. In the mornin."

"Could you get it now?"

"Now?"

"Aye. And what's the bill for the room and meals?"

He worked it out in his head. "Make it a round figure. Four pound."

"Write out a receipt when you're out there and I'll pay you for that too." She pushed the bedclothes down with one leg and spread the ransom for his inspection.

"Holy Christ," he said. "Y'ony done it once w'one wee boy?"

"Aye."

"Y'never done it w'anybody else but your husband?"

"No." What was he scared of? Syphilis? "He was ony fourteen —a wee schoolboy."

"What made you do it w'him?"

He liked the details. "He was cryin for it. Poor wee crature, he wanted it that bad. So . . . I let him. My man come in."

"Christ. I'll ony be a wee minute." He ran.

She was spread as she had been when he came back, locked the door, laid her fare and her receipt on the dressing table, and dropped his pajamas on the floor. "You're a nice wee woman," he said, and scrambled onto the bed.

She lay, passive. Almighty bloody God! A poor wee man with a danglin belly and a soft cock, haughin away at her for four pound and her fare to Belfast. It was started already. She cried.

He panted, "Is somethin wrong, dear?"

"No." She lay in his sweat and thought of Danny O'Connell. Danny slept hither and yon with a gun in his bed, but his wife and the seven wains were always in the same wee house they'd lived in since he married her. Mrs. O'Connell'd be dyin of grief and murder and chokin for revenge. I'm sorry, Pat. I just loved you, that's all. Her mind hopped from thing to thing. She was half-winded with the breath bursting out of her and the wee fat manager bouncing on her belly. We love our Protestant neighbors, Mrs. Machin yelled for the reporters, and they cheered her and went howling down the streets, screaming obscenities and hurling stones at the soldiers, luxuriating in the Irish ecstasy of hate. I just loved you, that's all. Instant transitions. Venomous transitions. Absolute transitions. Mrs. O'Connell's the first stop when I get to the Falls, she decided. "Pat Powers it was that killed your Danny, Mrs. O'Connell," she'd say to her. "Tell your fellas he's over the Border, huntin young Johnny McManus." There'd be a list, all right. Pat Powers would be on it, all right.

"Are you near done?" she said to the half-blown little laborer on her stomach.

"Soon," he croaked breathlessly, and with desperate fury and for his own pride's sake, tried to bring the matter to an issue.

When at last the issue was accomplished, Mary Connors heaved him off, stepped out of the bed, and unlocked the door. "All right. You're paid," she said. "Away on." She'd scored a point.

"Is that all?" he said, "for four pound ten?" He went sourly through the door, carrying his pajamas. "You're not worth four pound ten," he said, looking deeply aggrieved. He turned back and stabbed a short finger at her. "And another thing—it doesn't cover your breakfast." He'd scored a point.

She lay in the sweat-wet bed and cried, and composed her little speech for Mrs. Danny O'Connell. Powers'd find out who else was Irish, by God. He'd find out all right, by God. She'd score a few points, she would. By God, she would. That was Irish too.

TEN

McMANUS came to his senses and heard kitchen sounds. He was a child in his own bed, curled securely in a safe and familiar place, enclosed in safe and familiar sounds. The bedclothes were deep and warm and reassuring. "Mammy," he said. To himself, not to be heard. That was comforting too. His mother was close. He would call. He could hear. She would hear. She always heard.

He opened his eyes and was not in a safe and familiar place. He did not know where he was and was afraid.

He had been dreaming? Terrifying dreams; or were they real and had they found him and beaten him unconscious? He was sore, everywhere. There was a woman with pink jellyfish eyes that grew and shrank.

She was standing in the bedroom doorway, drying her hands on a towel. Wearing steel-rimmed eyeglasses that glittered. Or the eyes behind them glittered. It was hard to breathe and impossible to call out.

"There, child," the woman said, "don't fret. You've been sick." She came down the room slowly the way she would come catching a cat. Don't run, her sly movement said, I'll not hurt you.

She sat on the edge of the bed near the foot. "I'm Mrs. Burke," she said. "This is my house. You fell in over my half-door—a very sick child."

Child? Yes, he thought vaguely, I'm a child.

The woman's voice was gentle, but she didn't smile. That face didn't do much smiling. "I was just going to wash you," she said, as if she always washed him. "You've sweated something terrible."

She was big. No, not really big; tall, as tall as he was himself. His mind absorbed her in fragments, not in general. A bun at the back, brown hair, a little gray, mere traces of gray; a grayish dress, square like a flour sack with holes cut for the neck and arms. Strong arms, big hands. The face was narrow, plain, full of force. And tired. There were dark circles under the eyes. They reached well below the glasses.

"I'll get the things," she said, and left him to wonder what things. Strong legs. Big feet. She came back carrying the things; an enamel basin, steaming, towels over her shoulder; and pulled up a chair with a big foot and put everything on it.

"Now." He couldn't move when she reached with a big hand and slowly drew back the bedclothes. "You'll feel the air," she said.

He felt the air, all over his body. Not cold; fresh. He was naked.

She washed him from head to feet, the way his mother did when he was very young, and sick. She soaped a face cloth and went over him slowly, very gently. Then she dried him the same way, in all the same places. She turned him over, washed the other side, and dried him, and said, "Don't want bedsores, do we?" and rubbed cold fluid on his back and buttocks and it stung a little, freshly, then glowed on his skin. Then she turned him on his front again. His fears had gone. She was gentle, kind, motherly. She wouldn't harm him. She covered him and took the things away.

When she came back she said, "Want me to talk to you?"

"Yes."

She pulled a chair to the edge of the bed, drew his arm from under the covers, and held his hand in both of hers. "You collapsed at the door three days ago. Do you remember anything of the past three days?"

"Only your glasses."

154 ((

"That's interesting," she said like a kindergarten teacher. That's what she was like—a schoolteacher. Like old Moll McCullough who used to hide the cane when the Inspector came, and Paddy Gallagher who made his own fiddles knew where she kept it, and brought it out where the Inspector could see it. Moll whaled him with it afterwards, when the Inspector left.

"What made you smile?" the woman said.

"Moll McCullough."

"Who's she?"

"Schoolteacher."

"Did I remind you of her?"

"Yes."

"That's good. I was a schoolteacher once. We've been pouring penicillin into you," she said. "You've had pneumonia. You'll be fine now."

If she'd known Moll McCullough she wouldn't have thought it was good, and if she thought it was good why didn't she smile? Only her voice smiled. Or her voice sang at him, as if he were an infant.

"I'm going to give you a little clear soup. I'll fix your pillows. The doctor said only a little clear soup. We'll do as he says. He's a very good doctor." More infant tones.

She sat close to him, on the edge of the bed, pulled him up to her with one strong arm and with the other raised his pillows, patted them, and then put both arms about him and cradled him. "My poor child," she said, and held his face against her; against her breast. He could feel her nipple through the dress, against his mouth. His mother did that when he was sick, and he'd wondered years later whether she'd been wishing him back to infancy. But this woman pressed his face so hard against her breast that he coughed for want of breath. "Poor child," she said, and lowered him down on his pillows. I hope she does that again, he thought; she gave him a safe feeling. An odd thought occurred to him. She can do that to me, he thought, she's known me for three days. I've never really seen her before.

She brought the soup and fed him, wiped the spills from his chin and chest. "Take your pills," she said. "They'll keep you sleepy and you'll be fine in no time." She lowered his pillows, covered his shoulders. "I'll leave you now. Sleep some more, child. You'll mend quick."

He woke and slept and woke and it was like climbing a terraced hill on a crisp day. He felt better every time he turned to look about him. From soup to scrambled eggs. A week, maybe two weeks, waking and sleeping, taking pills and being washed. Two more days, in fact. On the third day time became measurable again, but by then he was enveloped in timeless kindness.

It was today, while the washing was going on, that he lay in pleasant acceptance, his eyes on the bun on the back of her neck and remembered what Pat McGladdery said one day in school about Miss Martin, who had hair like that. "She's got very sexy hair—that's pillow hair, Johnny boy." It had fixed an erotic image in his mind and women in his fastasies had long hair that flowed on pillows. Mrs. Burke was washing his upper thighs when his penis rose.

His embarrassment colored him. "Don't fret, child," she said, and moved her face cloth a little higher as if everything was normal. "God made you whole. Thank Him." Her voice was flat.

He sneaked a glance at her face. It was as severe as ever and as cold as the face of a spinster vigilante beating the village bushes for sin.

But she didn't wash him again. "You can take a bath tomorrow," she said. "I'll help you in and out in case you slip, but you're coming on fine." She put him in warm pajamas when the washing was done, and piled pillows behind him. "The doctor's coming,"

156 ((

she said. "You were sleeping when he came yesterday. He just took your pulse. Sit up and we'll talk." She helped him, then was busy about the room, tidying the tidy.

"Tell the doctor you're fine," she said, lifting and laying about the room, and not looking at him. "Would you like to go to a hospital?"

"No. No." It was too urgent. "No," he said calmly. They could get at him easily in a hospital. "If you can stand me," he said.

"All right, child. You'll stay. You need a mother."

Did that explain her? She came suddenly and sat on the bed. "Before he comes, we need to have a frank talk."

She was in a hurry. It harshened her voice and her look. "You raved a lot," she said. "There's two paperback books in your pack. You're John McManus. Your name's in them."

"Yes." Her urgency frightened him.

"Was Maureen your sweetheart?"

She knew it all, one way and another. What in God's name had he been saying? Raving. Hopelessly, he decided he'd told her too much to lie. "My sister."

"A man by the name of Powers? He killed her?"

"I think so."

"You said a lot of names—this man Powers, McCann, Clune, McCandless. Everybody knows who they are. They must be the only television stars the law can't find. Were you a Provo too?"

"Yes."

"You're not the kind."

"No." Bull Baillie saw it. She saw it. Powers and Clune saw it. Everybody saw it but him. Maureen would be alive if he'd seen it.

"Did you turn informer?"

That was the life-and-death question. The way she spoke, though? About Clune and McCann and the law?

"Not till they killed my sister."

She was about to say something and closed her mouth. "How

old are you?" she said instead. He knew she'd been going to say something else, something more important.

"Twenty-two."

"Do you know what's going on in the North this past week?"

"No."

"There's been nothing else in the papers or on the air for a week. The army got a big haul of Provos, bomb factories, a Catholic doctor by the name of McDermott and a lot of guns and ammunition. The same night twelve Officials were shot, including their top man in Belfast. The Provos issued a statement. They claimed they did it. They said the Officials informed on them and they gave them twenty-four hours to get out of the North. They've been killing one another for a week. The civil war the Provos wanted to start has started—but it's between Catholics. Again." She stared at him steadily, from a cold, thin face.

His head was heavy. He could barely hold it up. He didn't want to hold it up. What was it he told the policeman when he phoned home? Houses, factories? Jesus, when they understood there'd be hundreds of them after him.

"Maybe you're wrong," she said. "Maybe they're not hunting you. It's the Officials they're after."

"No. They decided to give me the black cap before any of that. I was quitting. They tried for me and it went wrong. They killed my sister . . . they'll keep after me. They never stop."

"You're for England?"

"If I ever reach it."

"Your gun's in the dresser. Top right-hand drawer. With your money."

She was in a great hurry now, giving the room a last look over for anything out of place. "I'm making trouble for you," he said.

"That's enough," she said sharply, and put her big hands on her big hips, bracing her shoulders as if to ease her back. "Lie down."

She had made up her mind about something. She punched his pillows. "Give the doctor no more than the time of day," she said brusquely. "Just yes and no. No talk." She covered his shoulders. "I'm Mrs. Burke."

"Yes."

"Yes, I told you that. He's Sullivan. Dr. Seamus Sullivan. He married my sister. She'll be here too, but you won't see her. Nobody else in Ireland knows you're here. The three of us listened to you raving." She was nervous, building something inside herself. "She'll be here because Seamus comes almost every day." She looked at him cannily. "You see what I mean?"

"No."

"If a brother-in-law who's a doctor visits his sister-in-law almost every day, either she's sick or she has somebody in the house that's sick—or he's going to bed with her. Anybody who saw him would take the third choice. So my sister comes too." She rushed away from that. "You were reading one of Thomas Burke's books." He grasped at a change of thought like a change of step.

"Yes. I was re-reading it."

"Good," she said, and the corners of her mouth creased a little. She bent suddenly and kissed his head. "That's a good child. I'm Thomas Burke's widow."

Then the doctor's car came and with it, he feared, hostility. So he braced for the strain, burning up energy, and Mrs. Burke went out to meet them.

There was talk in the next room among the three of them. It made him feel like a specimen.

"How is he, Kate?" A big deep voice. Not unpleasant.

"Sleeping. A bit better, poor child."

"Child? He's a full-grown man." A woman's voice, not far from Mrs. Burke's, but harsher. "Some child!" That had overtones, and he thought with guilt and pleasure of his erection in Mrs. Burke's hard fingers.

"I'll get him into the Schull Hospital," the doctor said firmly, making decisions for Mrs. Burke

"Am I a useless old woman? Is that it, Seamus?"

"That's the bloody point. You're not an old woman at all. That's what has your sister worried. That 'child' you're talking about has all his parts, full size."

"Watch your tongue," Mrs. Burke said, but it wasn't a rebuke.

"Where do you sleep, Kate?" the sister asked sharply.

"You've got the mind of a horny curate," Mrs. Burke said, as if her sister amused her.

"*Kate!*"

"By God, I think you need an invalid in the house, Kate," the doctor said. "Can't you do without a patient?"

"Go and see the child, Seamus."

McManus closed his eyes and waited for the doctor.

He was a hefty man with a weathered face. He probably spent as much time with a rod in his hand as he did at bedsides. "You're the great sleeper," he said to McManus, and took his wrist and stuffed a thermometer in his mouth. "And you have the constitution of a horse."

McManus did as Mrs. Burke had told him to do. "You talked a lot," the doctor said.

"Sir?"

"Why did you run to here?"

"It was far."

"Nowhere's far in Ireland. It's a big saucer. Didn't they teach you that in school?"

"Yes, sir."

"The Civil War was over fifty years ago. The last revenge killing that came out of it was only done a few years ago."

"Yes, sir."

"I'm sure you'll get the point I'm about to make. The Irish have

160 ((

a lot of unlovely things in their heads and hearts. So as soon as you're ready to move, I'm going to move you. *Out* of here. I'm not referring to Mrs. Burke's house, boy. I'm referring to the whole of West Cork. Right *out*. I'll smuggle you to the Cork Airport, and I'll leave you there. After that it's sink or swim. Do you follow me?"

"Yes, sir."

"Fair enough?"

"Yes, sir."

"We don't want them around here. They *are* here. But their guns aren't going and we don't *want* them going. We don't want executions, black caps—none of that stuff here. Keep it in the North. Have you got me?"

"Yes."

"I won't labor the point." But he labored it. "The minute you can move, I move you. Clear?"

"Yes, sir."

"Seamus," Mrs. Burke said from the bedroom door, "there's plenty of sick people in Schull."

"Do you want that fuzz off your jaw?" the doctor asked him.

"No, sir."

"Holy God, d'you think that'll hide you?"

"Schull, Seamus!" said Mrs. Burke.

"What the hell got into you, boyo? You're not a back-street gunman. . . ."

"Seamus!"

McManus watched her at the door with them. She waved them away with thanks and closed the half-door and shut the snib on the incongruous Yale lock. There was the first and odd little smile on her face. It was like the little smile he used to see on his father's face when evening came and he locked up the house and came to them and said with a great sweetness and contentment in his voice, "Well, the world's shut out." The family's private world was waiting and secure.

A rich sense of safety and of home flowed in him.

She came again into the room, her narrow face softened and private and warm, as if from some small victory. "We—ll," she said, and brought him a woolen dressing gown. "Come and rock by a nice turf fire and we'll talk a bit, child."

And he thought, I like the way she calls me child.

She was excited in a quiet fashion. The sign wasn't on her face; faintly in her voice, maybe; mostly in her talk. She chattered as she whipped eggs in a bowl; the chatter was idle in a way, but it all turned on one subject, purposefully he thought: Thomas Burke. She didn't call him Tom, or my late husband. It was always Thomas Burke.

Thomas Burke was a Name when McManus was fifteen and wandering the summer hills with more books than clothes in his pack. Burke was a Bad Name. His books were banned in Dublin, acclaimed everywhere else, and fought over in the Dublin press, "like mongrels at a meat bone," she said.

The banning started with Thomas Burke's first book, *Judas*. It was a book about political and social obscurantism, Catholic Nationalism masquerading as patriotic Republicanism, about devious Irish treachery, about politicians "whose only talent through the years of independence has been for talking out of both sides of their mouths," about malignant parochialism, malice and hungry sex. The book was a rejected lover's iconoclasm.

"Thomas Burke took me to America," she said, as if he had been a lover and not a husband. "He got to be a professor of English at New York University and I taught school. He wrote all his books in America. But he always wanted home to change Ireland and when the books made money, we bought this place and altered it, put in the electric, built on the bathroom and a pump

162 ((

and plumbing from the well. The little end room is his study." Is, she said.

The cottage had three rooms, the room with the bed, the electric kitchen, and the little end room full of books, a desk, a chair, and a cupboard. There was only one bed.

Where did she sleep? His sleeping bag was rolled up in a corner of the kitchen. His heart warmed to the lonely, generous woman. He slept in the good bed they brought back from America—Colonial, they called it?—and she slept on the floor in his bedroll. And didn't explain where she slept to the vigilant sister.

"He never wrote a good word in the end room," she said, and served scrambled eggs. "They killed him. It took him five years to die." She poured weak tea for McManus. "I nursed him," she said with peculiar tenderness.

That explained Dr. Sullivan's accusation that she needed an invalid of her own. It was almost funny in a sad sort of way: McManus and Mrs. Burke were being useful to one another. He heard himself say, "You loved Thomas Burke very much." She ate, her head down. He wondered whether Thomas Burke loved this narrow-faced, cold-faced, severe-faced woman. Was it with her that he learned the explicit things about sex they used to mark in his books and pass around? With her? No. She looked sexless. She was sexless.

"He cried himself to death," she said, and the phrase sat on his mind like a crow. "They screamed him to his grave. He couldn't think their thoughts or tell their lies. If you love Ireland your own way, it's treason, and if you're the wrong sort of Catholic, you're not an Irishman."

She cleared away. Her face was bleak.

"I want to thank you, Mrs. Burke," he said from the rocker and wondered at once why he had chosen this moment to say it.

"None of that," she said sharply. "Time for another pill." She gave it to him, with warm milk, and her hand brushed his hair.

"You'll be fine, child," she said, and washed the dishes. She had her invalid.

He felt better by the hour, hungrier, stronger. Dressed, he sat in a canvas chair in the fuchsia-walled garden and re-read the works of Thomas Burke. She fussed him, coddled him, shielded him from the doctor's fears and the sister's moral anxieties; gave him jobs to do, stretching his strength.

She pressed aside the fuchsia bushes to show him the land. Behind the hedge, a field of cut hay, and beyond it a mass of rock that rose four hundred feet, colored orange and mauve and violet and blue and yellow from the lichen and heather and rock flowers and gorse that grew from every crack and pocket of earth on its surface. At its foot were banks of fuchsia, honeysuckle, Michaelmas daisy, hawthorne, and buckey rose. There was a tiny copse of stunted oak. He could smell the honeysuckle across the width of the field, mingled with the scent of sweet new hay. The rock ridges rose beyond into rust and violet mountains and surrounded the house and its little afghan fields. And in front, through the green and crimson hedge, the glittering cove and a wider bay beyond it, and then the sea and a lighthouse, far out on a massive rock.

"That's Fastnet Light," he said.

"You know it?"

"Your cottage is in Toormore Bay," he said.

"You know it?"

"We used to take a house for the summer at Goleen, four miles west."

"You're at home," she said, and the gentleness in her voice made him look at her. The face was sharp and cold.

The road to Goleen to the west and Schull to the east, and Skibereen, and Cork must be behind the house and beyond the little fields, and beyond the first big ridge. He knew where he was. He was aware of the land again, of the mistress who was stream and hill and meadow and the spread limbs of the derry oak. They

164 ((

would never find him in this moon landscape of rock and gullies and green hollows and fern and thorn forests.

The warm air flowed through the flowering bushes. When she closed the hedge and shut off the moving air, the lawn was an enveloping warm cocoon. He was strong, he was safe. Time was in suspense. The world was very far and irrelevant. He drowsed in the little garden in hypnotic contentment and indolence lay on him like a layer of a dream, and in the evening she gave him his pills and they made him sleep deeply.

How old was she? Forty? Forty-five? Fifty? It varied by the day. He was a mother's boy and the mother cradled his head and put her braless nipple to his hungry mouth. Child, she called him.

Did he dream it in the sleep before sleep? The days slept also. Reality was a welcome distance away. The dream was real.

It was the first time he had wakened in the night. The pills were losing their power.

It was raining. Pouring. The wind was high, coming off the sea, beating the rain against the little, closed, front window. The big back window was open and the cool night air backed in and across the bed like a cool hand.

He was deeply rested, refreshed, life running in him, all his thought on his abundant good feeling. He stretched his legs, reached, and dragged on the head of the bed. It was a glorious feeling to extend a stronger body and feel the life in it.

It was the first rain for several days. The rains he had walked in in his sickness were vague or forgotten. He turned on his side and curled, contented as a cat, and reached his right arm across the wide bed, to sprawl, to sleep again.

Flesh. Warm human flesh. Round human flesh. He was disabled in body and mind and could not withdraw the hand. It was on a hip. She was lying half on her face, her legs stretched at length, the fullness of her hip under his palm. A large, firm, high hip. Slowly, the hand obeyed the head and came back to him.

He lay fearful of the sound of his rasping breath. She was naked in his bed. The sleeping bag on the hard floor must have done for her. Or had she used it? The pills that gave him deep sleep might have given her the chance for some sort of rest? She had to be a sexless middle-aged woman to lie in a man's bed—if she had been doing that? It was hard to believe. "Where do you sleep?" the sister kept asking, and he'd never heard her get an answer. Could a woman sleep beside a man and not . . . ? What did he knew about women? "God made you whole, child. Thank Him," she said to his erection and went on with her washing as if a hard penis was about the same as a piece of garden hose.

If he got up and sat in the rocking chair she'd know he knew. Then he'd have to go and he didn't want to. Was she naked? He reached cautiously for her back. Cloth. Her nightgown was gathered up about her waist. Frigid. A sexless widow in bed with a drugged child.

She always called him child.

Gently, as if the bed was rocking from his careful exertions, he perched his rigid body on the edge of the mattress, his back to her. He was erect again. Her hip was still warm in his hand as if he hadn't withdrawn it. The thought of it murdered him. Forty or fifty, she was a woman and he had never before had his hand on a woman's hip. If he turned in his sleep, hard and burning, he might press it against her and . . . by God, he couldn't allow himself even to think about that. He daren't go to sleep again in case. . . .

But he went to sleep again, and woke, still rigid in every limb, and aching in every muscle.

She was not there. There was no bruise on the pillow where her head must have been.

And the day was normal. She looked as severe as she had done

166 ((

all the days before. He began to doubt his senses and his recovery. She mothered him, gave him harder work to do, sent him to bed much later than usual, with his glass of warm milk and his pill.

It was still raining off the sea. He drank his milk by the big open window and shot his pill out into the rain. It would dissolve there just as readily as in his stomach. He wanted to wake in the night. He had been dreaming last night; some sort of relapse? Another sort of shroud?

It rained for three days. He had not been dreaming. There was no relapse. But maybe a new sort of shroud? She was there every night and gone early every morning. Sexless. He learned to sleep on the edge of the bed, his erections, sleeping or waking, pointed away from any cause of offense. And each day she was as she had been before. Kind. Severe.

The day the wind dried the ground she said, "It's time for you to walk beyond the garden. When it's dark. . . ."

They walked in the moonlight out over the little fields and up the narrow road to the first rock ridge. The moon flew in the sky and sailed on the sea. Far dogs bayed like women in childbirth.

"There, child, you're strong," she said, and he filled his lungs with the turf-scented air and loved the life in his limbs and the shadowed landscape of the mistress with hills like breasts and little fields like a soft, flat belly. How long was it, he asked himself, since he had *seen* her, really *seen* her? All his old emotions for her were alive.

"You're smiling," Mrs. Burke said. "Are you thinking about somebody?"

"Herself," he said, and swept his arm across the landscape. The clouds were banked like dark mountain ranges and between them light came from the molten pewter brilliance of the shining sky. "Look at her sky," he said, "it's like a furnace or an ice field."

"You're like Thomas Burke," she said, and laughed and started down the hill, holding his hand like a mother leading home her child. It was an odd, exultant little laugh, as if something had been accomplished. He had never heard her laugh. "Sleep well," she said in the house.

He went to bed at once.

He was half-wakened, no, less than half-wakened by the flaming delight flooding his body, swimming behind his heavy eyes, and was far down the adamantine road before the caressing fingers that made him moan softly were joined by the whispering voice that said, "God made you whole, child. Thank Him," and he was turning and still half-asleep and half-demented when the lips touched his and a tongue tip flickered in his mouth like a sugar-coated shock.

By then he was reaching for the woman and she was naked and talking softly and the hard fingers were magically gentle on his raging penis. "There child, there child," the voice coaxed, "do what you want. . . ." He was blind, the darkness was black, like a wall that shut in life and fire and sent the universe elsewhere about its alien and meaningless business. "It's all right'" the voice that touched his face whispered, "it's all right . . . do what you want to do, child," and there were no words in his mouth, none in his head; only whimpers of tearing passion and delight.

Gently she drew him and lay on her back, guiding his hand to her breasts, and his senses birled in his head. "I'm a country," she said, "feel my hills," and he grasped her breasts frantically and felt the hard erect nipples in his palm and took them in his fingertips and pulled his mouth from hers and suckled the nipples like a feeding infant. "Tease them with your teeth," she said, and what she said he did. She drew his hand to her belly and guided him over it, slowly, down, and "Do what you feel like, child," she said, left his hand where she wanted it, and "Come onto me," she coaxed. "Come on and I'll guide you, child," and her arm

168   ((

drew him onto her, plunging. "That's it, child," she said. "That's it, do what you want," and they cried their lust together.

When it was over, he lay on her and she held him hard with her thighs and caressed his hips with the soles of her feet, talking, crooning, whispering, her back still arched, her loins rising and falling gently, arms holding him on her breasts. "There child, there child, wonderful, child . . . wonderful, wonderful, wonderful . . ." filling him with immense pride, and peace and appetite. He found her mouth. It was like drinking cold spring water, he thought, and couldn't imagine her face, but her body was like a known country.

"Do everything you want, when you want, how you want," she coaxed.

"I've never done it before," he said.

"I know, I know, I know . . . my wonderful child. . . ."

There was no strangeness in him with her. There was no morning, and no light. She was there under him, teasing him, talking to him as if she had always been there. There was no age; a warm body, a warm voice, fingers like feathers, thighs that embraced him, a woman who whispered "my child" like a mother and made him feel safe beyond fear, and a woman who erupted under him and made his loins roar invincibly.

And insatiably. "I want more," he said. "I want everything."

"Everything is here," she said.

But in the morning everything was not there. Her mark on the pillow was not there. He saw her crossing the garden in the rain, with her egg basket, coming from the hen house in a gray raincoat, Wellington boots on her big feet, one of Thomas Burke's old tweed hats on her head, her face as narrowly severe as a village vigilante's.

And the day was like every other day between them; like the

day of a son in his young manhood and a mother in her middle life and not much need for talk between them.

He did his small services, brought turf from the barn, weeded and turned the few flower beds, looked out at the closing circles of rock hills, and tiny fields and the sea that encircled them, and there was nowhere he wanted to be but this place where he was.

Yet in spite of its ordinariness, there was about the day something not believed. "I'm a country. Feel my hills." Did that plain severe face really say something like that to him in the dark? Could those buttocks under that square flour bag and those breasts that were lost under its flat front really be as he thought he remembered them? In the bedroom he stared at the bed. His northern Jansenist mind knew they had been there and was not quite persuaded; or was not quite willing to believe. In this room? Wallowing between her thighs? Her voice? Her words? *Her?* That one out there? Did a murderer who went back to the scene of the crime really find the event real, solidly reconstructable? Were the battlefields revisited real after the battles? Was there more than one world to live in, and did they do more than cause their separate atmospheres to mingle as they passed? More and more as the day lengthened he thought of the night and his head warmed for the plain woman in the square dress.

Mrs. Burke did all day the things she had to do—washing, cooking, mending, dusting, dropping an odd word, sitting with a cup of strong tea for "a little crack," and "come to the table, child," and rocking before the fire when he went to bed. "Good night, child," she said when he passed her on his way to bed and touched his arm in a motherly gesture. "Sleep well, now," as if the light of day would be time enough to speak to him again. Did she really remember?

"Good night, Mrs. Burke," he said, and did not take his pajamas from under his pillow and lay on his own side of the bed with his eyes closed, waiting in the dark, insanely ready.

Then wildfire and lust under the velutinous night. "More, I want more, my darling darling child," she said with her lips cropping his and her tongue darting. "The morning's coming."

As if the clear light of day and clear sight were robbers of the things most precious and most real.

ELEVEN

AR O U N D and beyond the Irish customs post two men, Cullen the Garage and Heavey the Grocer, met Pat Powers and drove him to Stranorlar. The walk over the Border had cleansed Powers' mind of Mary Connors, the dirty connivin wee hoore.

He sat in the back seat of the car, harboring a fresh resentment.

Executions were secret things. Who knew who did them? Only the men who ordered them and the men who carried out the orders. That was meant to lower the risk of revenge killings by the dead man's friends, or his relatives. Before McManus got his, all Ireland was goin to know who done him. Powers would be passed on by the Stranorlar men to the Donegal town men, to the Sligo men— and wherever he caught up with McManus it would be known by a great crowd behind him that he done him.

And how many would he have to watch out for, from then on and forever after?

A better thought came, and there was space for only one at a time. McManus had no friends. Students, maybe, and Protestants. But nobody who mattered. T'hell w'that sort. He was tired and relieved by the thought of a friendless McManus. He relaxed and slumped.

"Don't give McManus another thought till you've had a good sleep and a good feed," Heavey the Grocer said. "We'll put you right beside him in the mornin."

That was good enough. His bed was in the house of Cullen the

Garage, behind the big church, down by the bridge over the Finn to Ballybofey. He went to sleep with an empty mind.

He came down to his good feed in the morning rested and spilling over with noisy geniality. "Jasus, missus, you're tremenjous," he told Cullen's wife, and ladeled away bacon and eggs and fried bread and Cullen watched him nervously, hoping Heavey and the rest of them would get here before the man was full. Heavey was the talker and with this big fellow he would have to talk well.

"We got the word you're to wait," Heavey told Powers when he came. It didn't seem to Heavey that it would make much difference to this bull how he heard it, rough or smooth. "There's one comin over the Border from the Bogside. He's goin with you."

"Who?"

"Name of Kiernan. Sean Kiernan."

"D'you know him?"

"He's from here once."

"What's he comin for?"

He'd have to say it sooner or later; he might as well say it now. "To take charge." He was supposed to get this over and done before Kiernan got here. It was done now, but not over.

Powers felt the shock down to his heels. His silence was not restraint; it was stupefaction. He looked at them sitting round the table, their hands folded, or looped round their plates, or in their pockets, and their faces were full of cunning and deceit and unfriendliness. He could smell it.

He had no clear thoughts but he knew things. He knew without thought that Clune thought this one up. Jasus, Clune was a sleakid wee cunt. A vicious wee cunt. He can't do without me, by Jasus, but he can't keep his fuckin nails outa me. Spite. Jealousy. The wee bastard knows I should be in his job. Don't open your mouth. Get outside and wait. The table tilted with the violence of his rising and the men around it blocked sliding dishes and spilling milk and tea.

174 ((

Powers rolled out of the house like a boiler past danger point. He didn't think; his head and heart and belly boiled together like stew in a caldron. He walked, blind, over the bridge into Ballybofey, weaving in and out among the streets, back over the bridge into Stranorlar, in and out among the streets and over the bridge again, not because he meant to but because he came to it. Back and back again. And out of the two towns into the country; boiling, inchoate. He glared without seeing, out over the rolling country. "Fuckin country," he said, and for a moment saw Heavey clearly in his head. "Fuckin shopkeeper," and started like a pointer for his shop. Why was his shop so far away? Conspiracy, that was why; it wasn't a thought but knowledge in the guts, born whole. His rage whinnied in his throat and he stormed towards Heavey's, heel and toe, arms pumping, a shade short of a run.

Heavey was serving an old woman a tin of Fray Bentos bully beef. He gave her all his attention. Powers pushed her aside.

"Houl on," she protested.

"What's up, Heavey? Who done that t'me?"

"Done what?" The face was blank with careful innocence.

"Don't make funa me! By Jasus, don't make funa me." Powers wheeled and leapt for the street, his head boiling with destruction.

The old woman followed him to the door, laughed in her throat, and spat into the street. "Holy Jasus, Mr. Heavey . . . thons a one," she said, and came back for her bully beef.

The pubs were opening. Tired by fury, Powers went into one. "Porter," he said.

"Pint or a half?"

Even the fuckin glass-washers were tryin to push him. "Gimme a fuckin pint."

Kiernan, the man from the Bogside, got off the bus at noon and wanted to hear nothing about McManus till he had eaten.

"I'm always afearda starvin when I'm away from home," he said with a room-warming smile. "I get these terrible sore heads whenma stomach's empty."

He was very small, very spare, his jacket loose on him, his little legs making no impression on his trousers. They flapped around his shanks and when he sat and the trousers settled on his thighs, there seemed to be only the thigh bone under them. But his little face was full of impish and endearing charm. "I know y'won't begrudge a skinny wee crature a bita grub, Mr. Powers." He smiled into Powers' surly face and appeared to be unaware of strain. The Stranorlar men watched it without sign of their malicious pleasure and expectation. Smiler Kiernan was a bloody wee marvel. "Toro, Toro," said Heavey inside his head, and kept his own smile in there, not to spoil the thing.

Powers was not drunk, only distant with porter and faintly aerial. When their session began he attacked. "You don't even know Mc-Manus. How're y'gonta kill'm?"

"That's a good point, Mr. Powers," Kiernan admitted, "and you're right as well. I'm only here for company to make up for that Callaghan that was took. What good would I be without you?"

"Right y'are," Powers said. This poor wee shit had more sense than them that sent him. His assurance returned, entire. He took over. "All right, Heavey. Put me beside the bastard."

"He's away in the West," the shopkeeper said.

"Details." That's the way the Big Fellow always worked. Attention to details. No loose bloody talk.

"Well, when the word was out on him, we put the eyes to work and. . . ."

"Where is he, for Christ's sake?"

Kiernan said, sweetly helpful. "There's details to be told, is that it, Mr. Heavey?"

"That's it, Seaneen," Heavey said, for he kept a shop, and Kiernan, when he lived here, only worked on the roads and ditches for the county council; so Heavey was Mr. Heavey, but Kiernan was only little Sean. "You see, he was spotted at the hotel here, pack, painty clothes, and all that. You see? He slept all day and left at night. You see it? Sleep by day and walk by night. That's it?"

"That's it."

"Well, that's not it."

"Somethin else?" Kiernan encouraged.

"For Christ's sake." Powers protested the back-chat.

"Then there's no sign at all of a man with a pack and painty clothes goin through Donegal town, and them watchin for him. So we ask the drivers on the Letterkenny-Sligo run. He got on a bus on the other side of the Gap and went to Sligo."

"He's in Sligo?" Powers said, ready to go.

"He is not."

"For fuck's sake!"

"Somethin happened in Sligo?" Kiernan asked with understanding, being a talker himself.

"The Sligo men worked the pubs. Every damned one. That's *work*. He went to the Great Southern. No painty clothes now. Tweeds, by Jasus. New. He's askin about coach tours with Americans on them and one of the barmen fixes him up w'a man by the name of Charley Murphy, drivin for Fianna Tours. This barman fiddles a wee bit up the lega the oul cashier and she says there's a phone call on his bill, t'Belfast. Up in his room he's coughin and wailin and girnin about his sister that's dead but he's not goin home for the funeral. What d'you thinka that?"

"Aye." Kiernan gave it omnibus significance.

They're gettin at me, Powers thought with the certainty of guilty knowledge. "Where the fuck is he?" he bellowed.

"Coughin his guts out," Heavey said. "This Charley Murphy remembers the whole lot. He never speaks. Won't talk. Skulkin like a sick dog in the back seat. This wee American girl by the name of Brendine Healy is as horny as a cat and showin off her knickers, but he won't bite. Then they make a stop on Clew Bay and Murphy finds them fuckin away on the shore. When they get to Bantry McManus takes off, walkin west up the Bay, and she buys herself some gear and comes back and says to Murphy, can you hire bikes here? and quits the tour and takes off on the bike.

"And where is he?" Powers shouted.

"He walked west from Bantry, coughin and sweatin and shiverin . . . and another thing I near missed. Growing whiskers on his chin."

"Meetin up with the wee girl somewhere?" Kiernan said.

Heavey smiled. "Takin the cure?"

"That's it."

"We're lookin for him and a girl west of Bantry. That's the best y'can do?" Powers had expected more after so long a wait.

"That saved you a week's work," Heavey said impatiently.

"Away on," Powers said to Kiernan, and got up.

"One wee minute and I'm away, Mr. Powers," Kiernan said. "A wee recapitulation."

"A wee what?"

"Another wee ask," Kiernan explained, and to Heavey: "West of Bantry, yes? Sick, yes? Meetin an American girl on a bike, yes? Disguised, yes? The whiskers?"

"That's it."

"That's it." And for Powers, with a smiling flourish, "I'm in your hands, Mr. Powers."

Cullen the Garage said, "There's a car at the door. Y'can have it for a week."

Kiernan drove, peering out over the wheel like a tall midget, smiling. "Lovely country, Mr. Powers," he said.

Useless bloody wee smiler. Smiling bloody wee spy. Peepin for Clune the Cunt. Powers didn't reply.

The Stranorlar men watched them go. "That Kiernan," Cullen said, smiling, "would smile the balls off an ape."

178 ((

"He's got one with him," Heavey said, smiling. There were a lot of amusing things in the world. They did not think of McManus. They had not seen McManus and what they had to do about him had now been done. McManus was as good as dead, though they didn't think specifically about that either. What for would they think about it? If they had seen him? That would have been a different pigpen. He did not, they heard tell, think their thoughts their way. They would have had to hate him if they had met him. Freed from this burden of knowledge, they were free to forget him. Right men don't cumber their memories with things they don't hate.

Kiernan talked a lot, mostly about the wife and the wains. "How's the missus, Mr. Powers? The wains well?" He didn't always wait for answers. "It's hard on youse ones in Belfast, not sleepin at home. I live in the No-Go in the Bogside. No bother at all. No army, no polis. Sleep at home. How many wains have you, Mr. Powers?"

He's gettin at me again, Powers thought, and said shortly, "Not married."

"By Jasus, boyo, y'don't know what you're missin. Y'know what's great? Y'know what makes you feel better'n the king?"

"What?"

"Makin your oul woman pregnant." He glowed with honest pride. "I mean, look at me. No, take a look. Go on. I'm a wee skitter. Aye? Five-foot-two in m'stockin feet. She's five-foot-seven and twice the weighta me. Six wains, Mr. Powers. Six!" He shouted it like a winning score.

"Right y'are. Y'like fuckin. Who doesn't?"

"Fuckin?" Kiernan's astonishment was real. "I'm talkin about my oul woman. Y'don't fuck your oul woman." He waved a shocked, dismissive hand, not smiling. "Y'make love. I mean—you *mean* it." He chewed his lower lip for a while and drove faster, like an angry man. "I don't hold w'fuckin," he said emphatically. "I'm a Catholic." He was good-natured. Cooling. He slowed the pace a little. "You make wains." Safely round a series of tight bends he recovered his enthusiasm. "That's what makes y'feel great. Like a king. Look at me, for Christ's sake. Me? I make people! Y'ever thinka that?"

"Aye." Powers was thinking of it. He wasn't grateful to Kiernan for bringing Mary Connors back like a persistent infection.

"There's a right waya doin things," Kiernan said pontifically. "I mean, y'don't stand in fronta your oul woman and open your spare like some wee bugger up an entry. I mean, I want this job over quick so I can get home. We're gonta start the seventh, y'see?" His smiling warmth was back as he thought about it. It was a real smile—full, warm, devoted. "I'll say t'her, 'Right y'are, love, are y'ready to start number seven?' Then we'll do it maybe twice a night for a week t'make sure she takes, like." He entered a caveat for the uncertain times. "That's if I get home every night, o'course." He might have been a flyweight explaining his training schedule to a sporting priest.

Powers glowered morosely at the flying hedges. Christ!

But this was the mere biology of makin wains. There was a more important—certainly an equally important—ingredient. "That's not the big thing, Mr. Powers," Kiernan explained. "The big thing is your statea mind when you're doin it, y'know? To get good-lookin healthy wains y'have to have the right attitude, d'you see?"

"No."

"Well, look at it this way. When her and me was married the priest said t'us somethin like 'a chile'll be as beautiful as the moment of its conception.' What'd'you think that? That's somethin, isn't it?"

He waited. Powers waited, counting cows in an approaching field.

"Well, all the time we're at it I'm thinkin of all the good things I can think of about the wife—y'know? She's a good mother. She's good in the house. She's clean and she's a great temper. Very gentle, y'know? So I'm tellin her all the time what a smashin woman she is, and she's tellin me 'you're wonderful, Sean, you're great.' Y'know what happens?"

"What?"

"Y'get lovely wains. My six is the healthiest, happiest, best-lookin wains God every put guts in. What d'you think of that?"

"What?"

"What I told you." His face was eager, earnest, fully persuaded. His smile was expectant. He had let this man Powers into an important secret of his small life.

"Y'mean, you thinkin well of her and her thinkin well of you while you're up her? That's what gives you good-lookin wains?"

A little shadow crossed Kiernan's bright face. It wasn't the way to speak about it or his oul woman—but the man was what he was and knew no better. "Aye."

Powers shifted in his seat and half-turned to face Kiernan. He was smiling a small Michael Collins smile. He'd seen it on an old movie on the Irish telly.

"Tell me somethin, Kiernan," he said, looking down on the tiny man from under the roof of the car.

"What?"

"You're five-foot-two in your stockin feet?"

"Aye."

"What weight are you?"

"Seven stone."

"Well, tell me this, now. When they made you, whicha them was drunk—your da or your ma?"

Kiernan stopped the car slowly, letting it run a long way. He pulled in to a ditch, his neck stretching to give him a good sight of it. The car was tight against the bank of the roadside, under a high hedge. He seemed not to have heard Powers. He said, "Get out, if y'please, Mr. Powers. I want to show you somethin," and opened the door.

Powers opened his door and swung his legs out. His rump was

still in the seat, his back to Kiernan. For big men, gettin out of
these wee cars is a bloody struggle, and what was he gonta do
with the door half-caught in the bloody bank? A knife settled its
sharp point in the back of his neck and drove out of his head
whatever he was about to say.

Kiernan said, in a gently spitting voice, "Powers, you're a stupid
big cunt. You're a dirty fuckin stupid big cunt. But I was sent
t'work w'you and I'm gonta do it. If you open your fuckin mouth
again unless I let you, I'll cut your throat." He was kneeling on
the seat. He put his hand over Powers' shoulder and withdrew his
gun. With the agility of a lively boy he was over the seat, into
the back of the car. "Now slide back and drive. We're gonta the
southwest to kill another fuckin cunt. And in case them boys in
Stranorlar didn't tell you—*I'm in charge here.* Away on. . . ."

Powers saw Kiernan's face in the rear-view mirror. It was pale.
The lips were a little apart and drawn back and trembling. His
pupils seemed to fill his eye sockets and they were black with lust.

Powers didn't wonder if that was what Kiernan really looked
like in bed, joyously extolling the virtues of his wife when they
were making beautiful children. The things he knew about told
him what he saw.

And he was thinking: thon fuckin wee man's a killer. By Jasus,
the looka that wee smiler'd take y'in, all right.

He put the car in gear and moved it gently into the road, as
though to rock Kiernan might disturb his detonator.

Kiernan smiled and talked to the Donegal town men. He talked
to the Sligo men and the bartender at the Great Southern. He
found the shop where the man with the painty clothes bought a
tweed suit. They slept the night in Sligo and left in the morning,
Powers driving, Kiernan behind, thinking that maybe tomorrow he'd
be on his way back and number seven could be started. But all
the way to Bantry, the silence ticked like an alarm clock.

The Bantry men met in a back room at Dolan's. For years there had been three of them, middle-aged, ridiculous, and patient, waiting for The Day.

On The Day, the last English boot would be off the last Irish neck and even the Northern Protestants would find happiness and a new thing: Irish peace. It was only a failure of understanding and the cunning of English propaganda that kept the Northern Protestants from believing there was a boot, English or otherwise, on their necks. Understanding would come with freedom. Freedom was a mouthwash that killed the subtlest germs.

Daniel Sorahan the schoolmaster was one of the three. His father survived the War of Independence and the Civil War that followed it, and was murdered after the Civil War by a former comrade of the War of Independence who believed with the Grand Inquisitor that a man who fought on the wrong side in Ireland was better dead than in mortal error.

Daniel did not, of course, remember his father, only the manner of his dying and the oppressive burden of his mother's unforgetting, unforgiving bitterness.

He was a humorous and a devious man who believed himself to be almost miraculously longsighted. He agreed cheerfully with those who laughed at the Bantry men, that they were ridiculous keeping the old IRA alive "like a bunch of playactin schoolboys," when "that sort of thing was away out of date."

"You're right there, you're right there," Daniel always agreed, "but I'll tell you somethin worth knowin . . . you don't throw away your feet when you're not usin them in your sleep at night. You leave them on your ankles. Maybe you'll live through till the mornin and there they are. Or put it this way. The Jews put the Maccabees in a book and kept them there till somethin happened . . . the ovens in Germany. Then they took them out of the book and called them the Irgun, and there they are. They call the place Israel. I'll get you another pint. Guinness, isn't it? It's bein there when somethin happens, isn't it?"

Something had happened in the North and the three middle-aged men in Dolan's backroom were joined by young men waiting for something more to happen. Not killing. Not bombing. This part of Ireland was a mild and gentle land with mild and gentle people who spoke softly. They were waiting for nothing more definable than something.

Daniel lived in a semi-detached house in Bantry. It was the only place in the town where he ever said what he really thought and he said it only to his wife.

He still loved the woman. He found her teaching in the school where he started his own career and they spent their honeymoon in London. They were Catholics whose Catholicism was aesthetic and social and at times cautiously religious. So they agreed in London that if the best was to be got out of the occasion, Daniel should find one of those shops that displayed a little card reading "rubber goods." It was Liz Sorahan who said after a couple of nights, "Danny, I'm not goin through my whole married life thinkin we do it every night and all I've felt of the real Daniel Sorahan is a secondhand impression inside a rubber bag. I'm seein a doctor." So the Sorahans in quietness but in nobody else's confidence brought the Dutch cap to Bantry and every day hurried home from school and laughed a lot in bed. Their two planned sons were away in Dublin at Trinity College with twelve hundred other Catholics who ignored the hierarchy's ban on Catholic attendance at the old Protestant Ascendancy College. And as the fire smoldered more and flamed less, Daniel and Mrs. Elizabeth Sorahan found laughter and trusting talk a fair compensation for the loss of six of the week's seven nights. With one another, they were themselves. They were the kind of Irish who could usher in the new hoped-for Ireland, if ever they had the public courage to stand for it.

184 ((

The most violent thing Daniel Sorahan had done in his life was to catch and kill a salmon or a trout, a mackerel or a herring. He had a great fondness for the English and their ways. "In the broadest sense," he said, his rump extending towards his own fireplace and his eyes smiling at his wife, "the English are the most civilized people in the world." All he had against them, he liked to tell her, was that they came to Ireland too soon and stayed too long. "If they could have made Englishmen out of us, they'd have done us a great favor. They couldn't, and the best reason for gettin rid of them now is that they'll leave us nobody to blame but ourselves. That's the great wrong they did us," he liked to say to her, "they gave us somebody else to blame for what we are. When they're right out of Ireland entirely we'll have to start dealin with Ireland's biggest problem—the bloody Irish."

But he didn't say things like that in the back of Dolan's Pub. His shrewd eyes inspected his young men and he thought as he had thought often in the past few years: the North's the big wide screen and these Bantry boyos are only sittin in the cheap seats, watchin. They need somethin to do.

Well, there was something now to do. Find a deserter and possible informer from the North. It made him nervous. It was more directly human than he had had in mind. What he had in mind wasn't clear even to him. It came under the general heading of "something." In Ireland one didn't face such issues till they bruised the nose. His eyes inspected the executioners from the North, and he didn't care much for them. They were direct, like bulldozers at a barricade, with blinkered single-track heads.

He particularly disliked the big one, this Powers. He didn't like their harsh clipped voices. He thought more softly of Kiernan, but that smile made him wary. It was too Irish. There was too much of it. Kiernan was agreeable, flattering, grateful to excess, a decent little creature, he was certain; very likely the man had never kicked a dog. But deficient. In what? In the sense that there was

)) 185

something in there that poisoned the smile at its roots. It would show, maybe. Meanwhile they brought the young men a prospect of patriotic if not heroic labors—to hunt, find, and deliver to Powers and Kiernan, one McManus, a student.

A graduate. That also made Daniel Sorahan uneasy. This McManus was not an urbanized peasant, like Powers or Kiernan; a middle-class Catholic with, maybe, more delicate perceptions? Scruples also? With ideas in his head that never entered theirs; and critical faculties? Was that it? And he wondered what he himself would become if he were locked in an urban ghetto with urbanized peasants trained single-mindedly to kill and demolish? He loved to fish. He disliked the killing of his catch. And what was he to think of what they said about "the soft-bellied-educated?" Did that include himself and Liz? Sorahan had in fact never till now set eyes on urban guerrillas.

"What we've got is this," he said, and spoke to Kiernan across Dolan's back room. "Nobody like McManus saw any doctor around here. He didn't go near the hospital. He wasn't in any chemist's shop tryin to get medicine for whatever it is he's got. He just walked west out of town."

"Right y'are, right y'are, Mr. Sorahan now," Kiernan said gratefully. "What about the girl? Anythin on her?"

"She hired an old bike from Driscoll's, and left her bags at the Westlodge. That's the hotel the coach tours use in Bantry. She booked in there, packed a rucksack and said she'd be back in a couple of days."

"She went after McManus?"

"He went west. So did she. One of the boys was down at Kilcrohane and heard from the Garda there that a farmer by the name of Cusack found this man ravin on the rocks at Sheep's Head with a gun in his pack. But the Garda says Cusack and his wife's not sober more than a day a month. That's what we have for you."

186 ((

Powers said, "It's not much."

"It's more than you had when you came here," Sorahan said gently, "and it took time and people."

"Y're great, Mr. Sorahan, y're great," Kiernan said, smoothing waters and smiling and drawing smiles he tried to understand from the young men who stood and sat around the walls. They were big, red-faced young men with tumbling black hair and they were caught between discomfort in the presence of real executioners—a scuffle after a dance was the worst any of them had ever seen off the television screen—and cautious admiration for men who had faced "the enemy" for "the Cause." They could carry the deaths of soldiers in the forefront of their minds. Killing and dying were part of the life style of an army and the British army in the North was "the enemy." The civilian dead they shuffled behind a mental curtain as accidents to be regretted and not thought about.

Daniel Sorahan watched Kiernan watching his young men and was glad he had not explained to the little man that the mood and the history of West Cork were not quite like that of other places; that here there were Protestant peasant farmers, as well as Catholic, that here there had never been animus between the two, that here a tradition of violence and strife went no deeper than an occasional drunken brawl far less serious than the normal behavior of Scottish soccer fans, and that these young men were willing to collect money for Northern fighting men—who were in reality headlines and abstractions, even romantic illusions—but were unlikely to be open and trusting with harsh men with harsh accents who had actually killed other human beings and were here to kill. And "the enemy," the British, came here on their holidays as "the English," and yarned in pubs about soccer and asked questions about Gaelic football and hurley and meant the livelihood of most of these young men who were now, because the English no longer came, unemployed. West Cork was a harsh land of gentle people who believed in "the Cause" and had not for many decades met it in the flesh. So with slight smiles and deep curiosity they watched Kiernan perform and he distributed his praise, "Y're all great. Great. Great."

"When do we start beatin the bushes?" Powers said impatiently.

"The mornin will be time enough," Sorahan told him.

It was a soft statement, like the southwestern air, and criminally, even treacherously lax to an impatient northern mind. "What sorta talk is that?"

"Bantry talk," Sorahan said even more slowly, even more softly. "Out here we never look for anythin in the dark, unless we know where it is." He finished his pint with elaborate deliberateness, put down his glass on the bench, and stood up. "If you want to start west, in the dark, on your own, Mr. Powers . . ." It had the elusive hint of a threat or an insult in its tone and Powers lifted his head and waited for the rest of it like a listening bull, looking hard at Sorahan ". . . go ahead and good luck to you and we'll catch up with you in the mornin."

The young men around the wall grinned, tonguing the air for promising hostilities, their eyes darting from face to face like dogs sniffing trees for the taste of enmity and the odor of relief.

Kiernan lifted his five-feet-two off his bench and stretched it, watching the grins from behind his warming smile. "The mornin's fine w'me," he said.

The grins shifted to Powers, but he did not look at them. He drained his pint, watching Sorahan steadily over the rim of his glass. He put the glass down beside him and wiped his mouth. "Right y'are," he said, and sat where he was, with Sorahan in his sights all the way through the door. He saw his back long after it had left the doorway and gone into the night.

"Good night. Six in the mornin. Here."

"Night."

The night air was like damp black velvet. Their voices clung to it. The young men went home, smiling in their heads, doing in-

188 ((

tuitive emotional sums in their heads, calculating whether Powers would push Daniel Sorahan to a bit of sport when the drink was running. They were eager for the morning and the hunt.

But not yet for the kill. That was two steps away, and only the first one was yet allowed into their minds.

Three cars, several motor scooters, bikes, and binoculars. Bread, slabs of Irish cheddar, cold sausages, and beer in cardboard boxes. Wives and mothers made them ready; manhunters and their transport gathered in Wolfe Tone Square under the statue of St. Brendan the Navigator who, it was said, discovered America. They gathered under his outstretched arms. Brendan looked out over Bantry Bay to the Atlantic. The manhunters packed their food and drink into the trunk of Powers' car. There was no sense in being hungry or thirsty. The day might be long; even longer than that; it looked like rain.

Daniel Sorahan hadn't slept well, though here in the cool morning air he felt fine.

"Do I know what's on your mind, Danny-boy?" his wife Liz asked him in the night. That was what she always asked him when "it" was on her mind on an unscheduled night.

"You do not."

"Then what is it?"

"Go to sleep." For several years, Friday night had been sex night, when the week's work was done. This held good on school holidays and it was still only Thursday.

In the early morning she came into the bathroom while he shaved. "You didn't have a good night, Dan."

"I did not."

Prudently he ate a large breakfast and didn't talk, though he was a talker at the table.

At the door, he kissed her. He had never left the house without kissing her, even when it was up the street for tobacco, a minute and a half away. But he forgot to smack her bottom and he had done that too, for twenty-five years.

"There's somethin about this, Dan," she said.

"There is."

"What?"

"Well," he said, and remembered her bottom and smacked it. "It's nothin much."

She caught his wrist. She had strong hands. "It's somethin," she said.

"It is." He kissed her again. "They might find the boy," he said.

"Well," she said, and thought better of saying more. She knew her husband. Yesterday when those two men from the North were on their way, he had wanted them to find the informer. Now the informer was "the boy."

"I wouldn't want those two to slaughter my pig," he said, and kissed her again. "These Ulster people are a coarse breed of human." He waited for her comment.

"Well?" she said, gently steering a weaving spirit she knew as well as she knew her own. She held his face and kissed his cheek. "You're a gentle man, Dan," she said, and having loaded her dice went in abruptly and closed the door on him.

"Liz," she heard him call. She went to the kitchen to rattle the dishes against the sound of his voice. Dan drove in unhappy thought to Wolfe Tone Square.

They were, he thought, a cross between one of those motor-cycle gangs he'd read about and never seen, and a conflux of bird-watchers on bicycles. They stood beside their machines and listened more or less carefully to Powers' directions. T'would be the fine outing, anyway.

190 ((

Powers was, Kiernan declared, "acting field commander of this search and destroy operation;" then he wafted back to St. Brendan beside Sorahan like a wisp of lost cloud. "Mr. Powers likes the one-two-three stuff," Kiernan whispered. "The man's a born corporal."

They went down the thin accusing finger of the Sheep's Head peninsula that stabbed sharply at the Atlantic between Bantry Bay and Dunmanus Bay. They went like an infestation of Bertha worms, covering the ground and chewing the stalks that might cover "a boy and a girl," as Sorahan had them now insistently in his head. From the hills they probed the hollows with their field glasses, knocked on doors, followed farmers over small fields, open hills, and into byres and chicken houses.

"Did y'see . . . ?"

"A girl, on a bike, with a pack on her back . . . ?"

"Campers wantin to sleep on your land . . . ?"

"A man and a girl, with one bike between them and two packs . . . ?"

They varied the questions as they thought about their search and their quarry.

The replies were elusive. "They'd be friends of yours I'm thinkin . . . ?"

"There's plenty like that, now. . . ."

"There's always a bike on the road. . . ."

Sly evasions; eyes wandering to give suspicious minds time to wonder. Two of them, the eyes seemed to say, askin questions in my yard now, and up there on the hill two more of them is it, at Curley's? And a head tilted to look past them, to see better the two men against the whitewashed wall of a distant cottage. " 'Tis a windy place now. You don't hear much when your back's turned." Enclosed faces, sheltering half-smiles, shifting eyes; it was like trying to keep a hold on the belly of a wet salmon.

And the English in their cabins that had been converted into retirement cottages, looking blank and asking courteously for more detail. "I'd like to be able to help you. A boy and a girl? Are they lost? Could you describe them? Oh, they can't get lost here. All the roads lead somewhere. I wouldn't worry too much. I wish I could be of more help to you. I'm sorry. . . ."

And the hours passing and the thirst growing and the stomach full of little but wind. You'd think, in the name of God, that somebody'd see somebody and the place only the width of a donkey's thigh.

Powers roamed the peninsula in Cullen's car, rolling out of it and pounding the earth like a dray stallion as he spotted searchers. "What'd y'get? What'd y'get? Jasus Chirst, you could see if y'were blind in this bloody place. . . ." But the blind had not seen. They were getting tired and bored and hungry and thirsty and the cases of beer and the cardboard boxes of food were in Powers' car and Powers was fierce and relentless and tireless. It was not the way these young men lived or thought or felt. The replies he got shortened and the surliness thickened and Powers did not see it.

He stormed the hollows and hills with implacable energy, barking, bawling, like an embodied shadow of the lowering clouds that rolled their mass across the sky, full of crushing turbulence and annihilating anger. "Find the fucker!" he raged, and rolled into the car and crashed gears and thumped the car over farm tracks and fields and stony hills to find other searchers and yell other maledictions.

And the dementia lurking behind the young men's eyes seeped to the front. A shy small youth named Barney said, "D'you think that big Ulster boar's right in the head?"

His hulking companion whose name was Colum sniffed the wind off Dunmanus Bay like a horse at a gate and said, "We'll find out when we get to the drink," and knocked with crusty knuckles on another door.

192 ((

Kiernan drove with Daniel Sorahan along the north shore of the peninsula. Sorahan was, he thought, like himself, a dacent man. He liked the lean, stooped schoolteacher. There was something kindly in his angular face, and in the graying black hair and white temples there was an air of gentility; something to trust? Was that it? He wasn't sure. What he knew was that there was somethin confusin, alien, foreign, deceitful about the people they questioned at doors and in the fields and on the hills . . . the wee smiles, the eyes that were always just leavin your face when you looked at them, the sly wee peeks when they thought you weren't watchin, the squints over your shoulder to give them time to think up evasions and questions of their own. . . . The ground under him was soft, the air around him thick and alive with strangeness. He couldn't name it, but he knew it—a slippery insecurity. He could understand an Orangeman in the North shoutin "Fuck the Pope" better than he understood these southern people. Foreigners they were; they made you feel as if you couldn't swim and were wadin up to your neck in a shore swell, not able to move where you wanted to, with your feet hard to keep on the bottom. *Answer a simple question, for Christ's sake!* But not bloody likely, O God no! He yearned nervously for the forthright North; lying back in his seat fitting it like a tall little boy. He said, "That farmer y'were talkin about that saw the ravin man w'the gun in his pack. Where's he?"

"Cusack? Sheep's Head. The Garda said he was likely drunk."

"Aye. I've seen a lota funny things when I was drunk. Go to Cusack." It was an order. Sorahan swung the car off the north shore road and up over the Goat's Path that intersected the thin peninsula at about its middle and went west on the south shore road, hurrying to Sheep's Head to find the cottage of Cusack the drunk. Well, it was activity anyway. He was paying his dues to the new revolution.

The sky was dark. The wind came in off Bantry Bay, carrying

rain. It squalled at first, then came steadily, driving across the peninsula.

"The boys'll get wet," Sorahan said.

"In the North, the boys're gettin killed," Kiernan said bitterly, forgetting his smile.

They climbed the narrow weaving road up the back of the Head and the wind and rain brought the cloud down on them. So they crept, peering for the edges of the road. Sometimes there were sheer drops to their left and worked-out peat bogs flooded and shrouded in ghostly white and green water lilies to their right. It took them an hour to reach the tourist car park at the last navigable point on the Head's back. They got out to walk in the lashing rain, and to find Cusack's cottage in a smothering blanket of musty dripping cotton wool.

From the car park they went steeply downhill over a short rocky road that turned sharply towards a seventy-degree drop down to the cliffs and the ocean-churning rocks. The rain drove into them, the wind staggered them. They stumbled down.

"Nobody lives here," Kiernan shouted against the wind, and came off the falling slope onto a broad ledge with three cottages huddling together like diminutive row houses. They were closed against the storm.

Hammering brought a man to the door of the first cottage. He opened the door a crack, holding it against the wind, and Sorahan shouted, *"Cusack?"*

"By himself. On the right," the man yelled back, and jerked a thumb. "Windy day," he shouted, and closed the door.

There was nothing to see on the right, but they went right and found a branching track onto a broad knob on the steep slope, and the ghost of a cottage with its back to the hill. They hammered again and got no answer. There was no light in the window. They tried the latch and went in. The place was dark.

"Gimme a match," Kiernan said.

194 ((

"They're soakin. I'm wet through to the skin."

The ashes of a peat fire glowed. Beside the fire a darker bulk. Sorahan groped at it, shook it, and said, "It's human."

"It's a woman." Kiernan stirred the ashes. There was a corked half-full lemonade bottle in her lap. It had no label. "She's drunk." They found the light switch. Even in remotest Ireland as the young pour out to England the Electricity Supply Board pours power in. In weather like this it often stopped pouring for long periods. It flickered uncertainly at the best of times. Now it lightened and darkened like a divided mind.

They shook the woman awake. She grinned sleepily, without surprise, and handed them her bottle. Sorahan put it back in her lap. "Mrs. Cusack?"

"Aye." The bottle reached out again.

"Where's your husband?"

"After the cattle."

"Where?"

"North Slope."

"In this rain?"

"In shelter." She was happy, only half aware, grinning like a gargoyle.

"Do you remember the young man with the gun in his pack? Your husband took it out."

The grin dimmed and died. Her fuddled eyes shifted from face to face. She wrapped her forearms around the bottle and held it against her belly. Slowly she fell back in her rocking chair and closed her eyes. Maybe she had fallen asleep again.

"Wake her up," Kiernan said impatiently, and didn't wait. He grabbed her arm and shook. Maybe she was asleep. The arm was as hard as a man's and tense. Her eyes stayed shut. Maybe she was asleep.

"Forget her. If you want Cusack you'll have to find him." Sorahan didn't care whether he found him or not. He was wet, cold, miserable, and Ireland's trouble could wait so far as he was concerned. He wanted a hot bath and dry warm clothes and Liz to talk to by the fire more than a united Ireland. The whole search was ridiculous. In this rain, in these clothes, the whole bloody dispute was ridiculous. He wondered ruefully how many Irish conspiracies, rebellions, heroic enterprises wilted and died in the Irish rain? Didn't Frank O'Connor in the story of his youth have a ludicrous tale about the Civil War and Erskine Childers with a woman's little gun "like a flower" pinned over his heart to his braces, and a wet night and an artillery piece nobody knew how to fire, and Irish Civil War enemies lost entirely and stumbling over one another by accident and running like Dolan's donkey, from one another and with one another and anything else that moved? "Find him by yourself," Sorahan said to Kiernan. "I'm chitterin to death."

The Electricity Supply Board stopped pouring and in the sudden darkness Sorahan bent and coughed to the surprising force of the skinny little man's gun in his stomach. "Get our in the fuckin rain, Mr. Sorahan," Kiernan said savagely. "You can walk off when yer not wanted."

Obediently, Sorahan stepped out into the wind and rain. They threatened jurymen. Below, the Atlantic charged the rocks, snarling and growling. What would be left of him?

Kiernan jammed the cottage door open with the kitchen table. The wind and rain whipped in on the woman.

"Why?" Sorahan asked him.

"Drunken oul bitch. She's not sleepin."

Meanness. Pointless, mindless meanness. Sorahan went up the slope, leaning against the wind, shuddering under the lashing rain, trying not to think; ashamed to think. But his thoughts gnawed at him. Weren't he and Liz the great pair? Was it thirty years ago they did their midwife's share at the long labor of the new Ireland; didn't they get a Dutch cap fitted in London, against the law of the church and the law of the land? Didn't they plan their family of two boys and to hell with the rhythm method? Didn't they support Dr. Noel Browne and Dr. Conor Cruise O'Brien and their Labor Party with money sent quietly? Quietly. Never a word in public though. But a vote in the secret ballot. Silent midwives. Reform in the privacy of the imagination. Hope and pray. And they were old Republicans too. Weren't all proper Irishmen old Republicans wearing two hats? One Ireland. A lovely feeling in the imagination. The imagination. A united Ireland would be nice, wouldn't it? he said to Liz, but it's a long way off, maybe. Think about it, talk about it, keep it alive in the imagination. That was the Irish genius, wasn't it? Imagination. The man behind him wasn't in the imagination. What did the imagination do, for God's sake? It refrigerated the mind and you thawed out at fifty, in the lashin wind and rain on Sheep's Head, and knew you were still only twenty and scared to death, and reality was an ugly thing like the taste of too much whiskey in the mouth in the morning; and the stomach that went with it.

"Cuuu—saaack!" Kiernan yelled, and the wind whipped his voice away in shreds.

Sorahan looked round at him and stepped on air and fell and fell and hit heavily and rolled downhill. He was blind with shock and panic, tearing at short grass that slipped from his fingers and cut them. He came up hard against a boulder and lay winded and hurting and helpless and trembling wildly.

"Jasus," Kiernan said beside him with genuine concern, "I thought you were a gonner. You walked off the ledge."

Painfully and slowly they scrambled and crawled back up the treacherous slope. "In here," Kiernan said. "There's shelter." Clucking like a mother, he guided Sorahan under the rock overhang he had stepped off. There was somebody under it already. Kiernan's gun was out and waving. "Who is it?"

"Name's Cusack." The man was sitting, his back against the rock wall. "It's a bad old day."

"We're lookin for you."

"Oh."

Kiernan put his gun away. "We'll not waste time on a wet day," he said. "We want to know about the young fella w'the gun in his pack. You told the Garda about him."

"Aye. He told me I was drunk. I was too."

Kiernan waited for a festering moment. "Mister," he said, "I come a long way for you. Don't give me any shit. Tell me about the young fella."

"Why's everybody askin for that one?"

"Who's everybody?"

"The young Yank girl. She went to the Garda after him. She came here too."

"Wantin what?"

"Where he was. She paid a pound."

Kiernan grinned slyly and gave him a pound. "Tell us about him."

"He was down there, where that one fell. Sleepin under that rock. Sick. Right bad."

"Beard?"

"Whiskers anyway."

"How sick?"

"Ravin. Shoutin."

"About what?"

"Maureen."

"What?"

"That's all I made out. Maureen. That'd be the Yank girl, wouldn't it?"

"Where'd he go?"

"Along the slope."

"Which way along the slope?"

"Car park way—off the Head."

"And away?"

198   ((

"Don't know. Didn't see him that far. He was staggerin round. I seen him fall, twice."

"Where?"

"Down the slope."

"And come up?"

"I didn't see. He had that gun."

Kiernan held out his hand. "Gimme the pound back."

"I told you," Cusack said, and didn't move.

"I'm tellin you. Cough up the quid." The gun was out again. The infallible persuader. Cusack handed over the pound. "Now, you lead us off this fuckin rock," Kiernan said, "all the way to the car park." The gun was still waving.

The going was easier on the way off the Head. Cusack knew the sheep and cattle tracks and Sorahan stumbled forward and feared for his ankles but he was steadier when they reached the car. "Go on home," Kiernan said, and Cusack disappeared into the cloud.

"The last gun that one saw, he told the Garda," Sorahan said.

"He knows this one could go off. I'll drive." Kiernan was very much in charge. They crawled in silence down out of the cloud to the road on the south shore.

"Does Maureen mean anything?" Sorahan asked when they were safe.

"She's the sister. She helped McManus get away. She's dead."

Sorahan's apprehension reared like a shock. He tried to skirt the question in his mind. His stomach couldn't take it yet. "McManus was very sick. He's likely in the sea," he said weakly. That would be the end of this. He was chilled to his backbone and shivering.

"He's alive."

"You don't know."

"The Yank girl found him. She has him somewhere."

"You don't know."

"Right y'are. So we'll keep lookin till I do."

Going through Kilcrohane he asked his question about Maureen. "How did she die?"

"Powers killed her. She wouldn't tell where the brother went. We couldn't let her off." There was nothing much to it. A punishment.

"And Powers is sent to kill the brother too?" Bitterly Sorahan said, "Isn't one enough, for Christ's sake? Why two?"

"Three," Kiernan said, staring out at the rain.

"Three?"

"Aye. He raped her before he killed her."

"Raped her? Jesus Christ!" Sorahan felt sick. Perhaps it was the fall. "And you're goin to help him kill the brother?"

"Aye."

"You mean that's the kind of scum I got these young fellows out to help?"

"Aye."

"Don't depend on it, Kiernan!"

"Aye, well, I will, Mr. Sorahan. I will. You're all in this army like the rest of us. I mean, they're in, Mr. Sorahan, and they don't walk out and in as if they joined some oul women's social club, do they now? You and me knows that. You've all been sittin on your arses down here, doin nothin but raisin pennies while our boys is gettin killed and crippled. I'll depend on you and the young fellas. I will, Mr. Sorahan." The threat was in his voice, not in his gnomish look.

"Don't try to scare us. There's not a man among us who'd lift a finger to help a bastard like that."

"If it makes you feel any better I'll tell you somethin, Mr. Sorahan."

"You can't make me feel better. You've already made me feel I want to vomit."

"I can try, Mr. Sorahan. The story's this, sur. Powers was in charge of a tar-and-feather job and he got one of his men shot

200 ((

dead. He said McManus wusta blame for disobeying orders, then one of the women that was there let out that it was Powers sent McManus off the job. So that's one man lost and a bloody lie to cover it. Then he lost McManus the day he was supposed to kill him. Then afore he started after him he had t'have a night on a wee widow-woman up the street and his mate was took by the British army and he niver lifted a finger. He was seen comin outa the widow's house by a sick oul woman lookin out the window in the house across the street. Then he took the wee widow with him t'Strabane on his way here and they had a dirty-mouthed shoutin match in the hotel after he'd been up her till the cook said he was shakin the house. The polis is keepin the rape outa the papers, but they sneak wee things out when it suits their book and we got the word. They'll niver find Powers and they know we'll save them a wee bita work."

"You said three?"

"Aye. I did. That's it. You twigged on quick. He has t'finish the job w'McManus, Mr. Sorahan. I have the black cap for him when that's done. That's one thing y'can say for us, Mr. Sorahan, we're terrible hard on bad morals. The only help I'll need from y'is a good place to bury Powers. That makes y'feel better, doesn't it, sur?" Kiernan had found his smile again.

"Christ!" Sorahan waited in his country school for twenty-five years. He waited through all the years for The Day. Now he had it, raw and close. He opened the car window to let the rain blow on his face and wished he could talk to his wife Liz.

"Don't let nothin bother you a bit, Mr. Sorahan," Kiernan said comfortably, and meant it sincerely. "When Powers is done w'Mc-Manus, you and your young fellas is off duty. I'll do the rest of it." He seemed to think he had pronounced a benediction.

When they came on the pack in a farmer's field beyond Foilakill, the wind had fallen away and the rain was a thick, gentle drizzle—a soft day, warm and clammy.

The men were huddled under a drystone wall and behind two cars and the motorcycles, getting what shelter they could.

Kiernan parked the car among them and did not get out. The food cartons were in the open trunk of the Stranorlar car, covered by a large plastic sheet that hung to the ground. The beer cases were on the grass. The eating was over, the drinking well begun. Powers paced impatiently among the young men, scowling at their miserable leisure. Young Barney brought food and beer to Sorahan and Kiernan and hurried back to the wall beside his hulking friend Colum. They were all past talking. They had found no trace of McManus and were soaked to the skin, chilled on a warm day. What commitment they might have had was gone. Powers had turned it to resentment, the rain had added misery.

The sheep dog came cautiously towards them from the farmer's cottage in the next field. It walked into the circle and stopped beside the plastic sheet, its head up. The men watched it with cold curiosity. It was something better to look at than their mutual discomfort. The dog jumped into the open trunk and sniffed about. Then, intelligently, it jumped to the ground and took the hanging edge of the sheet in its mouth. Tossing its head from side to side, it backed away and slowly dragged the sheet from the cardboard cartons.

Powers was pacing away from the car. When he turned, the dog was back in the trunk, its head among the sausages. "Get that bloody dog outa there," he bellowed.

Nobody moved. They were smiling slyly. It wasn't great entertainment, but it was mild relief.

"Get the dog out!"

Colum heaved his bulk from under the wall and crossed the circle. He did not move the dog. He patted its wet rump, bent down, and pulled two bottles of beer from a case.

"Put them back and move the bloody dog," Powers yelled at him.

"Move it yourself." Colum walked back towards the wall. He was as big as Powers, but much younger; and cold, and full of his strength.

Powers blocked his way. "You've had enough," he said, "put the beer back." He was suspended between two problems, Colum and the dog that was now busy eating the sausages. Powers was not good at dealing with problems in pairs.

"I'll tell you what I've had enough of. I've had enough of your big mouth," Colum said deliberately, and evidence of warmer life ran through the cold circle.

"Mr. Powers," Kiernan shouted from the dry comfort of Sorahan's car, but Powers could hear only the sound of Colum's voice.

"Put the beer back and take the bloody dog where it belongs. That's an order," Powers said.

"I'm drinkin the beer. Take the dog back yourself. You've been shoutin orders all day. You've been barkin like a mangy dog yourself, playin the bloody general or the bloody corporal till we're all sick of you. Give it a rest, you silly bloody playactor. We've all been wonderin just who the hell you think you are and who the hell you think you're talkin to. . . ." He wanted to go on, full of a resentful spleen that spoke for all of them. They weren't revolting against an idea or an objective but against being wet and bullied and abused and especially by an Ulsterman and no bloody matter whether he was Catholic or Protestant, he was a hard-nosed, hard-tongued, pushy, bullying bloody northerner. . . . The young man stood where he was, waiting for Powers to swing at him. . . . But that was the naïve expectation of a man not greedy for short answers.

Powers drew his gun.

"Mr. Powers!" Kiernan was out of the car.

But Powers was not listening. Colum's voice was roaring in his head. The dog jumped down from the boot with its mouth full of sausages and Powers shot it as it landed. The sound of the shot rolled down to the heaving seas. The men sat still, staring at Powers or the dog.

Sorahan was watching the dog. It lay on its side, its eyes open and the meat beside the open mouth on the grass. It cried quietly for a moment and then was silent. Blood came gently in a small stream from its mouth, staining the wet grass. Sorahan thought it looked like lava.

"Now put the beer down and carry the dog back to the farmer," Powers said.

"Put the gun away and make me."

Kiernan was beside Powers, his own gun pressing. "I'll take the gun, Mr. Powers," he said, and snatched it from Powers' hand.

Colum dropped his beer and charged. He had been waiting most of the morning to make the charge. He had been drinking all through their lunch break to make ready for the charge.

But when he reached Powers the man was not there. His great right hand dug into Colum just above the groin and the huge boy went over, double, crying out in agony. He went down on his face like a sack of dropped potatoes from a swinging thump on the back of his falling head. He felt the boot in his side, felt himself lifted and propped against the wall, and briefly but distantly felt the sledgehammers that beat his face, and he fell, feeling nothing, his face in the grass. Powers didn't want to shoot him. He wanted to beat him, see him bleed, feel the flesh giving under his knuckles, feel the shrill joy that shrieked in him when his hands dug into the belly and his bone cracked on splitting skin over bone. He threw Colum up onto the wall and flailed away. . . .

Then suddenly he stopped and turned slowly and looked around the circle of huddling young men with fear in their faces. His power leapt in his head. He was a foot off the ground, levitating on a cushion of supporting air. He screamed, *"You'll take orders!"*

and turned like a figure on a turntable, to see all their faces and taste their young fear.

His eyes came to the ridiculous and scanty little figure of Kiernan, who stood in the center of the circle, his gun pointing at Powers' stomach. "What the fuckin hell d'you think you are?" Powers screamed at him.

Kiernan's voice was as soft as the rain. "Pick up the dog, Mr. Powers," he said, "and carry it back to the farmer, and pay him his price. Or I'll put you down beside it."

Powers saw the face he had seen in the car when he made the little man angry on the way down. This was not the time and this poor little shit was not the man. There was no glory, no ballad in this scrawny weed's gun. His head cooled. He tried to remember what he had said to Kiernan in the car, to make him so angry. He couldn't remember. He said to himself with detachment, "Thon wee man's a fuckin killer," and picked up the dog and walked before Kiernan to the little farmhouse in the next field.

The farmer stood in his doorway and stared without expression at the dead dog in the big man's arms, and at the little man with a gun that looked far too big for him. He said nothing.

"He shot your dog," Kiernan said. "He'll pay you what it's worth."

Powers laid the dog carefully on the ground, wiped his bloodied hands on his clothes, and dug his money from his trouser pocket.

The farmer stated the price, Powers paid it, and went before Kiernan back over the field.

The farmer did not watch them go. He left the dead dog on the ground, stepped back quickly into his house, closed the door, and laid the bar in its slots. Then he stood in the middle of his kitchen, silent, staring into the slow-burning turf in his fire.

Daniel Sorahan leaned on his car and watched Kiernan and

Powers approaching across the field. "I want to ask you a question," he said to his young men, thinking like a schoolmaster. "Have any of you ever raped a woman?"

"In the name of God, Dan," one of them said, "has that bloody madman put you out of your head?"

"I want to ask you another question. What would you feel like doin if I raped your sister or your wife?"

"I'd shoot you the way that black bastard shot the poor bloody dog," one of them said.

"In that case," Sorahan said, "we'll go on home and get into dry clothes and meet at Father Heenan's house at four—without these two liberators from the North. There's things I'm goin to tell you. Then we'll talk."

When Kiernan came back to the quiet circle, he said, "Mc-Manus is not here. We'll join the Skibereen men tomorrow and work our way all the way down to Mizen Head if we have to. Away on home and get dry."

Then he got carefully into the back seat of the Stranorlar car, with his gun in his hand. He said, his face in the window, "I am very sorry indeed, Mr. Sorahan, about this incident." It was stiff, formal, an official apology. "I am very fond of dogs myself." The young men were folding Colum onto the back seat of Daniel Sorahan's car.

Kiernan said sternly in a loud voice to the back of Powers' head, "Drive on!" and flashed his gun so that he could be seen to be ready, willing, and able to handle dangerous situations till they cooled.

TWELVE

McMANUS was safe. He felt safe. They walked in the twilight, down between the rock ridges and over the lower ones, to the little bay. Mrs. Burke always determined the routes they took. When he tried to choose the paths, climbing to the higher ridges, she said no, too high, and she knew best. He was content. She pointed to a tall thin rock standing alone on a ridge. It looked like a man. It stood out in the twilight in a harsh silhouette. That's what we'd look like, she said, and he knew she was wise. The rocks and ridges and the mountains behind them closed in, the little fields closed in, the sea closed in. He was safe. England was almost forgotten; the run from Ballycastle was almost forgotten; the American girl on the coach—what was her name?—was almost forgotten. Powers and the Provos lurked, but they were in the North and he was in this fortress and the longer he stayed here the more baffled they would be—then England. But not yet. When the thought that he should go crossed his mind, he put it away; nervously. It disarmed him.

The first night they sat on the shore, listening to the retreating tide, he saw the sailing dinghy lashed to its moorings, high and dry on the wet sand. "It's mine," she told him. "The mackerel run just outside the bay. Sometimes I fish. When it's safe, we can fish." We. She said we a lot now. They were together day and night.

In the day he thought more and more of the night. It was never spoken of. He called her Mrs. Burke. She called him child. Mother in the day, mistress in the night. But he thought more and more of the night and his lust for her grew. He closed his eyes and could not see her, but he felt her, soft and warm and lustfully inciting. It was his first fulfilled lust. It made him dependent. He wished the days away.

The doctor and his wife brought their groceries. The doctor hinted, his wife nagged, and Mrs. Burke sent McManus to the garden while they argued. He could hear them. He heard them the day the doctor's wife said they would bring no more groceries. "Get rid of him! How'll you explain your double rations to Jim O'Keeffe at the shop?" she asked as if she had played her joker.

"There's more than one shop in Schull."

It upset McManus, but only till they left. Mrs. Burke always wore her little smile when they left. It was the flag she flew to celebrate small victories, and his cocoon rewove itself. Sometimes, the notion that it was all unreal crept into his head and he put it away. The real was cold; this was warm.

The morning after the doctor's wife said there would be no more groceries, Mrs. Burke took the bus to Schull "to lay in supplies," she said.

"You should have a car," McManus said, thinking of being alone. "You'd be quicker."

"The bus is fine."

"Don't be long." He felt feebly dependent.

She laid a long rough forefinger on the back of his hand. "Why, child?" The face was severe, the voice a little above a whisper. It was her approach to tenderness in the daylight.

"I want you back," he said, and because it was more than he meant to say he said more. "You'll be seeing the doctor and your sister."

"Oh, yes." She picked up her handbag, a worn old thing scuffed at the edges.

"She'll ask you where you. . . ." It was not a daylight question. "Yes, she will." She shrugged awkwardly and took his hand and turned the thing away. "Walk me to the hedge." At the gate she said, "Don't be seen now. Don't answer the door." In the time he had been in the house nobody but the doctor and his wife had come to the door.

"No," he assured her. She was away, striding down the lane. He watched her to the corner where the lane turned between honeysuckle hedges and in another hundred yards reached the road. She was out of sight. He went back to the house and closed the door. It was the first time he had been alone since he came to the house and a lost uneasiness nagged him. The clock slowed down. He wandered the little house and the little garden, tried to read, to lie still on the bed, to see Mrs. Burke on it in the light of day, and all he could realize was her absence. He expected her back long before it was possible; not hungry, for something to occupy his time he ate the stew she left for him in the oven, washed the dishes, made tea, was too impatient for her return to make more tea when the notion occurred to him. He went again and again to the gate to stare up the lane.

Then she was late, well past the reasonable time for her return and uneasiness turned to anxiety, and anxiety to irritation, and irritation to anger. She had no right. He was alone. She was the only human connection he had. The doctor and his wife brought groceries yesterday; why the hell did she need to go into Schull for more today? What was she doing anyway? Making it up with her sister and brother-in-law? They were more important to her than he was. What was he to her anyway? Little more than a schoolboy, with a woman of . . . what, fifty? What did she want with him? Why did her in-laws nag about him? Why did the doctor keep telling her she needed an invalid of her own? Why did the sister go on about where she slept? They knew something he didn't? That maybe she did things that frightened them? Maybe behind the severe, secret face of the widow of Thomas Burke was a middle-aged woman sick with lust and she saw him as the relief she wanted? Resentful son and jealous lover, when twilight came and there was no sign of her, "To hell with her," he said, "if she can go out for the day then by God I can look over the wall."

He went out and walked to the rock ridge across the fields behind the house. They called it The Hill. He had never been on top of it. She had never allowed him. He scrambled up now, through gorse and heather and lichen and bramble and the shock of what he saw brought him to his knees in a bed of ferns.

His isolation was an illusion.

He traced the course of their land to where it disappeared between the honeysuckle hedges and emerged at the road. At their junction were three houses, one of them a grocer's shop. To the left, below the road and concealed from ground level by the ridges between, was another little house, and up on the slope of the mountain that rose like a great brown rock half a mile to the north was a cluster of green and yellow fields and, on their edge, a white cabin. A man appeared from nowhere on the bus road. He had a pack on his back and wore a tweed suit and a tweed hat and as he walked he swung a thorn stick. His head was down as if his thoughts were far off. McManus crept back among the ferns and scrambled halfway down the slope of the hill.

The woman had neighbors. Why did they not pass, or call? There was a crossroads grocer's shop less than a quarter of a mile from the house. Why did she not buy there? How did he reach her house? By the road? Stumbling over the ridges? Who saw him? Why did he not break his neck, or a leg, or an arm? He wanted the woman back, urgently. Anger flew, dependence seeped through him. The dark seeped over him. He went up to the crest of the hill again, and sat among the ferns, watching in the sudden blackness where the road should be, for the lights of the evening bus. She had to be on that one. It was the last of the few.

He was full of apprehension. Small life moved on the hill, making him start. Field mice, he thought, or rabbits; reassuring himself.

The voice behind him said, "Don't move. I'll not hurt you." It was a northern voice.

The silence felt very long. His heart swelled and pounded. In the dark, on the hill, unseen and sneaking, a northern voice that said "I'll not hurt you" sounded like a threat. The voice said, "I'm comin to sit down behind you."

He heard the feet among the ferns, just above him, and the body settling. "Sit right still," the voice said, "I can see you clear and my gun would blow a hole out through your front a foot wide." I'll not hurt you? McManus felt ill with fear.

"You're McManus."

What good would denials do? "Yes." He was resigned, as if he had collapsed inside. A sort of sadness took him over. He wasn't the kind. He was too soft. He wasn't like McGuinness, the Provos' military leader in the Bogside who was his age but not his kind. McGuinness would despise him and wouldn't understand him, anymore than he could understand McGuinness, now that he had met the kind. Fear was pointless. They were here. The whole stupid escapade would be over in minutes. More grief for his father and mother. The sadness was for them, not for himself. In his deep sense of defeat he didn't care about himself, but his father and mother had only one life work, their children, and they'd soon both be dead. He was thinking of how they would survive this second stage of what he had brought on them when the man spoke again.

"I mean you no harm, son."

He didn't hear. "What?"

"I said, I mean you no harm."

"All right."

"I have questions. Answer them up sharp. I don't want to have to make you."

"All right."

"Who's Mary Connors?"

"She's a widow in the Falls."

"Was she Pat Powers' fancy woman?"

"I don't know."

"But you think?"

"I thought that's where he was some nights."

"Who's Val Cleery?"

"He's Danny O'Connell's number two in the Belfast Officials."

"Ever see him?"

"On Divis Street once. Powers pointed him out to me."

"Would you know him again?"

"Yes." Now he was puzzled.

"What was your sister's name?"

What was? Now the man was cutting at the bone. His questions were bewildering; frightening in their pointlessness. Devious. But to what end?

"Powers killed her," the man said.

The shock was more shattering than the first sound of his voice. Why was he talking about Maureen? "I know," he said.

"You know?"

"I thought so. He missed me. She helped me." What did it matter? "You'd have to kill somebody, wouldn't you?" he said bitterly. And, "You're that kind of scum."

It didn't bring retribution. "He killed her fella too. Broke his neck up the Glens."

McManus said nothing. He was trembling. How did he kill Maureen? His mind was the color of blood.

"He choked your sister to death."

So they were going to drag out his entrails before they killed him. They were like that. Jesus Christ, they'd killed a Catholic truck driver from Newry. The man wouldn't join them, wouldn't use his job to spy for them, wouldn't use his truck for them, wouldn't pay tribute to be left in peace. So they jumped him one night, took him across the Border, broke all the bones in his face, shot him down both arms, four times in each, shot him in the knees, then in his stomach, and only then in the head. The last sweet ounce of venom was squeezed out of his death. McManus couldn't imagine cruelty like that. That sort of cruelty was beyond imagination. But he could imagine his parents' pain. That was in the mind, in the head. His own death would be his own release. A queer little thought came into his head: If he was a Christian, was he supposed to be aware, after death, of his parents' suffering? It was queer, he thought, that with his Catholic upbringing, in a Christian country, he should think of his death as escape from the knowledge of his parents' agony.

The man behind him knew about the mind.

"She was found in Evish Lake."

He could hear the man's breathing.

"She was naked."

McManus was crumbling in the long silence between. He wanted to scream.

"He raped her."

"Don't, mister, don't." He was huddling among the ferns, hot needles in his nerves.

The man struck a match. "Look at me, son."

He was holding the match under the brim of his tweed hat when McManus turned his head. "I'm Val Cleery," he said. "I need help and I'll get it from you."

He was Cleery. The shape of his big gun stared into McManus's body. "Powers shot down Danny O'Connell, McManus. I'm here for him," Cleery said.

McManus turned his head away. Sweet relief ran in him. The lights of the bus came up the road from Schull and stopped at the three houses. She was coming. He got up and walked round Cleery, sat down again on the side of the hill facing the house, and paced her along the lane. She would take less than four minutes, with her stride.

"She's not right in the head," Cleery said.

"Who?"

"The woman. Thomas Burke's widow."

"What do you know about her?"

"The man in the shop at the corner told me. You've been in there all the time, haven't you?"

"Yes. I was sick. She looked after me."

"You were down at the foot of this hill the other night with her."

"Yes."

"I was up here, listening. What's she doing? Playing mother to you?"

"Yes."

"Is that all?"

"What do you mean?"

"You're not that young, McManus."

"You're dirty."

"Oh, it's not me, boyo. It's the man in the shop."

"He doesn't know I'm here."

"That's right. But he knows about the last young lad she had."

"I know nothing about her." He said it lamely, hating the man.

"They do, over the hill. Two years ago this summer this young lad came wandering this way with a pack. He took a notion to stay around here the rest of the summer till the university started again and nobody along the road wanted him for that long. He came down the road she's walking on this minute and stayed there. The doctor and her sister had the great rows with her about it."

"People take summer boarders."

"Not when they've only one bed in the house. The shop says she's not always right in the head. Never speaks to them since that time, he says."

"Who says . . . ?"

"Oh, they know at the crossroads. Every damn thing about everybody. They know everything she's got in the house. But I know anyway. I've been in when you and her were down on the shore."

"Well, I sleep in my sleeping bag, if it's any of your business." It sounded childish, even to him.

"It's none of my business. You're right. Powers is my business. . . ."

He heard the gate squeaking on its hinges. The lights went on in the house. The back light went on in the yard and the back door opened and she was there.

Cleery touched him on the arm with a pair of night glasses. McManus took them. He watched her in the garden, looking about, looking up to the hill. She pushed through the fuchsia hedge into the field, looking about. Then she went back into the garden, into the house. The yard light went off. All the lights went off. She had looked for him and he was not there. Poor woman. He felt a warm tenderness for her, pity maybe; he didn't try to analyze it. He wanted back to the house. Poor lonely soul. He stood up.

"Sit down." It was harsh.

McManus sat down. "What do you want?" he said.

Cleery took his binoculars and put them in his pack. "Powers is here, son."

"Where?"

"He was with a wee runt by the name of Kiernan from the Bogside and another man, trying the chemists and doctors in Skibereen and Ballydehob. I didn't know why, but if you were sick, as you say, they know it. They have their Bantry men beating the bushes for you, coming this way."

"They won't find me."

"Oh, but they will, boyo, they will." It was more than expectation. It was conviction. He didn't say he would see to it, and McManus didn't hear that in the man's certainty. Daniel Sorahan would have heard it, Kiernan would have heard it. McManus let it slide over his mind. "When he does, I'll be waiting for him."

"How did you find me?"

"By accident. You weren't the kind, son. You shouldn't have been with the Provos. You should have been with us. So I went and talked to your mother and told her why, straight out. Son, your mother wants Powers dead."

He could believe it. In his months in the Belfast ghettos he had come to believe that the killing would stop when the terrible warlike women of Ulster decided it must; not before. They conceived hatred and vengefulness as they conceived children, and passed the venom in their blood. He could believe that his mother wanted Powers dead.

"She told us your family used to spend the summers at Goleen, up the road from here. She said we wouldn't find you on any dung heap."

That was his mother all right. He was running for his life, but she knew he wouldn't do anything low-class. Like any middle-class Ulster Protestant, she was implacably better-class.

"We tried the cottages for rent, the let ones and the empty ones, from Goleen to Mizen Head, and watched all the good houses. I was watching this one with the glasses a couple of days ago and you came out the back door."

"We?"

"There's three of us. Danny O'Connell's brother and Danny's eldest son. Danny's widow said the boy had to come. They're away keeping track of Powers and his dogs."

Forty years from now somebody would still be taking vengeance for these days, and Irish Christians disdained the Moslem Arabs

216   ((

and their blood feuds. I have to go from here, McManus thought. "I can't help you," he said.

"You'll help. You'll remember your sister. We promised your mother we'd get you out. The price we didn't tell her because we didn't know. We know now. He'll come here for you and I want to be in the top floor of the wee stone barn at the back. The one with the hens on the ground floor."

"It's her home. I can't promise you anything."

"Then we'll just have to go down and talk to her."

"She's not in this."

"She was in it from the minute she took you in. She'll stay in it till I kill Pat Powers. Go on away down now."

They went carefully down the rocky hill, across the little field and through the fuchsia bushes into the garden.

Cleery stopped him. "You're going to help, McManus. Go in and tell her what we want. And you remember this, you'll get nothing for nothing. Your mother wants Powers dead. Danny's widow wants him dead, and I want him dead. And I'm not codding you, you get that woman to agree or I'll come in and do more than talk. I want the top part of the barn, and I want food and water up there and I want her to bring it. You'll stay in the house. If you want help to leave here alive, you'll get me all I want from her. Go on in and don't take long. If she's not out to talk, and right quick, by God, I'll come in."

McManus went into the house.

He switched on the kitchen light. She was not there. There was no sound in the house. "Mrs. Burke?" She did not answer. He looked into the bedroom and didn't see her at first. She was sitting in the dark room in an armchair pushed back against the wall.

"Mrs. Burke."

"You only went out."

"You were long."

"I had reason."

"What's wrong?"

"I thought you were away." She got up and came to him, standing in the doorway. Her rough fingers touched his face. "We'll have to be careful, child." She squeezed past him sideways into the kitchen, her fingers lingering on him. "It was dangerous to go out by yourself. We'll have to keep the windows shut and snibbed. When I go to the hen house or the garbage you'll have to lock the door behind me and I'll knock to get in. You're not to look out the windows. We have tons of food and we can do without milk and I got Springtime evaporated milk for our tea. . . ."

He watched her pace the kitchen as she talked and for the first time noticed the crammed rucksack on the floor by the table. He hefted it. It must have weighed forty pounds. He cut in on her chattering. "'You could have hurt yourself carrying that. . . .'" He had never seen her like this before, without cold composure. He had never seen her smile as she did now, her face paler, her eyes excited. Or nervous? He didn't know enough about eyes or states of mind in middle-aged women to know. He saw only the brightness, and the smile, and they made the narrow face almost handsome.

"Och, no! I'm strong," she said and lifted the rucksack from the floor. "I'll lock up," she said.

"No."

The smile went. Her cheeks seemed to sink. Standing under the light, the bone structure of her face shone. "What's wrong, child?" It was her kindergarten voice.

"There's a man outside. . . ."

"They're here?" It was a little cry.

"Who?"

"Them that's after you." It was the most Irish she'd sounded since he first heard her voice. This time he understood: her schoolteacher's control was slipping.

"What happened in Schull, Mrs. Burke?" he said. He wondered

how much longer Cleery would wait outside before he smashed in waving his big gun.

"Kate," she said. He couldn't tell what was important to her. She was flitting now; thing to thing in her head.

"Kate."

"Them that's after you. They were asking Seamus. A big fellow, rough, red. . . ."

"Powers."

". . . and a little man. His trousers were too big for him. And another one I knew, Dan Sorahan of Bantry. . . . Seamus said they described you . . . this big man did, down to your eyebrows, your tweed suit, your pack, your stick, and your sickness. . . ." She locked her hands. ". . . and a girl that was with you. American, they told him." She sounded huffy. "Where's she now?"

"I don't know. I only saw her on the coach. I can't even remember her name."

"Brendine Healy, they said."

"That's it. Mrs. Burke. . . ."

"Kate."

"Kate, please. There's a man. . . ."

"Sorahan said she left the bus with you. . . ."

"She didn't. There's a man. . . ."

The man opened the back door, waving his big gun. "What the hell's taking you, McManus?" he said.

"This is the man," McManus said to her. She stood very still, looking. She didn't appear to be thinking, merely staring, as if something bad had happened to stun and empty her mind.

"What does she say?"

"We hadn't got to it yet."

"Jesus Christ! You've a lot to talk about. Tell her now."

McManus told her. Nothing about her changed. Her face was empty, her stare not steady but fixed.

"And then you'll get him away?" she said to Cleery, when it was all told, and her voice was empty.

"If we can."

"All right," she said. It was spiritless, as if it had no meaning, as if she had not understood what was said to her or what she said to them. "All right."

Cleery was crisp, commanding. Sandwiches, he said. A flask of coffee. Two if she had them. He turned out her groceries on the table. Sandwich spread, that'll do fine; Brand's beef spread, that'll do; cooked ham, that'll do and hurry it up. Butter some soda bread too, and a cup of tea now. He sat at the kitchen table and drank his tea and ate soda bread as she buttered it.

She buttered more as he ate, wrapped what he did not eat, put his coffee in a flask, and his bread and sandwiches in a paper bag, and walked into the bedroom. The door closed behind her.

"I'll take your sleeping bag," Cleery said, and tucked it under his arm.

"You're going to wait for all these men with an old .45?" McManus asked him.

"Jesus, no. We've had the new ironware stowed up in her barn loft for two nights, son." Cleery was amused. "We'll be in for our breakfast in the morning—early," he said.

"We?"

"Aye. They'll be here as soon as Powers and his tame tigers start beating the bushes on this side of Schull." He went out, leaving McManus to close the door.

She was lying on the bed in her gray flour-sack dress, her broad shoes on the floor, her glasses on the dressing table. It was the first time he had noticed that her eyes were deep brown. Whether she saw more than the ceiling she stared at, he couldn't know. "Coming to bed, child?" she said at the ceiling.

Go to sleep, Mrs. Burke. Go to sleep, Cleery: all of you, for the love of God, and let me make a run for it.

220   ((

"Yes." He closed the curtains over the big window. Cleery out there, are you watching to see how I'm doing without my sleeping bag? So you know now. Wrong in the head, is she, by God? Harbored a wandering student, did she, in a house with only one bed? She's like me, she's empty and lonely and needs somebody to touch. Do you know the feeling, you stupid bastards? Spread the word from the crossroads to any bloody questioner who asks about Thomas Burke's queer widow, but I know how she feels. Go to sleep and let me run for my bloody life. . . .

"Your face is angry," she said.

"Yes."

"About him?"

"Yes." About all of them. And you too, Mrs. Burke. You need me at the wrong time. I know how you feel, but it's my time to run again. Don't you know we're always running away in this God-damned country; from one thing or another?

"Taking you away?"

"Yes." She was entitled to a lie, and its feelings, and whatever hopes were in it. And she'd sleep quicker.

"They wouldn't have found you."

"I know." He warmed to her. Pity or affection? He didn't ask himself. It didn't occur to him to ask himself. He was as young now as when he joined the Provos. I'm sorry, Mrs. Burke. I'm sorry, I'm sorry. I have to run away again.

"Come to bed, child."

He reached for the light switch.

"No." She got off the bed in an awkward movement and he saw the movement. Its awkwardness warmed his warmth for her, a kind of pity; he knew that; affection was better; sometimes it grew out of pity, didn't it? He owed her affection. "Could you stand me in the light?" she said.

"Don't talk like that. It's nonsense."

"Then take off my clothes."

Now? Waiting for the guns to go? With my mind on running? She turned the back buttons of her dress to him, waiting. I can get hard: All right, by God, I'll give her a ride that'll make her sleep. A long last one, Mrs. Burke, for both of us. He could see her smiling, listening to the fussing of his clothes and shoes as he took them off. He laid the gift of God against her. He had learned a lot in the dark. He unbuttoned her dress and raised her skirt slowly, kissing her neck. It was a long neck, and that he hadn't noticed either. His fingertips traced patterns on her hips and he felt her shiver. She pulled her dress over her head and threw it on the floor. "That's Knocknamadree," she said, smiling the way he'd never seen her smile, with her head on the tilt looking at him when his fingers ran over her soaring left hip, and "that's Gabriel," she said when he caressed the right one and he knew she could hear the voice of Thomas Burke. . . . Holy God, she lived in Thomas Burke's books. She was created in books and poems and lived in them. What she said was from a seduction scene in a little stone barn in Burke's *Carry Your Own Coffin,* a novel about love and girls and young men and priests in Ireland, and Cleery was out there in the original little stone barn and Knocknamadree was the mountain beyond The Hill and Gabriel was the mountain behind Schull. It was a passage they used to read with the book hidden under their desks in school. Their Protestant friends said they hid the book behind their Bibles and read it in Church and Sunday school. The memory fired his lust. Maybe she lived in fantasies, but the same fantasies, from the same books, served them both in their own place and time. He knew how it went on; let her have it; make her fantasy real. Then she'd sleep. He drew her pants down slowly, kissing her back on the way, laying his face against her hips as she untangled the pants from her feet, and set her legs apart—how did Burke put it about the country girl standing like this on the hay in the little barn?—"like a standing mare"? It fed him blind, like a stud at a mare and tenderness bolted. He gripped her

belly and her breasts and chattered loving obscenities that her lusting laughter multiplied as he bundled her onto the bed and
mounted. Her big hands took God's gift and buried it, "Fuck me,
my sweet child," she said, and rutted to his brutal rhythm, clamp-
ing him in her great thighs, her hands full of his flesh. She came,
convulsing endlessly; presently her hips rose and fell gently and she
said, "Child, child, child, oh child, I've been well and truly fucked."

She wrapped him in her arms and legs and held him on her, and
he waited, saying nothing. Sleep would come. But she talked, rub-
bing his body.

"Do you think I'm a hoore of a woman?"

"No. I love you."

"I'm an old woman, though?"

"No, you're not."

"But I'm just a horny old widow lusting for young boys?"

"No. You're a glorious woman, a wonderful woman, and I love
you."

"That's what Thomas Burke said. You're not ashamed lying here
in the light this way?"

"It's wonderful."

She rutted at him, binding him with her arms and thighs. "Can
we do it in the day?"

"Like this. Every day." He wished it could be true.

"He was younger than me." She was with her maker again.
"He used to catch me in the barn, in the kitchen, in the fields, on
the shore. He never said, 'I want to make love to you, Kate.' He
never said, 'I want you' or 'I'm going to take you.' He lusted
after me something terrible and stripped me in the barn or in the
fields in the dark and he always said, 'I'm going to *fuck* you,
woman.' He fucked me naked in the cold dew. . . . Sometimes he
thought I wouldn't want him, that maybe I'd leave him, but oh
God, he could have fucked me all day and all night and I'd have
wanted more . . . oh God, how I love Thomas Burke . . . up

there at the grocer's shop on the corner they told Seamus I wasn't right in the head. . . . They all killed Thomas Burke." Her eyes were wet.

He listened, and wasn't sure now who killed Thomas Burke.

"Thomas Burke made up old tales about Ireland," she said, "and made out they were about me. I know them all by heart."

"Tell me one." She'll tire. She'll sleep. Then I'll run for my life. Forgive me. Her arms and thighs relaxed their hold. She spread her legs. "Stay on me, child, while I tell it. There was this time Goll McMorna set out on a journey before the light was up.

"When he reached the shore of the lake he lay down on his face to ease the dryness in him.

"This voice came at him while he was drinking and the first time he heard it he said, 'I heard a trout breaking the water.'

"It came to him the second time and he said, 'The birds are calling to the light.'

"The third time it came he said, 'The air is bending the grass.'

"Then the voice said, 'McMorna is the beautiful champion.'

"And the small man stood at his full height and said, 'I'm a diminutive creature, with no beauty at all.'

"The voice said, 'McMorna sings like the blackbird.'

"And McMorna said, 'My song frightens the corncrake.'

" 'Come up the bank to me,' the voice said, 'and I'll make you taller than Finn and your song sweeter than Cuchullain's.'

"McMorna went up the bank and there was this young girl, lying naked in the grass and her glowing like wrought gold.

" 'Take your pleasure and give me sons to give me sons,' she said, and McMorna swam like the salmon in a golden stream, taller than Finn, sweeter than Cuchullain.

"But when the light came the girl under him was an old wandering woman, her breasts the broken hills, her belly as creased and cracked as the Burren, her legs the dead willows, and he leapt off her like a frightened deer, and ran over the hills.

224 ((

"When the light was dying she was behind him shining like fine silver and he lay down to rest, the strength run out of him trying to leave the woman.

"In the dark she said to him, 'Suckle my two breasts, McMorna, aren't they the sweet green hills to cool your face on? Lie on my belly, McMorna. Isn't it as soft and rich as a meadow in Meath? Bound between my thighs, McMorna. Aren't they the young limbs of the oaks of Derry? Lay your mouth on my mouth, McMorna, for isn't my tongue the darting salmon of Shannon? Broach my womb, McMorna, and give me sons for me to haunt in the day and whore with when the night comes.'

"All the night McMorna whored with the shining girl and when the light was up there was no will in him to run from the old woman and they walked and whored together night and day from that time on.

" 'What name do you go by?' he asked her when the light was going down and they were looking for a place to lie down.

" 'The name they call me,' she said, 'is Cathleen the Whore-Mother.' "

Her voice was sleepy, her eyes were closed and wet, her body was soft and relaxed, her legs flat on the bed, her arms by her sides. Her face was old. He rose off her gently and settled beside her. She drifted, mumbled, and was gone.

He looked at her in the hard light. The face was tired. She was the only naked woman he had ever seen, the only woman he had ever loved, and the breasts were full, the belly white, the thighs long, and she was marvelous in his sight. She was kind and lonely. Her lust was glorious and she shared it with him. She was created by a poet and storyteller and she lived inside his poems and his stories and he didn't understand that. She was there, that was all. And, God forgive me, at the right time she's asleep. He bent over her and kissed her nipples. She smiled a little as if she knew. He was sorry for her. He was sorry to go.

Half an hour, he thought, and lay gently. The light was on. Cleery would be sleeping now. He could dress, and get his money and his gun and be far gone walking, before she woke. There'd be a lift on the road beyond Schull and Cleery could do nothing and Powers could do nothing and he'd be in England by the first plane out of Cork. He watched her with pity and gratitude and heard the key slip into the lock of the front door. His breath choked him.

"Kate!" he shook her and she smiled and curled towards him, more than half asleep.

"Kate! Who has a key to the house?"

"What?"

"Who has a key to the house?"

"My sister," she said sleepily, half holding him.

"She's got it in the door!"

Mrs. Burke shot upright in the bed, propped on hands that were a little behind her, her arms stiff, her breasts out, her eyes unfocused, and the doctor slammed the bedroom door back against the wall, standing in the doorway with the eyes of a charging bull.

"You hooring oul sow," he shouted. "By God, I knew you were at it again."

McManus hopped out onto the floor guilty, confounded, and overwhelmed by the vulnerability of the naked threatened by the fully clothed. To him the doctor's clothes and boots were as substantial as a suit of armor; he was fearful for his tender genitals and his naked feet. He could feel the impact on both, of the enraged doctor's boots. He snatched his trousers from the floor and didn't dare disarm himself by trying to get into them. All he could do was stand there, foolishly covered by his trousers, held foolishly in front of him.

"You dirty little shit," the doctor yelled. "That's what you stayed around for!"

"Don't dare talk like that in this house," Mrs. Burke said in a

226 ((

deep loud voice so full of righteous outrage that McManus risked a quick glance at her.

She was still propped stiff-armed on her hands, her back held straight, her breasts flaunting. Her head was high and her ankles crossed. She seemed unaware of her nakedness, aware only of stiff indignation. "You're jealous, Seamus. You've always had a grievance because you picked the frigid sister. Hand me my glasses. They're on the dressing table," she said curtly, "and get control of yourself."

"Holy Mother of God," the doctor said despairingly, "sitting there in your skin giving orders," and went round the end of the bed to get her glasses. When the man was safely across the bed, McManus stepped frantically into his jockey shorts and trousers and got his vest and shirt on. Watchfully, he sat down to put on his socks and shoes.

"She woke up in the middle of the night," the doctor said, and handed her her glasses, "yakking about the three men who came looking for this dirty bastard. 'Get her out of that house,' she says, so get up now and get out."

Mrs. Burke put on her glasses and stepped out of bed, naked in her spinsterish steel-rimmed spectacles. She reminded McManus of a thin man he had seen changing in a locker room, bushy-bearded, bespectacled, naked. The hairy head looked too large for the hairless body. Mrs. Burke's steel glasses seemed to bear some incongrous relation to her pubic bush and her belly did bulge and droop a bit. Merciless God, did everything end in farce? She was swelling with defiant confidence and dignity.

"You're my sister's monkey on a string, not me. We're not leaving. We'll cope. Away on with you." She walked round the bed and sat on the arm of McManus's chair, indifferent to her nakedness. "Off you go home, Seamus," she said briskly, and waved the doctor away.

"Holy Mother of God!" The doctor held out appealing hands.

"Kate, will you for Jesus sake put on your clothes and come home with me."

"No."

The doctor appealed to McManus. "All right, McManus, you have a lot of influence in this room. You ask her."

"Mrs. Burke," McManus began lamely. All he wanted to do was slip through the open door unseen, and run for it.

"Kate," Mrs. Burke corrected.

"Kate," McManus tried again.

"No." She was smiling her victory smile.

"He can come too. I'll get him out. I'll get him to Cork Airport. . . ." The doctor opened a cupboard and threw her dressing gown across the bed. "Put it on, Kate," he yelled.

She put it on. "We've settled all that." She looked confidently at McManus. "Do you want to go, child?" Her hand was on his head. Her face was certain of his answer.

"Yes." He felt treacherous.

The doctor saw daylight. "All right. Come on. The car's at the crossroads. . . ."

Mrs. Burke walked to the bed. Her face old and desolate. She stood silent for a moment, staring at the bed. "You want to go."

"They'll find me."

"No."

"Yes, they'll find me. They'll kill me. You come too."

She dropped the dressing gown at her feet. Her belly bulged, her breasts drooped, her hips were creased by skin from which past substance had retreated. She got into bed, "You too," she said, and pulled the covers up to her chin.

"I can't go without you, Kate. She'll eat me alive," the doctor pleaded, seeing only surfaces. "Please, Kate."

"Take him," she said.

"Take him where?" The voice from the kitchen made their nerves leap like plucked strings. Cleery and another man and a thin pale youth were standing inside the half-door. Cleery waved his big gun at them. "Who thinks he's going anywhere, missus?" His white face sweated bitterness. He stepped into the bedroom and tapped his gun carelessly on McManus's shoulder.

It was the combination of bitterness, carelessness, and strutting gun-power that petrified McManus. He had seen it in the Provos, in innumerable acts of intimidation against helpless Catholic families unwilling to have their houses used as snipers' nests, or when strutting boys were collecting dues for "the Cause" or hunting informers or doubters or critics, or defaulters or non-cooperators. . . . The Officials were a little more stable, a little more political, but the gun was their answer also when the skein of human behavior was even slightly tangled. So he said nothing, for he didn't know what answer would meet Cleery's need and the wrong answer could pull the trigger and resolve the doubts in Cleery's mind. There was no point in cold bravery, even if he had been capable of it, for bravery might humiliate Cleery and therefore enrage him beyond restraint, for courage placed a limit on their power to terrorize and that could not be endured; fear fed their contempt for the fearful . . . McManus merely looked and his heart boomed in his ears.

Mrs. Burke stared at the ceiling.

The doctor said, "My wife sent me to bring her sister home," and worked his tongue and his jaws to make saliva.

The three pale heads turned to the doctor who stared palely back, the russet gone from his face. McManus saw them all in a sort of disassociated tableau, still and peculiarly distant.

Cleery turned to McManus. "You were going to make a run for it."

"Yes."

"But not now."

"No."

"You're a gutless wee shit."

There is nothing to say when that is true. He said nothing.

"Y'are, aren't you?" Ram self-knowledge down the victim's gullet. "Yes."

That was a satisfying admission. Cleery nodded thoughtfully. "Your sister had more guts." Cleery knew more than Powers about the mind. He smiled when the tears of shame and pain started in Mc-Manus's eyes. "Didn't she?"

"Yes," McManus said like a little cry.

"Scum," Mrs. Burke said.

Cleery turned to her. She was glaring at him with scorn.

"He was all man in there w'you, missus, wasn't he?"

"Scum," she said, and turned her face to the ceiling.

"Gabby oul bag," Cleery said, his humor lightening with each victory. "There'll be no run for it." He prodded McManus. "Dead or alive, you're bait, boyo. You all stay here now till Powers gets here. . . ."

"My wife . . ." said the doctor, and decent fear for her safety stopped him.

"Fuck your wife . . . or get McManus t'do it." The doctor shriveled. "Your wife's sitting in thon grand Mercedes up at the crossroads. Let her sit. If she comes down here, she stays till we're done w'Powers." He nudged his head at the other man behind him. "He's Kevin O'Connell, Danny's brother. He'll stay in here t'keep you all quiet. And that's Danny's son, Diarmuid. When the shop opens, he's walking up there. D'you know what he's going to tell them, McManus?" Grinning, he turned away and led his little army into the kitchen. He walked with Diarmuid O'Connell out of the house and closed the door behind him.

"Relax," the man Cleery called Kevin said, and sat down in Thomas Burke's rocking chair by the kitchen fire.

Silence sat in the bedroom, dissected by the rhythmic creaking of the rocking chair.

"I'll show them something," Mrs. Burke said softly to the ceiling.

230 ((

Kevin came to the bedroom door. "You two," he said, "in here. Sit at the table. You, missus. You stay in bed. You look in the need of sleep." He waved them to their stations and closed the bedroom door. Mrs. Burke lay on her back, staring at the ceiling as if she intended to do it harm.

Time ticked by in the kitchen. The man Kevin watched it on his wrist in the stirring silence and seemed to judge the quarter-hours with uncanny precision. When an hour had passed he stood up. "He's sleeping by now," he said. "Away on. Quiet now."

"We can go?" the doctor asked with relieved astonishment.

"Quiet if you don't want shot," O'Connell said to McManus. "I know all about it, son, your sister and that. Powers murdered my brother Danny. All I want is Powers dead. As long as he thinks you're here, you don't need to be. I'll handle Cleery. Away on."

"Mrs. Burke too?" McManus said.

"Thons your desperate woman. I'd be glad to see the last of her."

McManus went back to the bedroom. "The man says we can go if we do it very quietly. Get dressed, Kate, and come away on," he said.

"Come here, child." Her face was even older, even more severe; there was no trace of a smile round the wide mouth or of humor in the eyes. The eyes were lifeless. "Sit here," she said, patting the bed beside her. He sat down and she took his hand. "Tell me honest, child, were you happy in this bed with me—in the dark?"

"Yes, Kate."

"In the light?"

"Yes, Kate. Get up and come on."

"You did my heart good, child."

"You mine, Kate."

"You're for England now."

"If I'm lucky."

"We have a brother there. He's rich."

"Come away with the doctor, Kate."

"He lives in East Grinstead."

"Never mind that, Kate. Get dressed and come on."

"Get me a folder from the bottom drawer over there."

O'Connell stood impatiently in the doorway, "Will you for God's sake cut it and get outa here?"

"Five minutes, sir," Mrs. Burke said, with surprising charm, and McManus brought her the folder. "My brother has no children," she said. "He and his wife go to Spain every summer. He's a stockbroker." She said it with naïve pride. "We can use his house anytime in the summer."

"Use it now, then."

She wrote on the pad from the folder and gave him what she had written. "There's a key at an estate agent's in the square in East Grimstead. Give him that. He'll give you the key. You'll be safe there."

He took the letter. "Thank you, Kate. Now come on."

"You're a gentle child. Stay gentle. Kiss me again."

He bent and kissed her.

"I'm always left, child. I'm always left."

O'Connell was back in the doorway. "For fuck sake, if that's what you want, get into bed and get it. Make up your bloody mind!"

McManus leapt from the bed. God, everything went sour, everything was ridiculous in the end. He was ridiculous. "Goodbye, Kate," he said in confusion and grabbed his money and his gun from the drawer and rushed from the room. "She won't come," he said to the doctor.

"Then let her stay."

O'Connell took the gun from McManus. "You won't need that. You should never have touched one. You're the great bloody pair," he said, "and by God, doctor, no polis or we'll come for you."

They went through the front fuchsia hedge to avoid the creaking gate, and down between the slate ridges and through the grassy hollows to the crossroads. The doctor's wife was asleep in the back seat.

"I'll drive," McManus said, and took the wheel. He thrashed the car through the narrow twisting roads and wakened the doctor's wife.

"Where's Kate?" she screeched.

"She wouldn't come," her husband said curtly.

"You should have made her come. Let her rot. I did all I could for the crazy woman. Why's he driving?" the woman whinnied.

"Shut up," the doctor said as if for the first time in his married life.

"Seamus!"

"Shut your bloody mouth!"

The Mercedes roared through Schull. *"Schull! Schull! Stop!"* the doctor shouted. "Where the hell do you think you're going?"

"Cork Airport." McManus didn't speak again. He was away. Again. Well away. He'd be in England in hours with a place to hide. Well away. Again. Thank you, Kate.

"I'm dying with sleep," Mrs. Sullivan complained, and joined in the exhausted silence.

The light came up. The brakes ground in the fourcourt of the airport. McManus got out without speaking and walked into the lobby. There was a Cambrian Air flight to Cardiff at a quarter to nine. Yes, there was space on it. Yes, he would take it. He would take anything to get away quickly.

"Hullo," the voice at his shoulder said.

He turned and said, "Brendine Healy of Boston."

"I tried to find you," she said. "You look all right now. I don't mean it that way. I mean you're looking well . . . not sick . . . you know?"

"Oh?" he said. "I see," he said, surprised at first and then surprised at the sudden relief that ran through him. Laughing, suddenly, for the nightmare, the unreality was shattered in his head, and the normal, the real was with him. He reached out his hand to touch it.

THIRTEEN

POWERS drove.

"This car," Kiernan said bitterly, "will do the main road from Schull to Mizen Head and everything we can see from it. Half a dozen take the coast road. The rest do back beyond the main road." He sat behind Powers.

Sorahan sat up beside Powers with little Barney behind him. Sorahan's head was full of smiles at the cause of Kiernan's bitterness. But he kept his smile inside his head.

"I don't know," Kiernan said broodingly for the fourth or fifth time. "I don't bloody know. Nobody from Skibereen? That's a bloody mystery."

It wasn't to Sorahan, and his smiles were harder to hold. He was doing well as a conspirator. But then, intrigue's second nature to us, he told himself happily. We do it better than anybody.

"Thon Sheehy of Skibereen," Kiernan said, "thons a sleekid man." (Sleekid, Sorahan explained to little Barney, was a northern word meaning slippery, deceitful, devious, untrustworthy.)

"Very busy he is," Barney said ambiguously.

Sheehy had been very busy. Sorahan phoned him at the end of the Bantry men's meeting at the house of the priest and they met early that night in the back of O'Keeffe's Bar in Schull. "I'll tell you what it is, Tim, and I'll ask you what you'll do and I hope you'll do nothing."

Sheehy listened. "That's the way of it?" he said at the end.
"That's the way of it."

"Rape?"

"Rape."

"Holy God." Sheehy folded his hands defensively over his crotch.
"That's the fearful thing."

"The worst."

"There was no call for that."

"No call at all."

"There'll be *two* killins here?"

"Two."

"Jasus. I thought they'd take the boy back and do it up North."

"No."

"Here?"

"Here."

"Jasus. Tis the wrong time o'year, Daniel. There's the Ballydehob
Annual Show, the Skibereen Gymkana, the Skibereen Festival, and
the Drinagh Harvest-Time Festival. All at the same time. Two
killins here would bugger the lot."

"That's the God's truth. T'would leave a bad taste."

"Very bad taste, Jasus, aye. Have you the time to follow me
into Skibereen and we'll knock doors and get the boys together?"

"I have all night, Tim." They looked quickly into one another's
eyes and the look conveyed all the things they had left unspoken,
and they smiled little glancing half-smiles as if them that weren't
meant to would hear whole ones and drove to Skibereen and
knocked doors and went into conference with the men of Skibereen.

It was a long meeting. The light was brushing the sky before
they went home for their breakfasts, having heard Sorahan recount
in detail what Kiernan told him about McManus and Powers and
Maureen McManus and Powers, and the dread word rape fell with
cunning from his schoolmasterly lips onto their early-morning nerves.
The word was not spoken again when he was done.

236 ((

"Then there's two killins at the time of the Ballydehob and the Festival and the Gymkana and the Harvest-Time . . ." Sheehy said wisely and looked from face to face ". . . tis ruinous timin," he said, and in their sidelong way they skirted their revulsion and renewed their loyalty to the Cause, containing each in separate compartments in the single and collective mind.

"Tis a busy old time," a circular man said from the floor, "and the least we can do for being so busy is send the boys in the North an extra collection this week." They went home to fried bacon or mackerel and sweet tea with their consciences as fresh as the new day's air.

When they met Kiernan and Powers later in the morning, the two frustrated and impatient men from the North listened to a careful recital of the responsibilities, this week of all weeks in the year, borne by men who were in charge of the Irish dancing and horse-jumping and the fish-and-chip and fried-sausage van, and the flower shop and the country craft work . . . and how would they explain runnin round the country with the Ballydehob and Drinagh and Skibereen annual festivals fallin apart from want of them? They had to live here, it is.

Defeated and with nothing to get a grip on, Kiernan said bitterly, "By Jasus, youse boys carry a heavy load. All our boys in the North have to do is die."

He could not hear Sheehy say in his head, "Well, God rest their souls but let them do it in the North."

And who has heard a smile? Sorahan's was behind his eyes. "Hunt two by two," he told his young Bantry men, "and them that finds the boy, say nothin—just get him to hell out of West Cork. Let them find him somewhere else, but not here." Death is less ghoulish out of sight and hearing and executioners are less of a bother in the North, or somewhere else far away from West Cork. . . . "And you, Barney," he said, "if *we* find him, maybe you'd slip off and phone the Garda . . . we'll think about that." That was the sour one. Sweet Christ, that was informing. That one would have to be thought about. But not yet; not now; "later" is the sweet refuge from bloody decision, thanks be to God.

Sorahan was pleased with his conspiracy and for all he knew when they reached the crossroads shop at seven in the evening, two of the Bantry boys could already have McManus on a bus, running him to Cork and comfort.

It was a simple country shop, smelling of potatoes and bacon and bread and Mr. Deasy was behind his counter, tall, scholarly, and bent like a question mark, ready to close for the day.

"What can I do for you gentlemen?" he said, and speculated on their source of life.

"Half a pound of bacon," Kiernan said. The others stood back among the lemonade cases on the floor, ordered to keep their mouths shut and leave the talk to an angry and impatient little man.

"Sliced or wrapped?"

"What?"

"Do you want it cut off the side or out of the fridge in a packet?"

"Oh. Wrapped."

Mr. Deasy went to the fridge by the door into his living quarters. "Nice old day."

"Fine."

"You're not from these parts."

"No. Do you happen t'know," Kiernan said indifferently, "a young fellow by the name of McManus who could be stayin round here?"

Mr. Deasy looked thoughtful. "No. I don't happen to know anybody by that name. Friend of yours?"

"I'm his uncle. Tryin to find him."

"Is he a tall one?"

"That's right. You've seen him?"

"No. Would he have a beard?"

"He has. Y've seen him."

238 ((

"No. A lot of young fellows have beards. Is he from the North?"

"He is. How would you happen to know that?"

"I don't. You're from the North. I suppose your nephew is too."

Jasus! Kiernan paid for his bacon and tried again. "He was walkin. W'a pack, you know."

"They all are."

"He might have had a girl with him."

"Likes the flesh, aye?"

"Well, he's young."

"McManus?"

"Aye."

"Haven't set eyes on him."

Kiernan turned and opened the door and rang the bell hanging from it.

"But I know where he is," Mr. Deasy said, enjoying himself. There wasn't much to entertain you here, and Mr. Deasy liked a little joke. What do you do here in the winter, Cleery had asked him. Well, there's table tennis, Mr. Deasy said, and watched Cleery's eyes with private pleasure. Now he watched the unfolding four-figure tableau fold back into position in front of the counter and among the lemonade bottles. He had said something magical, like pushing a button on television.

"Is that right now?" Very disciplined. Not eager. Kiernan told himself he was getting to know these West Cork foreigners.

"Likes the women?" Mr. Deasy said.

"That's right. Has he picked himself one round here?"

"Picked a hot one." Mr. Deasy wiped his counter with a cloth and then wiped the scale of his bacon-slicing machine with the same cloth. "She's not all there. But she likes young ones. He's her second."

They're talking about a man's life, Sorahan thought, and waited, his hand on Barney's arm.

"I was afearda that," Kiernan said. "Near here?"

"Down behind."

"Down behind what?"

"The hill behind the shop."

"But you've never seen him?"

"Not yet."

"Then how d'you know?"

"Three fellas that's been round here told me. They spoke to him. They've been in the woman's house. There's only one bed in the house." His sparkling eyes said, how's that? and isn't gossip the countryman's live theater in the head and no excise tax on it?

"These fellas? Where're they?"

"Left. They took off this mornin, early."

"Who's the woman?"

"Thomas Burke's widow."

"Who's he?"

"He was from here. You never heard of him?" Mr. Deasy had a rack of paperbook books behind the lemonade. Tim Pat Coogan's *The IRA*, J. Bowyer Bell's *The Secret Army*, Donald S. Connery's *The Irish*, Dan Breen's *My Fight for Irish Freedom*, Bernadette Devlin's *The Price of My Soul*, and a lot of old rubbish it is, he told his customers. But there was no Thomas Burke.

"Am I supposed t'have heard of him?"

"Ah, no. You're more for business than readin up North. Why don't you just shoot them old bombers and get on w'business?"

"How do you get to the woman's house?" There are enemies wherever you turn. This stupid oul duff was one of them. The country's full of them. Kiernan was no longer all that sure about Sorahan.

"She has a sister in Schull—that's the doctor's wife, that one. The one down here keeps them on the run, I'd say." Don't answer terminal questions till you have to. They end the play.

"The *doctor's* wife?"

"Sullivan. Down the coast road."

240   ((

Everything Kiernan feared was being confirmed. He was in a nest of vipers. The Skibereen men were *busy,* for the love of God. *Busy!* And this doctor. Sullivan told them he hadn't seen a soul. Nobody came near him for medicine, or treatment! Bloody liars. Worse, by God. "This doctor. Does he come to the sister's . . . the Burke woman's house at all?"

"For a while, all the time. Every day for a while lately. The wife too. With him every day down here. Well," he winked and nodded, "a doctor has to watch it, aye? With a horny sister-in-law like the Burke woman. . . . There's always people that like a nice old gossip."

"How do we get there?"

"He was here last night. Woke me up in the middle of the night. I got up and looked and his car was parked out front there. He woke me again in the small hours, roarin away like a motor racer. . . ."

"Thanks." Kiernan bustled them out of the shop. "Drive up the road," he told Powers.

"Wait a minute. I need fags," Sorahan shouted, and ran back into the shop, panic growing in his head. "Have you a phone here?" he asked Mr. Deasy, and then it was blind clear to him too late that all he needed to do was look for a lead-in wire from the telegraph poles. No need to create a situation. Christ! The things you had to remember.

"No. The only one round here's in the post office a quarter-mile down the road. You wanted to phone?"

"Which way down the road?"

"I'll show you."

"No! No need. Just tell me."

"No bother." Mr. Deasy was coming round the counter.

"No need! Left or right?"

"No bother at all." Mr. Deasy shoved Sorahan out through the door into Kiernan's hearing. "Down there. There's a dip in the road on a bend and the post office is in a private house on the right. You can't see it for the trees and the hedge. . . ."

"Thank you, thank you. . . ." Sorahan stumbled into the car.

Mr. Deasy rested his hands on the door. "There's one thing, though."

"Thank you, thank you. . . ."

"The postmaster's over eighty. Very crusty. Won't let anybody use the public phone after three, the poor old cripple. You're over four hours late, mister."

"Thank you, thank you. . . ."

"Away on," Kiernan said. "Along the road." He leaned towards Sorahan. "What was all that about?"

Sorahan's native talent for conspiracy was scrambling to save its face. "I was askin him about a phone. I have to call my wife when I get a chance," he said, because he couldn't think of anything else. His mind was spinning like a fly wheel and Kiernan looked very quiet. This necessity to lie in a hurry was the bad part.

"You went in for fags. You came out lookin for a phone," Kiernan said gently.

"Yes. I just forgot the fags when I remembered my wife."

"But the oul postmaster's a cripple and won't let you use the phone after three?"

"That's what he said."

"Then how'se you goin t'phone the wife?"

"I don't know." He knew nothing now.

Kiernan handed him an open packet of cigarettes. He hadn't smoked a cigarette for fifteen years. "I never seen you with a cigarette, Mr. Sorahan."

He lit it from Kiernan's match. "I do, sometimes," he said.

They stopped a short way up the road on a bend from which they could see The Hill. McManus was in reach. The end of the road was in sight, for McManus; for Powers.

242 ((

Kiernan said to Powers, "Are'y ready?"

"Fuckin right, I'm ready." He had been quiet, under restraint. His time had come. He could taste McManus. It gave him great pleasure.

Kiernan took binoculars from the dashboard pocket. "We'll take a look from up that rock."

They climbed The Hill and waded among the ferns and gorse and lay down on the crown. The little house lay white and quiet inside its fringe of fuchsia, like a cotton blouse. The white stone barn was at an angle to the gable of the house, on their left. It's one glassless window gaped out like a blind eye.

Sorahan saw the place with dismay. It was a peaceful sight. It was a killing ground. What the grocer said about Thomas Burke's widow didn't matter much to him. Once, he had thought of Thomas Burke as a prophet; now he was no more than a dead novelist still in print in paperback. The wives of living novelists mean nothing to anybody but the novelists; their widows mean nothing to anybody. Sorahan lived eighteen miles from this one, and wife or widow, he'd never known she breathed.

The grocer would know some of what he pretended to know. For the rest, gossip was the fleshing out of lean lives. Malice salted talk. Sometime or other the woman in that house had cut Deasy. His sly winking twinkle as he slid his knife in was the decoration on a cultural cake—the stage business in a living live theater. The grocer would know *who* the woman was. He would know who came and went about the place and how many beds were in the house. Who slept where in it or with whom, he would decide by what he would like to do in McManus's place. Maybe he'd tried for her himself and she's laughed at his years? Whatever it was, he would draw from it malice and humor—and drama. Life on the fringes of the island fringe of Europe was personal, drama in the mind. Missing lines improvised on the spot.

Sorahan didn't need to think about this. It was there, whole, in the mind. He was one of them.

His thoughts were of himself and his predicament. He had swung half-circle from his delight in the loved illusion of the native Irish genius for conspiracy and intrigue to alarm and despondency at his half-thought fecklessness. Conspiracy *in the mind*. It was part of the drama in the mind. Most literate Irishmen called it imagination. That's what Sorahan called it the other day. Today on this rock hill he called it fantasy. What in the name of God made him think he could find a phone easily in this landscape where he *knew* phones were five miles apart? What made him think he could call the Garda down on these men? Wasn't he, like more than half the nation, their passive but supporting bystander? What made him think he could *inform*? The gut instinct of the nation was against it. Fantasy. Wouldn't little Barney have a catatonic seizure if he tried to lift the phone? Drama in the mind it was. Irishmen young and middle-aged and old glancing forever off the shoulder of reality, never meeting it head-on. Myths; the masturbating emotions of myths; saints made out of schoolmastering windbags; martyrs made out of psychotic killers . . . heroic virtue pouring out of the barrel of a gun . . . we're a nation of political masturbators, he thought, and buried his sweating face in the ferns. That white quiet place down there is a killing ground and I've been playing with my political genitals like a thirteen-year-old but the real fuckers are here, beside me in this place, and when I see them open their political flies I'm sick at my stomach.

"What's eatin' you, Mr. Sorahan?" Kiernan asked him.

"I'm tired." I'm an Irish fantasist, he wanted to say, and I've walked into a brick wall with my face stuck out in front of me.

"Aye." It sounded contemptuous. "Not long now. It'll be over after it's dark and then y'can go away on home." It was open disdain. Kiernan rolled on his back and looked into the sky. "Nice quiet place this."

Powers was watching the house through the glasses. "I seen the woman," he said. "She's in the room w'the big window, lyin on the bed." He raised his head, grinning. "In her skin."

"Any sign of McManus?"

"Not yet. Why's she lyin naked?"

"Y'can ask her when it's dark."

"The oul fella in the shop's right. He's been fuckin her."

Barney lay apart like a staying retriever. Dirty jokes among his peers were funny and didn't mean anything. Dirty talk from older men made him feel dirty. He shut off hearing and felt lost and thought about his mother and father and wanted to be at home with them. There was a man in there goin to be killed. Murdered, he tried to say in his head and his mind wouldn't accept the word. He's not much older than me, he said. Jasus, it was great lyin in the hills in the warm sun and the bees singin, thinkin about dyin for Ireland but, piteous Jasus, it never crossed your mind that that meant killin for Ireland. Softly, he moved farther away, as if that made him safer, less part of the event. He loved Mr. Sorahan surely and he'd let nothin happen Barney couldn't face . . . but what could Mr. Sorahan do? He was only a schoolmaster.

"You won't be fuckin her," Kiernan said distantly, with the sky in his eyes.

"What d'ye mean . . . ?" Powers was up on one elbow.

"Get your stupid head down. . . ."

"You said somethin, Kiernan. By God, you'd better explain it." The man was gettin at him again. It was Maureen McManus he was talkin about. He'd forgotten Maureen McManus. What did Kiernan know? His mind darted fruitlessly. He didn't understand this little weasel of a man. . . .

"Explain *what?*" Waspishly, as if he wanted to explain it.

"About me not fu . . ." But it was hard to say. Maureen McManus was in his throat, in his eyes, and if Kiernan knew . . . the word shut off in his mouth. If it wasn't said, it wouldn't stay in Kiernan's mind. Powers didn't know what was in Kiernan's mind. It was hard, not to know. Not knowing started a peculiar trembling in the gut.

Kiernan turned on his side to face Powers. "Were you thinkin of fuckin her, Mr. Powers?"

The way he said "Mr. Powers." Mockin me. *"I was not,"* Powers said.

"Good," Kiernan said meanly, and rolled on his back again. "When the light goes, go on down and scout the place. Then come back and we'll see."

"I know how to do it."

"You're great. You're great." Kiernan's smiles were gone. Sorahan hadn't seen one of them for twelve hours or more. Kiernan's own moment was closer; he was sickening for it. He turned his head and looked at Powers. It was a covetous look. "Give Mr. Sorahan the glasses," he said. He knew the mind. He smiled at Sorahan when he had them and said, "You watch and keep us posted." Sorahan wished he hadn't seen the smile for another twelve hours.

The light died to twilight. "She's up," Sorahan said.

"What's she doin?"

"Putting on a dressing gown."

"That all? No clothes?"

"No."

"Any sign of McManus?"

"No."

"Keep lookin."

There wasn't much to look at. He could see the woman as a shape, through the kitchen window. She was working at the counter beside the sink. What she was doing he couldn't tell. Getting a meal?

He moved the glasses across the house to the right. Just beyond it a rock ridge rose about a hundred and fifty feet high. It must, he thought, overlook the front yard of the house, giving a line of sight over the fuchsia hedge. He searched the ridge idly as a welcome alternative to watching Mrs. Burke and saw the movement between two rocks. It was a man. He saw him shift a rifle from his left side to his right, and slide behind one of the rocks.

The glasses moved back to the kitchen window to think about the man on the ridge. A Garda? Had Dr. Sullivan reported their visit, knowing where McManus was? Was McManus there at all? Why was Mrs. Burke in sight and never McManus? Was he walking with these two men and little Barney into a police trap? What should he tell Kiernan? Nothing, he decided. Nothing. Not yet.

"What's she doin?"

"Making food, I think." There was no more sight of the man on the far ridge. The light died. The lights in the house went on. The yard light went on. The back door opened and Mrs. Burke came out, in her dressing gown, carrying a back pack and a jerry can.

She crossed the lawn slowly, her head down. "Gimme the glasses." Kiernan fixed them on her. "That'll be McManus's pack," he said. "Maybe he's in the barn." She went through the barn door.

"All them barns is the same," Powers said greedily. "I can get him in there."

"The way to do it," Kiernan said coldly, "if he's in there, is to get to the woman and make her call him out."

Powers said doggedly, "I can get him in there."

"And get shot." Kiernan had an execution of his own. He was not to be robbed of it. "Go on down and scout the place." He put down the glasses. "Go down this hill the way we come up it and circle the whole place—see, go round behind thon hump to the right of the house and check the place from the front. Then come back here." He said firmly, "Powers. Do nothin till I tell you. All I want to know is—is McManus in thon house."

"Aye." It had an angry guttural sound.

Sorahan still said nothing about the man on "thon hump," and Powers scrambled down the back of the hill.

The woman was a long time in the barn. When she came out she still had the pack, but it hung thinly from her hand. "He's in there," Kiernan said. "She took him somethin. Grub maybe." She did not have the jerry can. "There was water in it. He's in the barn."

She went into the house and closed the door. The front yard light went on.

"I hope Powers isn't buck stupid enough to walk into that light," Kiernan said like a man afraid of being cheated.

Mrs. Burke walked into the light in her bedroom and dropped the dressing gown to the floor. Naked she lay down again on the bed. Like a vigil, Sorahan thought; like a nude virgin on the altar at a black mass. She lay on her back, her legs straight down, her hands folded on her belly, like a Pharaoh's widow on a sarcophagus: nothing common, nothing mean; drama in the mind. McManus was in the barn. She took him food and water. He had been sick in there, raving and writhing in the hay. Dr. Sullivan had tended him there, in the hay. The poor woman had stayed his fever, cooled his brow. All this time he had been the hunted, his refuge among whatever dumb animals the woman had in there, with no soul to talk to but the woman . . . and yes, the three men the grocer mentioned, who had seen him and spoken to him. No, they had gone, the grocer said, they had no connection with the man on the ridge. The police were hidden around, the man on the ridge was one of them: Powers and Kiernan and himself had gone to see the doctor, looking for transient patients, "calling himself McManus, or something else, beard, pack, a girl with him maybe . . ." and the doctor knew the one they wanted, down there in his sister-in-law's barn. He told the police. Good. Sorahan no longer needed to. Absolution. It was done, *by a doctor*. A humane act. And Powers was walking into a police trap. Good. Soon he and

Barney could drift away in the darkness. The thing was all over bar the shouting. . . . Drama in the mind. He had it all worked out, comfortably.

Powers went far to the right from the bottom of the hill, then struck towards the sea. It was the wrong way to approach the house. He ought to have gone round the left side and come at the house under cover of the blind gable of the barn, because Kiernan told him to come at it from the right, round thon hump. He got bad orders from the stupid jealous wee cunt, so he'd improve on them. He went down all the way to the sea and then came left over the rocks above the shore. The nesting gulls on the rock faces cried warning and anger, took flight from their ledges, settled on the sea, scolding like coarse-throated shrews. He came up from the shore, hurrying now, climbing through the pockets of soil among the rocks, through stabbing gorse and thistles, and the sheep coughed and sneezed and rose and ba-a-a-d and moved stupidly ahead of him in single file, along the crowns of the rock ridges, announcing him to the night. There was one ridge more, thon hump. He climbed down to the grassy hollow that passed it and let into the lane that ran to the gate in the front fuchsia hedge.

That hedge was almost the end of the road. Beyond it, Mc-Manus, the cause of every trouble. There'd be no mistakes here. His heartbeat was faster, not from the climbing. There was sound in his head, high sound, pleasant sound, and a kind of sweet pleasure ran through his frame and into his groin. His mind was on killing. The pleasure deepened, swelling him. The sweetness was intense behind the eyes, like an itch. He rubbed his eyes and the pleasure was rich. He muttered obscenities, greedy, hungry obscenities, and eagerness roared in his chest and his head and delight sang in his throat.

The black mass of thon hump was on his left. He walked faster tight against its base, his step almost silenced by the sheep-cropped grass, and when the side of the ridge no longer sheltered him, made a crouching run over the hundred feet to the hedge. Not the gate. Gates have unoiled hinges. Through the hedge, slowly, gently. The hunter. He stood in the hedge, holding fuchsia bushes apart and saw her through the small front window, lying naked on the bed.

Holy fuckin Jasus! She's a l-o-n-g one.

His eyes lapped her body from her feet to her head.

Christ, lyin there naked in her glasses.

The steel-rimmed glasses touched something. He had to get closer. He moved along the circle of the hedge to the left gable of the house and slid along the wall to the little window.

He was open, in the little lake of red-ringed light.

The woman's eyes were closed. Sleepin. Them fuckin curtains on the big window were open. Kiernan would have the glasses on her, feedin his face. Jasus, she's a one. He could feel her thighs round his rump. Them glasses. They made him drunk. He could hear the delight in his throat.

When he was done w'McManus . . . McManus . . . it was a struggle to move from the window. He passed the door and slid across the little window of Thomas Burke's study. The light from the kitchen gave him all he needed. McManus was not there. The kitchen? He reached left-handed for the latch and knew it would be locked . . . the kitchen window at the back . . . his hand fell from the latch as he turned and heard the shot after the bullet spun him and came through the fleshy rump of his left shoulder and tore a hole in the door. He fell rolling, not hurting, his arm hanging numb from a thump, and heard three? four? more shots as he rolled at the hedge and felt his foot jerk from another violent thump. Then he was through the hedge and out of the lake of light and scrambling low, one good arm keeping him from falling on his face, the other arm dangling and warm-wet. He was among the rocks and ridges again, trying to see a course in his mind, from memory, back to the car. But he was going in the wrong direction and the arm was alive and hurting more with every unbalanced stride, the pain mounting up into his neck. It was a jolting run, shattering his head. His foot was not hurting, but the heel of his boot was gone and small stones and spiked vegetation pierced the thin leather skin under his heel. He broke into the lane beside the grocer's shop and knew where he was and made a limping run for the car. The arm was agony, burning hot, screaming in his head with every jarring stride, then he was in the car, fumbling, missing, ripping gears and away, half-blind with pain and nausea and bleeding. He whinnied in his nostrils, stifling screams.

"I *told* him *not* to," Kiernan said with the first shot. *"I told him not to!"* He thumped the ferns with his little fists. "I *told* him . . ." and four more quick shots rolled in the hollows and over the enclosed bay. *"It was a rifle!"* Then a sixth shot. Then the silence, and the after-shock of sea birds' complaints and sheeps' pitiful protests.

"It was a rifle," Kiernan said in a tiny voice. "There was no talk of McManus havin a rifle."

Little Barney slid farther down the back side of The Hill, dry in the mouth and weak in the legs.

Sorahan said nothing. He had been waiting for a voice, a challenge in the night. He had already fixed "Hands up" in his mind, a voice shouting, and it rhymed there. The shots stunned him.

"He got Powers," Kiernan said. "Holy Christ Jasus." He lay limp and still, robbed and puzzled. "He got Powers. That last one was a finisher." He rose to his knees and crouched in the ferns. "But where is he?" he said, bewildered, peering down at the house. "Where is he?" The little man was frightened. He lay down again and hugged the ground. "We'll wait and see," he said prudently.

Sorahan took the glasses from his hand and parted the ferns. Mrs. Burke was off the bed. Her movements were unhurried. She put on the dressing gown. He watched her appear in the kitchen and disappear. The back door opened. The birds were settled, the sheep were settled, the night rustled, and Mrs. Burke walked across the lawn slowly, in eerie undisturbed composure. She went into the barn and came out immediately, carrying the jerry can she had earlier carried in. She took from her dressing-gown pocket something that looked like a long cloth, a shirt sleeve, a towel, and stuffed it into the mouth of the can. Then she carried the can back into the barn, was inside for a little while, and came out, closing the door behind her.

"It's a fire-bomb, for Christ's sake," Kiernan said, and stood up. "She's gonta burn the place." The bullet fired from the blind eye of the barn took him in the chest. Mrs. Burke walked quickly into her house and closed the door.

The fire-bomb woofed like a howitzer.

They could hear the screaming hens as the barn door flew open and burning balls of bird were blown out and scattered like little scurrying campfires on the grass.

Kiernan fell across Sorahan as if he had been thrown. Sorahan thought he had thrown himself down. "That shot was from the barn," he said, and Kiernan, deadweight, lay across him.

"Barney," Sorahan yelled as a slight figure jumped from the barn window and landed heavily and tried desperately to get to his feet on a broken leg. Sorahan watched him drag himself on his belly, away from the flaming barn. The sea birds were scolding harshly, the sheep complaining, the barn roaring. "Barney!" Sorahan yelled again.

"I'm down here," Barney called.

252 ((

A man stood on the ridge to the right of the house, a black shape against the night sky. He leapt out of sight.

"Come up here and help me," Sorahan yelled, and pushed Kiernan's corpse away.

The man from the ridge came tearing around the left side of the barn, his rifle beating the air. He caught the crawling man by one arm and dragged him, running awkwardly, away from the fire, across the little field.

Like torment on torment the voice shrieked from the eyeless window.

"Kev-innnnnn. . . ."

A man with a hat on fire and his coattails flaming stood up in the window, leaned out, and jumped like a thrown torch. He landed and rolled, tearing the hat away and tumbling in the grass, beating himself. The man in front dropped the one he was dragging, dropped his rifle, and tore off his jacket as he ran. He beat the burning man with his jacket, flailing in the weird light like the reaper, then dragged away the burning coat and the smoldering man. He slung his rifle, towing the two men along the grass. Sorahan watched him till they disappeared through a gap in the drystone wall and wondered from what black well the Irish obsession with fire as a weapon was drawn. He heard voices, like the baying of dogs.

"I'm here, Mr. Sorahan," Barney said plaintively, his face against the ground. He lay, unawares, between Sorahan and Kiernan's corpse.

"That woman'll burn, Barney," Soranhan said. "I'll have to get her out. Stay here and stay down."

"Let *him* go, Mr. Sorahan," Barney whimpered.

"He's dead."

The boy crept back quickly from Kiernan's corpse. "Oh Holy Jasus . . . I want to go. . . ."

"You've got nowhere to go. Stay there, boy." Sorahan crawled forward and down the hill to the little field and rose and ran. He wasn't thinking, he wasn't afraid, he was merely running. The shooting began when he was halfway across the field. It was fast and vicious, flying vengeance. Sorahan wasn't thinking. Explanations were ready-made in his mind and he opened his lungs as he ran and yelled, *"Garda, Garda, Garda."* The lead sang . . . six, seven, eight . . . all he knew was that the stuff was pouring past him. He didn't count. He ran, crying "Garda," his coattails flying like wings on a crippled crow. The ninth bullet hit him in the left knee and he went feet over face and slammed the ground with his back and one leg stiff and another, slower, in separate movements, and dived into blackness.

And Barney, watching from the hill, held onto his slipping senses and said, "I'll get the grocer, sur, I'll get the grocer," and in a dry and desperate terror slid down the back of the hill and ran, whimpering.

And Mrs. Burke stood still and in some distant place, in her kitchen, in her steel-rimmed eyeglasses and Thomas Burke's old dressing gown and said to someone in the place where she was, "We were born to self-destruction, child."

Powers drove the car straight at Dr. Sullivan's wooden gate and took much of it on the twisted hood up to the doctor's front door. He was swimming on the edge of consciousness. The front door had glass panels in its top half. He staggered to it and smashed the panels with the butt of his gun. Mrs. Sullivan rushed into the hall and into the pit.

"Open it." His face was savage with pain.

She unlocked the door.

"Where is he?"

254 ((

"Over the road at the hospital." The gun wavered close to her face, almost purple with the pressure of fear.

"Call him back here."

"He has patients, I don't know. . . ."

"I fuckin know, missus. This is my blood. Get him back."

Fumbling and incompetent, she got her husband. Powers took the phone. "I'm bleedin to death, mister. I've got a gun in her back. No polis. Come back quick w'everythin y'need and fix a hole in me. No polis, mind."

"I'm coming."

Powers spilled blood in one of her best armchairs, propped his head up, his eyes open, and Mrs. Sullivan on the edge of the chair across the fireplace. The doctor took two minutes to reach him.

"Stop the blood and kill the pain," Powers said to the two weaving images in his eyes, "and no polis."

"No police."

They humped him to the surgery at the side of the house before he fainted and his gun dropped to the floor. The doctor kicked it aside and went to work.

"Get the Garda now," Mrs. Sullivan said, from panic, not courage.

"Christ, woman, I promised no police. Do you want to get shot?"

"He's unconscious, for God's sake."

"Behind him there's more. There's always more. Just shut up and help me."

"I'm calling the Garda."

"Try it," he said grimly. "We won't bugger about with this lot. We'll clean and patch him and he can go. Then we'll keep our bloody mouths shut."

"If he won't go?"

"Then you'll look after him and keep your mouth shut."

It would have been simple to lift the phone. The house of the Garda was up at the town end of the street, by the Munster and

Leinster bank. It would have been simple, but it was not easy. The thing would have been over. For the moment. Dr. Sullivan knew about punishments, jurymen knew about punishments, the wives of unarmed policemen knew about punishments, punishments hung over the minds of men like gray cheesecloth, inducing a mood of induced inattention. Dr. Sullivan cleaned and sewed and dressed with a professional mind professionally directed. This is a wound. This man is in pain and losing blood. I am doing my job. When it is done, I am minding my own business. This man can rest and go. Sew, dress, sling, bed down.

"Gunshot wounds are notifiable," his wife said anxiously.

"Will you, *please,* for God's sake, woman? This man never came here. Have you the wit to see that?"

"Yes, Seamus," she said to the desperation in his voice, and understanding dawned.

They humped him to a bed and watched and waited with him, awed less by the bulk and strength of the man than by the invisible lines that ran out from him—long, mindless, silent, and relentless. To where? To Belfast, to Dublin, to the bank on the corner . . . which clerk? . . . to the bars in the village . . . which bartender, which publican? . . . to what grocer's shop, to what fishing boat? Some were known and open, some were not . . . the ones who were not, they were the ones who turned the blood gray and nourished the national mood of inattention, look there, look yonder. Do not look here.

"We'll go to bed now," the doctor said when Powers came to.

"You'll stay where y'are. Where's my gun?"

Sullivan got it for him and humbly handed it over. "My wife's exhausted. Let her go and sleep."

"Put her chair in thon corner. She can sleep sittin up."

Mrs. Sullivan was propped up in her chair in the corner like a disinherited relation at a wake.

"Feed me, missus," Powers said, and she struggled to the kitchen.

He drank brandy and ate ham sandwiches. "You've no Guinness's? This stuff's poison."

"No."

Mrs. Sullivan took her place in the corner, her ankles crossed and her hands folded in her lap in a posture of rigid composure. The muscles in her neck ached, her face collapsed, and her eyes were wide with weariness.

Sullivan's forearms were on his knees, his face in his hands.

"We come to see you, mister. We ast about McManus. We described him to you. Did he come to you for medicine, we ast you. Y'told us no."

"Yes." He didn't look up. He had conspired against them. He couldn't look up.

"All the time y'were lookin after him at the widow-woman's house."

"Yes." The room was cold. Why in the name of God didn't 1 take that boy to the hospital, no matter what that crazy woman wanted? It's too late now and look where it's got us. One of them, *in the house. With a gun.*

"You and her was hidin McManus."

"No. He was sick. That's all."

"You said you didn't know him at all when we ast you!" . .

"He was sick. I'm a doctor."

"You're a liar." Powers saw them sitting there, a new and terrible clearness in his head. With the first shot at the widow-woman's, and the thump in his shoulder, his animal instinct suspended thought and he acted to live. Pain and instinct brought him here without thought. He knew the way, that was all. But now he could think. He had been shot at the house of the widow-woman. This man knew McManus was there. This man knew they were lookin for McManus. His mind hacked at the doctor and his wife like an ice pick. They stood out in his eye—ugly, hostile, treacherous, isolated images full of malignancy.

)) 257

"You give McManus a rifle."

"No. No. I have no rifle. No gun at all."

"Y'were out there last night. The grocer saw you. Y'took Mc-Manus a gun." Thon two was the enemy. The cunta'll pay for it. I can wait. I can rest. But they'll pay. They'll know. "McManus shot me. Waited for me. Knew I was comin. You knew I was comin. You told him I was comin. You gave him a rifle. The widow-woman kept up the blinds and lay on thon bed naked to draw me down into the light. He shot me. You shot me." It was very quiet. They were there. They were helpless. Their helplessness gave him pleasure. He felt the pleasure in his head, in his chest, in his genitals. It was as if parts of him were warm, parts of him cold. His mind was cold. His head was warm. His tongue was cold. His cock was warm. He touched it with the barrel of his gun and smiled.

The doctor saw the action and the smile and his stomach soured. "McManus isn't there," he said. "I was out there, trying to get my sister-in-law to come in here. Not McManus. Not McManus," he said as if he would betray Mcanus but not this man on the bed. Not that. "She wouldn't come. He jumped behind the wheel of my car and drove us all the way to Cork Airport." He said, with a sigh that promised absolution, "He's in England."

The room was very still. Powers sat, propped on pillows, the clothes cut away from his shoulders and chest, his left shoulder and part of his chest wrapped in bandages and tape. The fingers of his left hand were half-closed. The hand lay outside the tail of his sling; a ham. The fingers opened and closed slowly, like an experiment.

Sullivan felt some relief. He had told something. Not all. Shreds of self-respect clung about him. The three men at Kate's house, the O'Connell man who said to McManus, "It's Powers I want. . . ." *They* shot this man. They would find him. Let them find him. Survive. Let this one go. Let them find him. Let them kill

258 ((

one another. What could ordinary people do against Ireland's secret societies of secret killers who recognized no government, no courts, no parliaments, no rules but their own? What could ordinary people *do?* Cultivate a mood of inattention. That was all that was all that was all.

But nothing is simple. "Who shot me then, mister?"

Almighty God, I didn't think of that. You can't win. Desperately, Sullivan said, "Before God, I don't know. McManus isn't there. He took the plane." Stick to your point. But you're making it worse, for Jesus sake, and where's the way out?

Powers looked long at Sullivan. He looked long at Mrs. Sullivan. Long enough to paralyze them both. The phone rang. Sullivan went to the next room, his system re-shocked by the sound. He was trembling. Powers came behind him, stood behind him. "Yes?"

"Doctor," the nurse said, "there's somethin fearful. Can you come quick?"

"What is it?"

"Deasy the grocer. Toormore. He just brought in Daniel Sorahan, the schoolmaster at Bantry. Can you hear me?"

"Go on."

"Shot in the knee out at Mrs. Burke's. He's unconscious. Are you there?"

"Go on, girl."

"He's lost a lot of blood but the bleedin's stopped. There's more, doctor."

"What is it, girl?"

"Deasy and a boy from Bantry brought a dead body with them —a little man shot in the chest. And Mrs. Burke. . . ."

"No!"

"Her place is burned. Deasy said she wouldn't leave and he had to drag her out by the hair. Are y'comin?"

"I'm coming." He slammed the phone down. "Accident," he said, "one dead, one dying. I have to go across the road." Tell no more, tell no more. Hear more from Deasy. "I have to go," he shouted.

"No polis. She's stayin."

"No police. God, man, *I'm a doctor.*"

"Away on. I have her. Mind that. No fuckin polis."

"I *said* no police. I have to go." He ran.

"What is it, Seamus?" Mrs. Sullivan came, shouting.

"Accident. Back," Powers said, barring her way, "away in t'your perch." He was not in control. Doubt and confusion needled at him. He sat on the bed, watching Mrs. Sullivan, walking to the window to peer at the hospital across the road, back to the bed. "Too fuckin long," he said.

"You will not use those words," she said, salving some dignity.

"I beg your pardon, missus."

There were too many things at once, phones, people running out and in, questions, doubts: Who shot me? drifted away in the confusion. Where is McManus was his job. It stayed in his mind.

There was silence then for two hours. Powers rested, dozing and waking. Sullivan came back, gaunt, gray, worn to a thread. How much to tell, if he was pushed? What Deasy told him? What the frightened boy Barney told him? What Sorahan mumbled? *Nothing,* by God. The man knew nothing. Tell him nothing. A flame of pseudo-defiance flickered. Don't tell him what he has no way of knowing! Get him to go, *some* way, *any* way.

"He's dead," he said.

"Who's dead?"

"The man." It explained the unknown.

"Where's McManus in England?" That was the thing.

"I don't know. He didn't even speak to us on the way to Cork. He flew to England. That's all we know."

"Gon back in the bedroom."

Sullivan went obediently in and sat in his appointed place. Powers sat on the arm of Mrs. Sullivan's chair and laid the gun to her shoulder.

"You've heard tell of this," he said to the doctor. "I'm goin t'ask you, Where's McManus in England? Every time y'say I don't know, I'm gonta shoot this woman in the arm, all the way down t'her hand. You've heard tella that?"

"Yes."

"All right, then. You helped McManus. The widow-woman helped McManus. She was fuckin him, the grocer says. . . ."

"He's lying." Even in extremis Mrs. Sullivan salvaged some family dignity.

". . . and if y'helped him once between you, you'd help him twice. Where's McManus in England?"

"My wife," the doctor said, swallowing and watching the gun against his wife's shoulder, "has a brother in England." He looked to her eyes and quickly looked away. He had let McManus stay with her widowed sister, now he was sending this man to her brother in England. "McManus was alone with Mrs. Burke before he left the house. He had a letter . . . it might have had to do with my brother-in-law. Before God, that's all I can tell you. . . ." He looked like a beaten dog at his wife who looked and sent back her compassion. It was many years since they had felt so close to one another.

"She might have sent him there," Mrs. Sullivan said in support. Maybe the man would leave now? Go somewhere else?

"Write it down," Powers said, and the doctor wrote it down in block capitals.

"I want a doctor's bag n'food and drugs t'keep down the pain." They got it for him.

"I want all the money y'have in the house." They emptied their cash box and their pockets and purses. One hundred and twenty pounds in English ten-pound notes.

"I want another shot." He got it. The man was preparing for a journey. In his anguish the doctor had no mind for his brother-in-law's summer habits. He did not think of them. So he did not mention them. The man was going. Thanks be to God.

"Get your car out." The doctor brought it to the front door "You're drivin me to Cork Airport."

"Have some compassion, man. I have patients. They need me." There was Sorahan, who would be a cripple for life, dependent on the skill of a harassed country doctor. There was Mrs. Burke, sitting in Deasy's house like the plague.

"I *need* you, mister. The two of you away on, in the front. I'm gonta sleep in the back. If you stop or change speed, I'll wake up and beat the faces off you."

And at Cork Airport, he said, "By Jasus, I'm tellin you, no polis if you want to live till next week. *I'm tellin* you."

"No police." There were weeks and months and years to be conserved beyond next week. The man was going. The nightmare that fell over the widow-woman's half-door, half-dead, was going away.

He was flyin.

Soarin. L-e-a-p-in in the sky. The hound of fuckin heaven.

He sat very still, his head roaming. Disassociated. All that had been was not. They were not here they were there and he was not there therefore they were not. He was moving. Traveling. Away. Alone. He was the measure of all that was. His head roamed and sang and he closed his eyes and was feather-light. He could fly without this plane. He was smiling, not in the face, but inside his head. Seventy minutes of sweet levitation, Cork to Heathrow. His face and head full of sweet secrets. Ahhh, if you good people knew what I know . . . who I am . . . where I'm goin.

> *I know where I'm goin*
> *And I know who'll go with me!*

Courtesy on the ground, sweet courtesty, sweet syrup. I beg your pardon, m'am, my fault entirely. I'll pick it up. Victoria Station, if you please, driver. Thank you, driver. That was the grand bloody ride. Lovely fuckin weather.

Day return to East Grinstead, sir. Thank you, sir. The platform on the far right? *Thank* you, sir, *thank* you!

Euphoria by the bellyful. Wackadoo, wackadoo, wackadoo. Won't Mother England be surprised!

Judge Jeffreys' house, lunches, teas, dinners. Can I have lashins of scrambled eggs? The arm, y'see. Fell offa bridge on a Saturday night. . . . Gimme a spoon and H.P. sauce, missus. Judge Jeffreys lived in this house, is that a fact? The Hangin Judge? They abolished *him,* didn't they? Hangin Judge Outa Work!

Fuckin English bitch. Can't take a joke, by Jasus. Would that be funny in Belfast? Snippity-snip!

Stoneleigh House? That's one for the book—ask a bobby! Excuse me, officer, can you direct me to Stoneleigh House? First left past the parish church, the big house on the left on the edge of town? Thank you, officer. (Fuckers like you wouldn't last long on the Falls.)

The gate was open. It hadn't been closed for years. His euphoria sank into hardness. He stood in the gateway, looking up at the bend in the drive, looking at nothing, his mind settling to its work.

Then the hardness heated. The eyes warmed. McManus McManus McManus you Antrim Road cunt McManus McManus. He walked slowly up the drive and saw the house around the bend, a monument of stone, in a large open circle of gravel and grass. Aye, aye, it would be a place like this for you, boyo. High class. Like a Protestant fuckin squire. McManus McManus McManus. He was beginning to love the sound of it in his head. He went up the steps to the front door and put his gun in the sling.

The door was closed. In the column of the door frame, a small white button with PRESS on it. It was a wee bell for a big house.

Nobody answered it. He tried again and again. He leaned on the button. He could hear the bell inside, like an alarm clock in an empty packin case. Nobody rose to it.

He came down the steps and wandered round the house, through a well-trimmed hedge arch into a rose garden and beyond it a vegetable garden. An old man said from behind a box hedge to his right, "Was there somepin?"

"I was ringin the bell. Nobody came."

"Nobody'll come. They're away."

"Away where?"

"Spain."

"Spain?"

"Spain."

"What for?"

"Howzat?"

"For how long?"

"All summer. Every summer. They'll be back next month."

"There's nobody here?"

"Me."

"Who're you?"

"Gardener. You after a job?"

"I got a job. D'you live here?"

"I live a'tome."

The doctor got rid of him, lied to him, made a fool of him. His head was full of black, blacker than darkness but like a bloody empty hole with nothing but black in it. He couldn't see.

"Somepin wrong?" the old man asked him.

Powers didn't hear. He walked blind round the house lifting his feet by instinct and was at the road again. A cricket match was in progress in a field across the road. Perhaps he saw it. He went across to the field, sat down at the foot of a grass bank, and stared at the players. They were like white spots before his eyes. The doctor's face obstructed his vision, and the doctor's wife sitting in her corner and the doctor's wife's sister lying naked on the bed. There were no words in his head, only intentions. When the pain came hurrying back sight came with it and the cricketers had gone. He groped in his bag, opened his shirt, and cried out when the needle went into his shoulder. The pain sank and he sank with it. Massive dejection took him over, he was drowning in it, crying self-pity to the green grass, till he looked across the road at Stoneleigh House and felt the spurs of resentment and soon, revenge, and mounted on the wings of taloned eagles.

He walked into the town, bought a heavy clasp knife and went down the main street and at Sainsbury's bought four pounds of sliced ham, a pound of butter, a sliced loaf, a bunch of bananas, a packet of tea, and a bottle of milk. With his groceries in a paper shopping bag and his doctor's bag clutched in the same hand, he went to the movies.

When he came out, it was almost dark. He went back to Stoneleigh, found a short ladder in a garden shed, shot the latch on the kitchen window, locked it again behind him, went out the back door, put the ladder back, and took his possessions inside.

The house had three floors. He went up to the top; a billiard room and quarters for two maids. He had a place to sleep. On the second floor, a drawing room and the family's suite; four bedrooms, bathrooms, and a small kitchen for preparation of teas, snacks, and morning coffee. Handy for servants. Fuckin rich.

He scouted the ground floor for exits and the routes to them and went back upstairs. The small kitchen would do him. By candlelight he ate ham and bread and butter and drank tea, put his food in the fridge, cleaned his mess, and went to the attic and to bed.

He needed sleep.

In the mornin, back to that doctor, and his wife and thon fuckin widow-woman. . . .

On his right side. God, I'm wore out.

Ahhhhh. A long stretch, feet against the end-board. Jasus, that's lovely.

Then he drew his knees up to his belly. The fetal position. Sleep came at once.

FOURTEEN

McMANUS, suddenly, felt young. His age. Unencumbered. He laughed and wanted to laugh. Delight danced in his blood. It was quadrangle delight, campus delight, immediate, levitating.

He kept hold of her hand and forgot he had lately forgotten her name. "Brendine Healy of Boston," he said, "I've got to talk to you. I've got to apologize . . ." He guided her away from the ticket counter.

"Our tickets . . . ?"

"In a minute. There's a coffee place upstairs," he trundled her along. She was laughing.

"You were awfully sick," she was still laughing.

"Yes. Yes, I was. God, I'm glad to see you." He didn't know why. There was no need to know why. She was young. His own age. Another port. Not touched by . . . but put that out of mind. . . . "Sit down here. I'll fetch the coffee."

She watched him at the cafeteria counter, full of her own delight. Company. Somebody about her own age. She remembered how he had needed her. His beard was more like a beard now. It made him look younger. He was a nice-looking boy too. . . .

He brought the coffee. "Sugar?" Attentive.

"No. Figure. You know." They laughed at that too. With her figure, who would worry?

"Look." The going was a little harder here. He stirred his coffee. "Look. I feel bad . . . very badly . . . I'm . . ." He laid

)) 267

the spoon in his saucer "I'm going to tell you something. It's terrible. I'll explain. I want to apologize." He needed to tell. When up from the depths you arise, you need to tell, to talk, to shed bad blood like bad dreams.

"Tell me," she said. "I looked for you, you know."

"Thank you. I wish you'd found me."

He told her. Almost everything, from the beginning. "I meant well," he said at the end.

She stirred her sugarless coffee, looking into its little whirlpool. "Where are they now?"

"Still in West Cork, still searching for me, I suppose. But I've lost them now." Get thee behind me, Satan; I am out.

"We know it all, don't we? When we're young, I mean."

"I did. There were reasons, mind you. Don't think there weren't. But I'm a fool. God, the suffering I've caused. Such terrible trouble. . . . My sister, my parents . . . other people. . . ." like Mrs. Burke, and the doctor, and his wife . . . Mrs. Burke warmed his mind. . . .

"Don't think about it. It's over, isn't it?"

"Yes. Yes," he said, thinking of Mrs. Burke, looking at Brendine Healy of Boston.

Young lives, in need of young laughter.

She dipped her head, and tossed it and smiled shyly and said, "I never even *heard* your name."

"Johnny McManus."

"You wouldn't make a good gunman, Johnny. I don't think you're the kind." She sounded wisely immature, playing at maturity.

"No. No." It was known. "You agree with all the people I love."

"Look." She glanced about quickly, as if to make sure the coast was clear, and laid her hand on his. "Why don't we go by boat? I mean, the car ferry?"

"I haven't a car."

"We can hire one." She tightened her hold on his hand. "Why don't we? Come on." Little adventures; young laughter. The summer was almost over and there hadn't been much to show for it.

In a week or two she'd have to fly back to Boston and in another week she'd be slogging away at Boston U. There'd been something for the mind, but very little laughter. She could get an essay out of it; she couldn't curl up under the electric blanket and smile herself to sleep, remembering. "We were . . . you remember . . . we were going to. . . ."

"I have this house to go to," he said. "Mrs. Burke gave me a letter." He passed it to her. "You mean, drive to East Grinstead? All the way across Wales and southern England?"

"Why *don't* we?" Summer's dying, winter's coming.

"If we go halves on it."

"It'll be great fun. *Gosh,*" she said, very young. "Gosh, I'm glad I was here when you walked in. I was over there, just sitting . . . you looked so *cross* . . . I'm real glad I saw you. . . ." Eager and young. "Halves. I'll get the car ferry. You get the . . . meals . . . gas. Petrol." She hop-skipped beside him to her baggage. The car ferry would cost more. It wasn't halves, but he probably didn't have much money and Daddy wouldn't know the difference . . . children at play . . . they hired a bright blue two-door Opel from Cahill's on her international driver's license and she made the ferry reservations, happy little mother with something to do with somebody her own age and the car ferry didn't leave till eight and the day was bright and cool and glorious, and they had to spend it.

They spent it at Old Head of Kinsale, the button-head on a little peninsula jutting out into the ocean. They went down through soft Cork pastoral land of pale green and yellow in the summer's end. Not like the harsh stained-rock glory of West Cork, not gold and orange and red and white and rose and purple and brown, full of power, the crash of angry water on stubborn rock, the gang cries of sea birds, the lyrics of the wood pigeon, the crass squawk of the crow, the wind's howl; not the gorse and fern and thistle plucking spitefully at the legs. . . . Here, soft land and the flat and endless glaring ocean.

They ran barefoot on the beach, bought sandwiches at the hotel,

and threw bread to the gulls that were tame people-hangers waiting to be fed; beach bums on wings. Not like the wild things in
the western coves. Brendine lay on the shore, playing with the
sand—young, gentle, slender, safe, without spot or blemish, without
past or present. Sane. Sane. Sane. Not like Kate Burke—hard, severe, plain, full of power and lust and fear and courage and some
great wild beauty. Crazy. Go away, Kate. Out of my head, you de-
vouring old whore. . . .

Lying in the sand, on their backs, fingers woven, faces under
the sun, eyes closed against the glare, "What will you do, Johnny?"

"I don't know. I can't go home. I can't stay in Ireland at all."

"Do you care?"

"Oh yes. Oh yes."

She looked quickly at him, at the tightness of his lips, of his
eyes.

He pulled his hand free and turned on his face. "Oh yes. She's
the whore we never leave," he said, his eyes shut tight to filter
tears. "No matter where we go we're always here. Somebody called
her the old sow that eats her farrow. . . ."

"What does that mean?"

Christ! Kate Burke knows. "An old pig that eats her litter."

"I see," she said, and, in a small voice of apology. "I don't
really."

She was very young; honest; not one of us. But *we* understand.
Ourselves alone. "We talk at her and about her all the time," he
said. "Did you do Austin Clarke in that Irish literature course you
told me about?"

"I haven't met that name," she said solemnly, a Litt. One student for a sterile moment. Why do I have to read that stuff at
all, she wondered? I like arranging things, helping out. I'm good
at helping out, I'm not good at that stuff, really.

"He's a bitter man, an anti-clerical man, a poet," he said. "I
wish I could be a poet. I'd write the poems Austin Clarke wrote,

and this one most of all. . . ." He dug his fingers into the sand to grip and grind it.

Then he said, his eyes tight, his voice tight,

> *"On a holy day when sails were blowing southward*
> *A bishop sang the Mass at Irishmore,*
> *Men took one side their wives were on the other*
> *But I heard the woman coming from the shore:*
> *And wild in despair my parents cried aloud*
> *For they saw the vision draw me to the door.*

> *"Long had she lived in Rome when Popes were bad,*
> *The wealth of every age she makes her own,*
> *Yet smiled on me in eager admiration*
> *And for a summer taught me all I know.*
> *Banishing shame with her great laugh that rang*
> *As if a pillar caught it back alone.*

> *"I learned the prouder counsel of her throat*
> *My mind was growing bold as light in Greece;*
> *And when in sleep her stirring limbs were shown,*
> *I blessed the noonday rock that knew no tree:*
> *And for an hour the mountain was her throne,*
> *Although her eyes were bright with mockery. . . .*

> *"Awake or in my sleep, I have no peace now,*
> *Before the ball is struck, my breath has gone,*
> *And yet I tremble lest she may deceive me*
> *And leave me in this land where every mother's son*
> *Must carry his own coffin and believe,*
> *In dread, all that the clergy teach the young.*

"Come on. Time to go," he said, so that she might not speak, and sprang up and hauled her to her feet. "We're off to Philadelphia in the mornin." *Get out of my guts and my groin, Kate, you old whore.*

"Ours?" he said, leaning against the berth.

"I thought it would be cheaper," she said. "It's a nine-hour sea trip from Cork to Swansea. It's in my name. I wouldn't see you for hours if we were in separate cabins. You know? You should have company, Johnny." Little mother.

"I'll toss you for the bottom berth."

She won. They climbed to the top berth and sat with their backs to the bulkheads, their legs out, their hocks mingling. "We're off to Philadelphia in the *evenin,*" she said, pleased about something. "What will you do, Johnny?" Still with the same questions. Persistent.

"Find work," he said. "In 'the building,' likely."

"What building?"

"The building trade. That's what Irish immigrants call laboring in the English construction industry. It'll keep me alive till I can find a decent job."

"Johnny."

"Yes."

"I was thinking."

"What about?"

"Why don't you come to the States?"

"Four reasons. The fare, a job, a sponsor, the quota. They all add up to no visa."

"I could get Daddy to help."

"What does . . ." he almost said Daddy ". . . he do?"

"He has companies."

Ah. People have companies. Rich people have companies. Rich people have power. Except a grain of wheat fall and is watered in fertile ground it cannot grow?

"They have subsidiaries in Canada. Sometimes when he wants to bring people to the States, he gets them jobs in the companies in Canada and then has them transferred to the States. It's quick and easy that way, he says."

"I'd never really thought of going anywhere till this happened. . . . Let's go up and watch her leave."

They were through the channel, cutting the long swell. There she was, lying on her back, the cool evening air nibbling at her green paps. *Piteous Jesus, Kate, call me.* Sleight of voice. Sleight of mind. He lashed at his heart. "D'you know what Kavanagh said about us and that old whore over there?" It was almost a shout, a whip in the tongue to beat the past out of the head.

"Who is Kavanagh?"

"Another poet. They're the hardest working men in Ireland. He said, 'It would never be spring, always autumn.' In Ireland, you know. Us, you know? The way we talk. The way we think and feel. . . .

> *"It would never be spring, always autumn,*
> *After a harvest always lost,*
> *When Drake was winning seas for England*
> *We sailed in puddles of the past*
> *Chasing the ghost of Brendan's mast."*

"Who's Brendan?"

"A seafaring monk. They say he discovered America."

Sleight of voice. Sleight of mind. There's the word. America. "Why would you want me to go to America, Brendine?"

She took his arm and leaned her head against his shoulder and said nothing. Then she said, "It's cold. Let's go down."

Sleight of voice. Sleight of mind. He turned without looking again at her green paps, and they went below. America. Time future. No skull of Irish bard, no thigh of Irish chief there, no young sprout cursed for being in the way; time future. Tears to laughter.

"Do you think your father might?" God, that would be *something!* Leap from death to life. Leap from sorrow to joy. Leap from goal to goal. Leap from foot to foot. He closed the cabin door. "D'you think . . . ?"

"He would. His family came over on a coffin ship in the famine. I'll tell him what he has to know. They never forget. . . ." Little mother.

"I could kiss you."

"Why don't you, Johnny?"

He took her face in his hands and put his mouth gently to hers. Her mouth was sweet and soft. Smaller than Kate's. Not consuming like Kate's. *Get out of my head, Kate.*

"Johnny?"

"What?"

"Brendine Healy of Boston, are you a virgin? Remember?"

"Yes."

"I am." She kissed him, her arms round his waist. "Are you?"

He kept his mouth on hers, wondering. "No," he said.

"Many girls?"

"No." Exorcise Kate. "Mrs. Burke," he said. "She taught me." He nibbled her lips.

"Johnny?"

"Yes."

"Teach me."

"Yes."

Naked and a little shy, they went to bed in the bottom berth. The way you taught me, Kate. Yesterday was a long day, full of consuming anger and anxiety. Last night was a long night, full of Cleery's vengeance and Kate's consuming lust. Today was a long day, full of sleight of mind, sleight of voice.

"Johnny?"

He was asleep.

Very early in the morning, while it was yet dark, off Port Eynon Point on the run home into Swansea Bay, they stirred.

"Johnny? Now?" she whispered. "Please."

"Yes."

He was slow and gentle and careful.

She was not Kate. These were not Kate's strong cunning thighs, Kate's hips not these little hips were for lustful, luxurious wallowing, this little belly was not Kate's warm hungry belly, these little breasts . . . this was not Kate. Get out of my head, Kate. Let me go, Kate.

"Johnny? Did I please you?"

He lay on her belly. "Yes. Oh, yes." Make the voice right. Be kind.

"Johnny? Why don't we drive to the house today? Not stop anywhere. Tonight I'll be better. You tell me what you like. Tell me what to do. Yes?"

"Yes."

But it was a happy drive and a happy day. Leap from past to future, from land to land, from skull of bard and thigh of chief to daughter company to mother company, leap from foot to foot, from old to young, woman to woman. Leaping transitions, instant transitions. The day's laughter grew. Kate was distance. Brendine was presence. His warmth for her grew. On the phone the estate agent said, "Yes, well, bring Mrs. Burke's letter to my house and let me see. I have a key here."

At eleven, they turned the key in the door and filled the house with light. Yes, it would be better this time. Joy in their genitals, anticipation warm in their eyes.

"Do we eat first?"

"There's another floor up there."

"Leave it. Pick the bed you want to sleep in."

"You slept last night." Laughter. Kiss me. Hold me. Touch me.

"Let's not sleep much tonight."

"Look, there's ham and milk and bananas in this fridge. . . ."

They ate in the little kitchen. Lashings of ham, sliced bread, bananas, coffee. "We'll wash up later."

He undressed her slowly, scorched her with counseling words, flooded her with tenderness, loved her with passion, laughed with her jubilant thanks. Triumph. She held him hard for a long time. Then she said, "Let's wash the dishes and come back to bed." Loving little mother.

In a closet she found a large fat woman's dressing gown and paraded in it like a little girl dressing up. He put on his trousers. They washed the dishes, talking, laughing, full of young joy.

She said, believing it, "I've been in love with you, Johnny, since the day I met you. Daddy'll help. . . ."

Times past are past. Times to come are on the doorstep.

The pain was back wild and gnawing.

Powers groped in the dark for the black bag on the floor by the bed. He groped in it for another needle. An attic light in this house would shine out across the town like a beacon. He cursed his shoulder and felt sick and blind with pain. The needle went in clumsily and he moaned to stifle the screaming in his head. Laughing too. He could hear laughter in his head. I'm goin out of my fuckin mind.

Kneeling, head on the bed, he moaned away agony, waiting for relief. The laughter in his head troubled him. What he imagined it could mean troubled him. When relief came he lay down again, moaning now with sweet ease that grew steadily sweeter. But the laughter stayed in his head. He listened to it.

Not in my fuckin head at all. Downstairs. He's here. And he brought a piece of cunt with him. The gun, under the pillow. The doctor was right. The widow-woman sent him here. He apologized to the doctor and walked softly to the head of the attic stairs. Holy Jasus, washin the dishes! And her *laughin*.

Her laughter started the music in his head. It sang down into his throat, high sweet music down into his chest, through his belly into his groin. The swelling started. The pleasure of it! He could wait now. He knew how to do it. Wait till they finish the dishes. He stood back from the top of the stairs looking down into the lobby below. The little kitchen was off the lobby. They'd come out, cross the lobby into them big rooms. Then he'd go down. Quiet. McManus had a gun. But he knew how to do it.

The dishes were done. There was silence. Then soft laughter. They came across the lobby, arms around waists. No shirt, by God, and her in some big blue tent. He's been up her already

276 ((

and me sleepin! The door across the hall from the kitchen closed. He stood a while thinking of it. The pleasure of it.

Then he went down, testing every step.

They were not in the big drawing room. There were no voices, no sounds in it. He put the gun in his sling and turned the handle with herculean patience. It struck him for the first time—there were three doors into this big room. All of them were closed. And there were voices behind the one straight ahead. Soft laughin. Getting her up for a night's good fuckin.

Wackadoo wackadoo wackadoo.

Won't fuckin McManus be surprised. The music was exquisite; higher, sweeter; his groin harder.

What's better, Pat, killin or fuckin?

They're both about the same.

He crossed the room on the thickest carpet he had ever walked on. He took the gun from his sling. He stood outside the door. They were still laughin, soft-like, cuddlin laughin.

Knock or throw it open? They were good locks. Thon one in the door from the lobby opened like it was oiled every day. The hinges had no sound in them. He put the gun back in the sling. No knock. McManus had a gun. He'd have it close. He'd reach it before a knock died. But thon cuddlin would fill his head. Open the door and watch them. Who hears anythin when a woman has her fingers on your cock?

Slowly. Slower than before. It turned almost without movement. Push the door an inch, to clear the catch. Get the gun back in your fist. They're still cuddle-laughin. He pushed the door. It opened slowly, smoothly, silently; wide.

They were lying across the edge of the bed, their feet trailing to the floor. McManus's trousers were about his ankles. Brendine's voluminous splendor was pulled up to her thighs and McManus's hand was out of sight in the ample, bundled folds.

"Will you want to do this when I'm fifty, Johnny?" she asked him.

"There y'are, are ye, Johnny?" Powers said.

They shot off the bed, onto their feet, like figures in a Chaplin comedy. She stood frozen, terrified and lost in the smothering folds of a fat woman's dressing gown. McManus stood gawk-mouthed, paralyzed, his trousers about his ankles, to face his executioner.

"Never saw a cock go softer faster," Powers said.

"I have to inform you," he said with instant ludicrous formality and some difficulty, "that you, John McManus, has been lawfully condemned t'death by a proper court of the Irish Republican Army and I am here to carry out the sentence forthwith." He felt a certain pride. This was a formal action, an official act, for and on behalf of a greater power. He was an em . . . an emminisery.

The girl's scream hurt his head. He shot her through the face.

The bullet knocked her back onto the bed, her arms askew, her legs apart, her feet flat on the floor, a rag doll.

"The widow-woman told me I could get y'here, McManus."

"Piteous Jesus Kate no no no not you Kate," like the crying of a beaten dog.

Powers shot him through the heart. The bullet knocked him back onto the bed, splayed out beside Brendine. His face was deformed by an ancient anguish.

That was that.

Powers lifted the girl's skirt and dropped it. "Skinanbone," he said. He had done his duty. They said don't come back till y'kill him. And there he was, lookin a right bloody eejit w'his trousers round his shins. What way *would* he look? He never *was* anythin. "Y'was niver the kind," Powers said with contempt, and dismissed a life. The girl didn't come into this. "In war there's always people gettin kilt that shoulda been some other place," Clune always said. Fuck Clune too.

What else?

He looked about the room like a housewife finishing for the night. Aye, there was McManus's gun. The capture of enemy arms is a military virtue. It wasn't under the pillow where it shoulda

278 ((

been. Eejit. It wasn't anywhere obvious where it shoulda been. Right y'are, right y'are, Johnny, boyo. He took the clasp knife from his pocket and opened it with his teeth. The pillows first. He hacked at them with rising glee. There was no gun. He wasn't looking for any gun. There wasn't any gun. There was an ignorant eejit that didn't know his arse from his elbow. Hack for the hell of it, hack hack hack every fuckin thing in sight. The bed covers, the mattress them two was spread out on, the chairs . . . fuckin gold coverin . . . hack hack hack . . . what's in the closets? Rip rip rip. At the end of it, he sweated freely. That'd cost them somethin. He went upstairs to gather his things. Time to go. Taxi back to London. Find a hoore house and have as good a belt as the shoulder would let him. That's what he needed. Not the dead skinanbones down there, a livin fat fuck. . . .

The lights of a car far below touched the maid's room. He looked down onto the graveled drive. Polis. *Polis?* More of them, in cars, pourin out.

He sat down to watch them, coldly. Polis, like midgets, skitterin about down there. With rifles, some of them, by Jasus. Lights, by Jasus. Settin them up on the lawns and back there among the roses. They wanted to fight, by Jasus.

It struck him suddenly. *Who told them?* Kiernan? Not Kiernan. Sorahan? Maybe Sorahan, maybe the doctor, maybe his yatterin wife, maybe the fuckin widow-woman, maybe the Bantry men, maybe . . . Jasus, there was bloody dozens coulda informed. *Somebody told them.* Right y'are, *right y'are,* that'd wait. But it was likely the widow-woman . . . thon oul hoore.

Well, it was late in the day to get at her. But she'd get taken care of. Look at them. Thirty or forty of them. You'd think, by Jasus, there was twenty men in here, w'automatic rifles. There's only me, he said, smiling down at the policemen positioning themselves beyond the lights. They think I can't see them, he said, looking out over the lights focused on the ground floor. Bloody midgets. Midget heads.

Right y'are, right y'are, write a song for Patrick Powers. He died for Ireland fightin fuckin Forty to One . . . there was forty, anyway. Write a song for Patrick Powers. Forty to One? Anyway. There'd be Twenty before they carried him out. The Big Fella's way.

He stood up and said solemnly, "This I was born for."

But do it right. Big Mike Collins would do it right. Check the roof. Where's the trapdoor? He ran through the attic rooms, switching on lights, scanning ceilings, and found it on the landing, with a folding ladder pulled down by a chain. He went up to the roof. He could keep the fuckin forty all night, holed up on this roof . . . wee nests, golops of cover . . . leave the ladder down.

He ran down to the ground floor and found a long broom. Switch on every fuckin light in the house. Smash the bulbs. With system, he worked his way upstairs, up to the attic again. Smashing lights. They'd have to use lights to winkle him out. Lights make nice targets.

He waited in the drawing room, watching the preparations for his destruction and a thought dealt his head a heavy blow. He scrambled to the attic.

There were no cars in the road beyond. No polis controllin curious crowds. Polis motors only, on the gravel below. No crowd over the road in the cricket field. One in the morning, for Jasus sake. Dirty English bastards. *No reporters?*

Then who will tell the story? Some policeman at a cornorer's inquest? "On August 29, at approximately midnight, I proceeded. . . ." Not bloody likely!

Y'needed reporters in this warfare. Half your armament is reporters. No television, no reporters, and all you've got is half a bloody war and anonymous death.

He opened an attic window and yelled, "Where's your fuckin reporters?"

The police went quietly about their business. He didn't even see one lookin up.

280   ((

"Where's the fuckin BBC?" he yelled.

Y'might as well talk to a cartloada monkeys.

He sat down to consider these dishonest English tactics. He thought also of checking his gun. Four in the clip. Reload. Where the . . . ? Holy Jasus, he had four bullets. All the rest, two boxes, were in the dashboard pocket of the car and it was bashed up in the doctor's front yard! Four bullets! Four polis! W'rifles.

The Song died.

The bullhorn outside called to him. "Patrick Powers. We know you are inside. We know you have a gun. We know you have no extra ammunition."

There y'are, by Christ. It was the doctor. He called the Garda. They called the English. Fuckin informers. Fuckin *traitors! They* found the ammunition. "We don't think he has more than one clip." He could hear the craven bastards tellin it. "Come down and open the front door and throw out the gun. Then come out with your hands above your head."

He yelled out the window, "I'm a soldier of the IRA. I'm not comin out w'my hands up."

A bored voice said on the bullhorn. "I don't care if you come out sliding on your arse, chum. Just come on out and let's all get some sleep."

He heard the polis laughin all over the gravel and the grass.

Mockery mockery mockery mockery mockery fuckin English mockery doesn't every Irish schoolboy know the English think we're trash? Don't we learn that in school?

"Righty'are, righty'are."

Leap!

Leap from Death unto Life. Leap from the Dungeon to the Sky. Leap from Goal to Goal. Hop from Foot to Foot. He lashed himself with a compensating thought. Instant transitions.

Escape! Aren't we the greatest escapers there ever was in the world? Was the jail ever made that could hold us? Aren't we the

)) 281

darin, dashin, darlin boys? The world sits on the edge of its chair waitin for news that another one's out and the English can't hold us. The pages of glory. Escapers' glory.

Write a Song. "The Great Escape of Patrick Powers."

He threw his gun out the window and watched it turn in the air till it hit the gravel. It discharged and polis all over the place scuttled.

"Stick it up your arses," he yelled. "I'm comin out."

For a wee while. He lashed his spirit. It rose, soarin, on the wings of fuckin eagles.

They handcuffed him to a bald and portly bobby. The Black Maria came up the drive. Two of the polis got in with him.

"Where we goin?"

"London."

"Scrubs?"

"Yes."

"I'll not be long there." No reply. "Why d'they call this thing the Black Maria?"

"Who cares?"

"D'ye know why the Yanks calls theirs the Paddy Wagon? Because they used it t'round up the Paddies *us, us, us,* the bloody Irish and throw us in jail. Y'know what we done? *Us!* The Paddies? We took over the fuckin States! We took over the fuckin White House. *Kennedy.* Y'heard the name? That's *us!* Put us down. Put your foot on our necks. Y'know what we do? We eat your fuckin leg off."

Perhaps the bobbies weren't listening. His was the only voice. The tires whistled. The engine purred. Powers lashed his spirit.

"Y'ever heara Jimmy Steele, Paddy Donnelly, Eddie Maguire, Liam Graham, Jimmy O'Hagan? Yes, y'hearda them. Y'couldn't hold them in Crumlin Jail or Derry. McAteer? Y'couldn't hold him. Patrick Powers? Y'can't hold him! *Y'can't hold us!* Y'ever hear what Jimmy Steele wrote in jail? A poem. Y'ever hear it? Your fuckin Shakespeare! *Jimmy Steele's your man. . . ."*

282 ((

His own song leaped into his head, full grown, ringin w'glory. He said it in his head,

> "Come sing a song for Patrick Powers
> No English jail could hold him
> And while they dragged him to the Scrubs
> By God that's what he told them."

Tell the bastards. Tell the words t'them.

They were gone. They came, whole. They went, whole. The head is a treacherous friend.

Tell them what Jimmy Steele wrote in Crumlin Jail.

"Listen," he said. "Listen. Here's what Jimmy Steele wrote in Crumlin Jail. Hear it, y'fuckin English cunts, and then try keepin your feet on our necks. Listen to it. . . .

> "O, Sacred Heart of Jasus!
> We pray to Thee today,
> To aid our sufferin Motherland
> Upon her bloodstained way.
> For loyalty to serve her,
> For strength to set her free,
> O, Sacred Heart of Jasus!
> We send our prayer to Thee.

> "O, Sacred Heart of Jasus!
> Look down on us today,
> Make us strong fearless soldiers,
> Ever ready for the fray,
> 'Gainst Thine and Ireland's enemies,
> Wherever they may be,
> O, Sacred Heart of Jasus!
> We put our trust in Thee."

He laid his head back against the wall of the Black Maria. "Y'can't

)) 283

hold me. Y'can't beat the Sacred Heart of Jasus, boyo. And we have it."

Softly, the portly bobby said, "Was it the Sacred Heart killed the two in the house back there, Powers?"

Powers sighed desperately. "Jasus, y'can't *talk* to them. Y'can't *talk* to the fuckin English. . . ." His head was beating.

McManus was in his head, standin there w'his soft cock hangin and his face twisted, lookin like an eejit, and the widow-woman was with him and the doctor and his yatterin wife and Sorahan and one-eyed Clune and Kiernan and Mary Connors and a great cloud of witnesses and McManus was shoutin,

"Pietous Jesus Kate no no no not you Kate. . . ." . .

Powers held the top of his beating head with his one good hand. The pain was shrieking in his shoulder. His nerves marched like an army with drummers. He screamed, *"Get out of my head, McManus!"*